D1236204

EVELYN WAUGH: NEW DIRECTIONS

EVELYN WAUGH
New Directions

Edited by

Alain Blayac
Professor of English
University Paul Valéry, Montpellier

MACMILLAN

First published 1992

Published by
MACMILLAN ACADEMIC AND PROFESSIONAL LTD
Houndmills, Basingstoke, Hampshire RG21 2XS
and London
Companies and representatives
throughout the world

Printed in Hong Kong

British Library Cataloguing–in–Publication Data

Evelyn Waugh: New directions.
  I. Blayac, Alain
  823

ISBN 0–333–53839–0

To Ariane, Claudie and Dorothée

To Ariane, Claudie and Dorothée

Contents

Acknowledgements

The editor and publishers wish to thank the following who have kindly given permission for the use of copyright material: the Written Archives Department of the BBC for the permission to quote from their material; P.A. Doyle for his permission to quote from the *Evelyn Waugh Newsletter*; Harman Grisewood for permission to quote from his correspondence; the Harry Ransom Humanities Research Center and the Iconography Collection, University of Texas at Austin, for their permission to use material from their files; Rayner Heppenstall for his permission to quote from his *Journals*; Little, Brown and Co. (Boston) for the permission to quote from *Brideshead Revisited*; G. McCartney and Indiana University Press for permission to use material from *Confused Roaring: Evelyn Waugh and the Modernist Tradition*, (Bloomington and Indianapolis: Indiana University Press, 1987); the Peters, Fraser and Dunlop Group for permission to quote from the writings of Evelyn Waugh; Auberon Waugh on behalf of the Evelyn Waugh Trust and the Laura Waugh estate.

Notes on the Contributors

Alain Blayac, President of Société d'Études Anglaises Contemporaines (SEAC), wrote his doctoral thesis on Evelyn Waugh. He has published essays on Bennett, Waugh, Joyce, Lawrence and Valéry in French, English and American magazines. His research currently focuses on British fiction, culture and mentalities. He teaches at the University Paul Valéry, Montpellier.

Winnifred M. Bogaards is a Professor of English at the University of New Brunswick in St John, Canada. One of the compilers of *A Bibliography of Evelyn Waugh* (Whitston, 1986), her research interests are primarily in British and Canadian prose fiction.

Jean-Louis Chevalier is a Professor of English at the University of Caen. After his doctoral thesis on Denton Welch, he specialised in nineteenth and twentieth century literature. He has published articles on Sterne, Dickens Virginia Woolf, Orwell and A.S. Byatt and has translated Arnold, Yeats, Katherine Raine and Iris Murdoch among others.

Robert M. Davis is the author of *Evelyn Waugh, Writer* (Pilgrim, 1981), editor of *Evelyn Waugh, Apprentice* (Pilgrim, 1985) and author of seven other books on modern authors. He has written more than eighty critical and bibliographical essays. He is now Professor of English and Director of Graduate Studies at the University of Oklahoma.

Donat Gallagher has published numerous critical and bibliographical essays on Waugh. One of the compilers of *A Bibliography of Evelyn Waugh* (Whitston, 1986), he has also edited *The Essays, Reviews and Articles of Evelyn Waugh* (Methuen, 1983). He teaches at James Cook University, Queensland, Australia.

Leszek S. Kolek specialises in the theory and history of literature (British fiction, modes and genres, semiotic approaches to literary theory). His doctoral thesis was entitled 'Evelyn Waugh's Writings: From Joke to Comic Fiction'. He teaches at the Marie Curie-

Sklodowska University in Lublin, Poland, and currently works on semiotics and poetics.

George McCartney teaches at St John's University in New York City. His articles have appeared in various publications, including the *National Review* and *The American Scholar*. Parts of his essay have been adapted from his book, *Confused Roaring: Evelyn Waugh and the Modernist Tradition* (Bloomington and Indianapolis: Indiana University Press, 1987).

Introduction

I discovered long ago that the most satisfactory research – from a sentimental standpoint at least – must always link people sharing common ideas and principles. Several years of studying in France, England and America allowed me to meet a number of Waugh scholars, some of whom in the course of time became my friends. From then on it was not difficult to find collaborators for a project born of our admiration for Evelyn Waugh. We all shared the idea that such an enterprise should explore new directions and take into account recent critical trends. I then decided to juxtapose biographical essays on essential – but little-known or badly distorted – aspects of the writer's private and professional life with more literary approaches.

At the same time, I wanted to bring together critics from the whole international community of Waugh studies: Winnifred Bogaards (Canada), Donat Gallagher (Australia), Robert M. Davis and George McCartney (USA) for the 'New' continents, Leszek Kolek (Poland), J.L. Chevalier and myself (France) for the old. The team thus composed would make me think I've been true to my ambitions, were it not for the absence of a British contributor – the result of a last-minute (and much deplored) impediment – and for the obligation to leave aside so many eligible specialists. Bogaards and Gallagher proposed biographical essays, the rest of us decided on more literary articles.

Professor Bogaards traces with her usual rigour the passionate, tempestuous – and barely known – relationship of Evelyn Waugh with the BBC. In the process she discloses scores of new elements of that venture and provides fresh insights into complicated dealings that lasted for some thirty-odd years. Her expertise, her relentless pursuit of the facts, and the systematic use she made of all the sources available combine to present what is, in my view, the definitive account of this facet of Waugh's life. Her account offers us lively portraits of the writer, his interlocutors and of the developing BBC.

Donat Gallagher, whose *Essays, Reviews and Articles of Evelyn Waugh* was a landmark in Waugh studies, delves into a subject which no one could disentangle better than he – Vatican legal procedures. His 'Evelyn Waugh and Vatican Divorce' exposes the clichés and misconceptions that still encumber this most controversial issue. Written 'in the interests of accurate biography', it sets right the ungrounded arguments that the annulment was a 'Catholic legal fiction', clarifies the nature of a divorce often thought fishy and indissolubly linked with 'privilege' in people's minds. In the course of his demonstration, Gallagher analyses the arcana of Guglielmo Marconi's and the Duke of Marlborough's divorces, draws on a variety of testimonies, gives a detailed chronicle of the facts of the divorce and explains the complex rules of canon law. Gallagher concludes that Waugh was 'moderately lucky' to gain his decree of nullity.

George McCartney situates Waugh in the intellectual and aesthetic contexts of his times. He relates the novelist's writings to the battle of ideas about Bergson's philosophy so heartily combated by Wyndham Lewis. He underlines Lewis's misreadings and demonstrates that Waugh adhered to the ideas of Bergson for whom the ceaseless process of evolutionary growth (Becoming) is a reality while the timeless Being of the essentialist philosophers remains a pure fictional construct. According to Waugh, life eludes our static categories. McCartney's essay, starting from an analysis of Picabia's and Ernst's paintings as metaphors of the modern world, offers a stimulating approach to Waugh's writings, while a minute analysis of futurism is linked with his Christian commitment. It finally provides *Helena* with a new status, and pleads for Evelyn Waugh's place as a major thinker and aesthete of his time.

Robert M. Davis's 'Imagined Space in *Brideshead Revisited*' brilliantly analyses the underlying structural unity of the novel. It examines Charles Ryder's position and contrasts the problem of a mature narrator who is sometimes uncharitable and often unpleasant with the immature and moving actor. The essay centers not only on the 'now and then', but also the 'here and there', space being for Charles divisible into circumscribed and mutually exclusive areas. In the course of his study, Davis shows how Ryder has matured learning to see all places and actions in light of a larger purpose, eventually being able to 'fit together the tiny bits – artist, lover, soldier – into a whole, Captain Charles Ryder'.

As I said before, I wished the volume to reflect the development of Waugh studies throughout the world and desired to include scholars from non-English-speaking countries whose works deserved a wider audience. Leszek Kolek's semiotic approach to *Black*

Mischief undoubtedly belongs in this category. It gives a fine illustration of 'European' criticism both classically theoretical and ironically personal. Let me thank him for having completed his essay in a year so fertile in dramatic events and so crucial to the history of Poland and Eastern Europe.

J.L. Chevalier brings his encyclopaedic culture to the study of Arcadia in *Brideshead Revisited*. His originality and acumen allow him to link Waugh and his novel with a whole literary world. His highly personal essay casts a somewhat new light on a major novel and shows its relationship with many other international works. His versatile method draws upon intertextuality, narratology and hermeneutics in a convincing and enlightening vision of the novel.

As for the editor of the volume, he has tried to define humour in relation to Waugh's personality and fiction, an elusive phenomenon which the French find typically English and baffling to Cartesian minds. He strove to analyse its mechanism and nature by applying the theoretical definitions to the study of Waugh's texts.

Let me finally thank all the contributors to the volume who accepted my requirements, complied with my schedules, answered my queries, and put up with my impatience in a most un-Waughian, but highly appreciated, spirit of tolerance.

Alain Blayac
Université Montpellier III

1

Black Mischief as a Comic Structure
Leszek S. Kolek

A recent Soviet anthology of critical studies in English literature contains, among others, a popular introduction to Evelyn Waugh and reports a fact which might have surprised even the novelist himself: he turns out to be one of the favourite English writers in – out of all places – Siberian houses of culture, where copies of his translated works are reputedly disintegrating after so many readings by the workers. Waugh is reported to have won there a popularity equal almost to that of Dickens, although the Soviet scholar describes no Siberian equivalent of the protagonist of 'The Man Who Liked Dickens'.[1]

This paradoxical finding could serve as a pretext for reflections on such a flagrant failure of ideological indoctrination, but that should better be left for people acquainted with the reading public in Siberia. The fact is interesting for us because it proves that Waugh's ideas, aristocratic characters and the allegedly insular English sense of humour do not constitute insurmountable barriers in the reception of his works in Siberia or other exotic places. Although one cannot exclude a possibility that his novels may be read analogically to the ingenious interpretation of the birth-control posters in *Black Mischief*, the comic aspect of his writings is perceived everywhere. The laughter will probably differ; it may occur at 'wrong' moments or result from different cultural associations; its occurrence is also obviously dependent on the work of the translator. Yet, Waugh's works evidently contain a kind of humour generating mechanism that proves universal, perhaps as universal as the great classical comedies of past ages. And it is precisely that aspect of Waugh's novels that will be our concern in this essay.

A brief digression should make my purpose clearer. A joke about Mr X does not necessarily fail to produce laughter when the recipient has no idea about who or what Mr X is. It may be more

1

poignant for somebody personally acquainted with Mr X, but if it is based on some peculiar trait of character, ignorance or presumption, it will remain comic because Mr X is then accepted as a representative of a certain class, race etc. or simply as a human being. Although there are jokes clearly depending on some expert or inside knowledge, surprisingly many texts of this kind survive this process of abstracting and retain their ability to produce laughter. Moreover, it is easier to 'get the point' of a joke occurring in a larger narrative because the context provides then the knowledge necessary for the comprehension and appreciation of its basic incongruity.

The purpose of this digression will become evident when we put forward a hypothesis that a comic narrative contains at least one structure analogical to the joke. Joke patterns actually appear on many levels, in various forms, and serve a large number of functions.[2]

The theoretical assumptions of the hypothesis are based on the semiotic nature of literary communication. The latter is understood as a dynamic process of providing bits of information of which the reader constructs signs of a higher order (initially empty, then progressively filled with attributes through concretisation), which then become components of still higher complexes, thus creating a semiotic hierarchy of the text. One may therefore speak of signs of the verbal medium, of the fictional world (characters, spatial-temporal setting), of situations, events, plot, up to the highest level of main ideas. Each sign on every level is perceived both as a (relatively) autonomous whole (the self-assertive aspect) and as a constituent of a higher sign or a larger narrative unit (the integrative aspect). The signs on all the levels are generated by means of narrative units which also make up a hierarchy of growing complexity, such as verbal units, presentational modes, the so-called simple forms (*einfache Formen*),[3] stylistic-generic codes, and literary conventions.

If we add now that the simple forms include the category of the joke, the significance of the digression will become evident. The underlying assumption is that – at least theoretically – it should be easier to identify the effects of a single joke than those of a complex text, a short story or a novel. According to aestheticians, every element of the semiotic hierarchy is endowed with aesthetic qualities, so what happens in its reception may be described as an 'algebra' of partial aesthetic-emotional effects, both inherent and emergent, producing sequences of aesthetic modulations. At the same time the approach should also allow a deeper insight into Waugh's technique of writing as reflected in his finished works.[4]

Black Mischief has been chosen for the examination mainly because it is Waugh's first novel with a foreign setting, exploiting one of the ancient sources of comedy, the clash of cultures (thus bringing us back to the opening paragraph and the problem of the universality of appeal). An even more relevant reason is connected with the proposed approach and the position of this novel in Waugh's *œuvre*. Written between *Vile Bodies* and *A Handful of Dust*, it seems to constitute a distinct stage in the evolution of Waugh the writer and an important contribution to his poetics, thus making possible the generally acknowledged success of several later novels.

The analysis will therefore begin with the examination of the generative process in *Black Mischief*, paying special attention to jokes on particular levels of the semiotic hierarchy, and it will end with the novel perceived as a single, complex sign in its integrative aspect, i.e. as a component of Waugh's *œuvre*.

THE WORLD OF AZANIA

The opening sentence in *Black Mischief* already illustrates perhaps the most characteristic feature of the generative process, namely, multifunctionality. It appears to be a quotation (italics) and indirectly creates only one sign, Seth, with a number of highly heterogeneous attributes which function on several levels: *referentially*, they concretise the figure of Seth and, indirectly, place him in some setting; *aesthetic* effects result from self-contradictory attributes (e.g. both feudal and democratic claims to legitimacy); the *symbolic* function is evident in the juxtaposition between exoticism or barbarism and civilisation; finally, the *structural* role is manifested by interrupting the 'quotation' just before its subject is revealed.

All these functions prove significant as an initial context, necessary for subsequent joke structures. The very next sentence shows a trick with presentational modes by turning the 'quotation' into dictation, i.e. a dramatic mode or 'speech'. Mentioning Seth's action (looking out of the window), the narrator then generates the setting in an almost lyrical description – 'harbour . . . the fresh breeze of early morning . . . the last dhow setting sail for the open sea'.[5] But the terms used in Seth's utterance ('rats', 'stinking curs') destroy the poetic quality and reveal a specific, though enigmatic, fact; the last dhow actually carries refugees escaping from some danger.

The 'lyrical' description becomes therefore a 'misleading index', a device typical of joke structures, and its mechanism is based precisely on the process of concretisation, on making a general fact more specific: the reader is offered minute details which merely imply a higher sign, i.e. Seth's general situation, and the latter, together with the subject of the proclamation and the reasons for the escape create an extended puzzle. Such deliberate manipulations disturb text coherence and form joke structures which simultaneously generate the first signs of the semiotic hierarchy.

The remaining part of scene 1 (pp. 7–8) contains more instances of such manipulations. From the dialogue between Seth and Ali the reader can get no idea about Marx, but his connection with the wireless implies modernity and its unreliability. On the other hand, the enigmatic, recurring reference to 'the hills' consolidates the sense of some impending danger. Yet, comic effects are obviously predominant. Particularly effective is the perfect joke in Ali's phrase 'the last eight words of reproof', referring to Seth's outburst closing the first paragraph, a device forcing the reader to return to the original 'reproof'. But structurally the most important joke is the continuation of the dictation and the finally disclosed aim of the proclamation, namely, 'amnesty and free pardon'. The pompous formulation, though quite in keeping with the opening sentence, not only undermines the claim to 'the unanimous voice of our people' but also betrays the utter futility of Seth's endeavour. The significance of the dictation is therefore modified again and the last sentences refer directly to the opening statement, in this way framing the construction of scene 1 and providing 'a punchline' for its underlying joke pattern. It should be noted that, as in most jokes, the effects are achieved primarily by the appropriate ordering of information, withholding solutions and piling up specific details which force the reader to guess their full significance.

The characteristics of the generative process described above seem negated by scene 2 (pp. 8–15). Not only is it several times longer but its sole presentational mode is a fully coherent 'report' by the third-person narrator who provides a general background for the preceding scene, describing the country and its history, while preserving the puzzle about the nature of the crisis. On closer examination, however, one discovers manipulations similar to those observed above.

Waugh's purposeful selection of details serving several functions at once may be exemplified by the linking passage. It generates a minor, though significant element of the setting, the old Portuguese fortress, and the 'historical' incident of the relieving fleet coming too late to save the besieged. The passage continues the same mood of impending doom, while contributing to a fuller generation of the setting to follow.

The narrative in scene 2 strikes a new tone because comic effects seem to disappear. The narrative provides a detached and factual description that might almost come from a travel book, if it were not for the specific criteria of selection with emphasis on the ugly, primitive and brutal (cf. the Sakuyu, their cattle, past outbreaks of violence). The narrative code in this and other passages concerning the same subject acquires features typical not so much of realism but of naturalism. Waugh clearly avoids codes which are aesthetically neutral and prefers extreme effects, either comic or grim.

Yet, when the narrator passes on to the repeated attempts to introduce civilisation into the country, the two codes, naturalism in the generation of barbarism, and absurd comedy connected with characters attempting to civilise Azania, are superimposed and produce effects typical of the grotesque and black humour. The latter is best exemplified by the rule of Amurath whose conquests are described in the naturalistic code, as are his ruthlessness and cruelty, whereas the reforms he tries to introduce are strictly absurd (ranks, titles, religion, technology etc.) The same clash of codes occurs in the construction of the railway line, involving both macabre loss of life and comic, ingenious uses for the steel sleepers and copper wire by the natives (a variation on a theme continued throughout the novel), culminating in the grotesque first journey of the train (pp. 11–12).

Naturally, scene 2 makes Azania a much more concrete country, endowed with a number of attributes significant in several dimensions, so that it is much more than a mere place for the action to develop. First of all, it seems crucial that the two codes are clearly linked with different sections of the generated reality, an association continued throughout the novel. Secondly, the historical aspect of Azania implies an evident element of cyclicity, of alternating periods of chaos caused by an invasion of civilisation, followed by relative equilibrium. The resulting world is thus turned into a dynamic system whose main opposition concerns barbarism and civilisation. The scene provides a rich context for the preceding dramatic part, yet in a way which avoids solving any suspended puzzles, concentrating instead on the creation of a whole system.

Moreover, scene 2 is placed between two fragments of Seth's dictation, so that the historical-geographical section is offered as a kind of substitute for the simultaneous action apparently taking place elsewhere: the narrator chooses to leave Seth's hopeless and (presumably) repetitious dictation, and provides 'more pertinent' information. The manner of inserting scene 2 creates a joke structure on the level of construction, since it is a disclosure of the narrator's deliberate interference and his attitude towards Seth's activity.

In the remaining scenes of the chapter joke structures again become more numerous and functional especially on the plane of the action, which is developed along two parallel lines, both finding a climax in the last scene.

The subplot involving secondary characters (Ali, Youkoumian, Major Joab) constitutes a good example of a pattern of a string of joke structures based on the same incongruity, namely, that of one rascal outwitting another. The result is a cumulative series of comic reversals producing almost identical aesthetic effects that might be described as low burlesque, if it were not for the rascals' ruthlessness, involving beating, tortures, killing, and an attempted hanging, which endow the whole with the features of black humour.

Quite similar in its aesthetic effects is the overlapping plot of Seth although it is based on a different mechanism. His plot is less eventful but it displays a clear progression of effects when his position becomes increasingly desperate, when he is betrayed, surrounded by traitors, and finally left completely alone. The ultimate nightmare is summed up in a symbolically revealing statement by the narrator:

> Seth lay awake and alone, his eyes wild with the inherited terror of the jungle, desperate with the acquired loneliness of civilisation.
>
> (p. 26)

Thus, the main opposition reappears, now enriched with the pathos of a character trapped between barbarism and civilisation and having the worst of the two. However, this increasingly grim development is not only overlapping with the sequence of jokes mentioned above but it also creates its own comic effects, based on exposing Seth's further absurdities – his unshakable belief in all things European, 'the Tank', Progress, Evolution, the Oxford Union, Shaw, Priestley etc. Thus, black humour predominates again, although, contrary to the subplot of the rascals, in Seth's case it is achieved differently.

Comic solutions to all the puzzles scattered over the chapter are typically supplied in the last scene (pp. 32–44). The vital hint is again given by way of concretisation: the sign which has so far been known merely as *an* army 'in the hills' becomes now *the* army and the information affects at once all the levels of the semiotic hierarchy generated so far.

In its immediate context Seth's victory constitutes the final reversal in the subplot of the rascals. Initially a victim of a plot (and his own cunning), Youkoumian now emerges victorious and the efforts of other fugitives, all the suffering, pain and death, are rendered unnecessary.

Throughout the chapter the idea of imminent defeat has repeatedly been impressed on the reader by both the narrator and the characters who, contrary to Seth, have been shown as eminently pragmatic. Hence, on a higher plane, Seth's triumph turns into a victory of the absurd over common sense, of the grotesque dreamer over scheming, hardened blackguards.

The latter conclusion is consolidated by the long and detailed description of Connolly's army, continuing the same mixture of naturalism and the absurd (e.g. the soldiers re-enacting their deeds of valour and literally killing their comrades-in-arms, p. 36). Structurally, the description is a device delaying the final revelations in the dialogue between Seth and Connolly.

As in a typical joke, it opens with another of Seth's absurd monologues and only then can Connolly report the real cause of the victory, namely, primitive (i.e. barbaric) superstitions. The narrator then provides a necessary component of black humour in a long and macabre description of the final massacre, and then allows the final revelation, the concretisation of the sign of Seyid, Seth's opponent, mentioned by name before, yet without revealing his relation to Seth; the latter is exposed in Seth's casual remark:

> They should not have eaten him – after all, he was my father . . .
> It is so . . . so barbarous.   (p. 43)

At this point a typical joke, intended mainly to provoke laughter, would end, since the statement contains a sudden disclosure, sufficiently macabre to create black humour, and inhibits potential emotional response by Seth's obsession. Breaking the narrative at this point would also make it easier for the reader to reconstruct the nature of the conflict, i.e. the son fighting against his father in a war of succession.

But *Black Mischief* employs joke structures for a deeper purpose and, instead of an abrupt end of the chapter, there follows another outburst of Seth's. One consequence of this extended ending is the exposure of Seth's insensitivity towards his father, similar to Youkoumian's attitude towards his wife: both are characterised by an unthinking acceptance and infliction of suffering, i.e. a feature typical of barbarism. The ending also emphasises the black comic mode of presentation and, finally, it shows that exposition is still the main function of the chapter.

Seen as a whole, Chapter 1 reveals its underlying pattern as a complex of joke structures based mainly on the concretisation of both the world and the main event. The jokes are laid out in a specific sequence: (1) the last dhow, fugitives, and the proclamation; (2) happenings 'in the hills'; (3) an army in the hills; (4) Seth's army; (5) the victory and its dubious cause; (6) the fate of the opponent, his identity, the cause of the conflict (civil war) as motivation of the escape, explaining item (1). The crucial aspect of the sequence is the ordering of information, typical of any joke. Thanks to the geographical-historical section all these signs can now be placed within the overall, cyclical dynamic system and the narrative now passes on to the generation of the other pole of the main opposition, namely, civilisation.

THE WORLD OF CIVILISATION

The examination of Chapter 1 has taken much space because of the nature of the generative process, so multifunctional and rich in aesthetic-emotional effects. Subsequent chapters may be discussed more briefly because the analysis will concentrate on progressively higher levels.

When Chapter 2 is perceived as a whole, it seems inconsequential, hardly adding anything to the plot and apparently lacking any overall joke structure. Yet, on closer examination of the generative process and the order of creating signs there emerges a certain analogy in introducing, first, two initially anonymous characters, then providing a wider background, and, finally, showing a given action. Thus, both chapters reveal a similar narrative strategy, additionally confirmed by temporal simultaneity (cf. pp. 57, 63–4 and the time span of Chapters 1 and 2).

The aim of the strategy is clear since it indirectly enforces a comparison between the two worlds. Having shown an enthusiast dreaming of introducing civilisation into his barbaric country, the narrative now presents the representatives of this civilisation. What the strategy achieves is, first, the demonstration of the absolute separation of the two worlds and, secondly, the exposure of what Waugh himself called 'the attendant and deplorable ills'[6] of civilisation. It is precisely the narrative strategy that realises the satirical intentions, because the 'points' of the numerous joke structures in Chapter 2 produce a radical shift in aesthetic-emotional effects towards those kinds of comedy which apparently lack the satirical impulse.

The shift is abrupt since the chapter opens at once with a playful, nonsensical dialogue of a light erotic comedy (cf. presupposition in 'they rolled apart', 'the stinging thing' on William's neck becoming 'two things', 'the butterfly kiss', etc., pp. 44–6). The farcical entertainment that develops creates quite a different world, although the setting is the same country – 'on the crest of the little hills above Debra Dowa' (p. 44). In the second world barbarism is reduced merely to some naturalistic hints, e.g. the indifference of 'the priest's youngest child . . . to the flies which settled on the corners of his mouth' (p. 44), an ironic equivalent of 'the butterfly kiss'; with the gradual disclosure of temporal simultaneity the irony becomes stronger and is deepened by the aesthetic contrast between the two narrative codes.

In the next scene (pp. 46–55), corresponding to the geographical-historical passage in Chapter 1, the comedy is further modified. There are satirical touches in the narrator's presentation of the diplomats, especially of Mr Schonbaum, in the comic narrative trick with M. Ballon, provided only with one attribute ('the Freemason'), or in the grotesque career of Sir Samson. If the description of the British Legation still contains some hints of the barbaric character of the country, the action that follows turns into pure social comedy based on exaggerated stereotypes, English manners and the traditional rivalry between the British and the French.

Perhaps the most paradoxical, though ideologically fully motivated, aspect of the world generated in Chapter 2 is the total lack of difference which a change of the setting could be expected to make in the life style of the representatives of civilisation. The paradox consists in Seth's admiration deriving from the original life style of civilisation, while its resistance to change automatically implies its closed character and precludes any hope of assistance. Moreover, contrary to Seth, who has only too many numerous ideas, the British are shown as lacking any ideas whatsoever, being entirely preoccupied with pleasures, from erotic amusements to Sir Samson's infantile fantasies in his bath. The contrast is double-edged: not only does it expose the barrenness of the civilisation but it also emphasises the absurdity of Seth's aspirations. It becomes increasingly clear that the civilisation he wants to introduce is worthless and materialistic, and even its pleasures are too often boring. Simply by juxtaposing the two worlds the narrative exposes and ridicules the representatives of civilisation, while avoiding the code of explicit satire.

Indifference is also the key note at the beginning of Chapter 3, when the narrative moves to England, the seat of civilisation. The narrator's understatement of 'very little impression' made by the news of Seth's victory could equally well refer to both the Legation and London, though in the latter case the sentence is followed by a series of 'illustrations' in the form of several specific, comic reactions of anonymous people. The device turns into a 'guessing game', inviting the reader to discover the identity of the speaker by what he or she says, while stressing the general ignorance, cynicism, and condescension of the British.

The reaction of the last reported recipient of the news is not specified; instead we are told of Basil Seal cashing a bad cheque (p. 67), a typically incongruous piece of information, comically disturbing text coherence and switching to a new sign. The latter is generated in a series of Basil's visits, talks, and his journey to Azania, each episode creating a joke structure; each also reveals or confirms his peculiar attributes – audacity, careless dishonesty, instability, opposition to the ideals of the older generation, lack of emotional involvement, and love of 'rackets'. At the same time, these joke structures generate other figures, such as Basil's father, Rex Monomark, Lady Seal or Jo Mannering who, with several other named and nameless characters, constitute the 'social background' and complete the presentation of the world of London high society or 'Metroland', a familiar ground to any Waugh reader.

The chapter also raises a problem important for the whole plot, namely, the motivation of Basil's decision to go to Azania. His talk in the club reveals his interest in that country. We are also offered Basil's opinion about London being 'hell' and the comment (actually a quotation) of the club member – 'Fellow who's tired of London is tired of life' (p. 68). Although these facts are disclosed in joke structures, they might imply something as serious as a 'death wish', a feeling not unknown to 'the Bright Young People' from *Vile Bodies*. Since London seems to offer no more 'rackets' exciting enough, Basil is facing perhaps the worst prospect, namely, boredom.

The observation concerns not only Basil but the whole world of civilisation, thus complementing the picture created in Chapter 2. Some parallels are, indeed, quite deliberate, e.g. the William-Prudence and Basil-Angela affairs, both introduced by means of the same comic device of ellipsis whose effects depend on presupposition (comp. pp. 44 and 87); apart from hedonism and lack of emotional involvement, both reveal the constant presence of boredom. Moreover, the world of civilisation is not entirely free from barbarism, either, as indicated by the attractiveness of Basil's unshaven dirty appearance for two fascinated girls at the party (pp. 70–71) or the dogs in the Trumpingtons' bed (pp. 78–9). Seen against the background of Azania, the relations seem to be reversed: in Azania barbarism is a real power, primaeval and all-pervading, while in London it is reduced to mere mannerisms, making pleasure more refreshing or perverse.

Apart from concretising the world of civilisation, the main contribution of Chapter 3 is the generation of Basil who, like Seth, has a full chapter devoted to his presentation, a clear signal that he has an important role to play. But for an analysis of his function in the pattern of the whole novel we must now pass on to the higher level of the semiotic hierarchy, namely, the plot.

THE PATTERN OF THE PLOT

Although the first three chapters abound in events, their pre-dominant function is the generation of the fictional reality as a dynamic system based on the opposition between barbarism and civilisation. Still, the configuration of the main components of this system foretells a possible course of future events. Brought together, these elements resemble some traditional narratives based on the following pattern: (1) an enlightened ruler comes to power; (2) he finds some progressive and loyal characters who help him in (3) his attempts to introduce reforms; (4) the attempts provoke conservative opposition and the conflict between the two results in: (5a) either the victory of the reformer who can now carry out his plans (5b) or the triumph of the conservative forces, the reformer being defeated, but his progressive ideas living on in others.

The pattern is known from many realisations whose origin could probably be traced back to the myth of Prometheus, but which may involve any sort of noble reformer of religion, science, politics, etc. In semiotic terms the scheme constitutes what C. Segre calls 'the usual course of events', as opposed to a contrived or perverted course in comic narratives.[7] By comparing the scheme suggested above with the plot of *Black Mischief* we may discover the set of manipulations carried out on the underlying pattern to turn it into a comic structure.

Thus, (1) in the scheme has already been discussed above in terms of joke structures in the generation of the two signs, 'the enlightened ruler' and his coming to power, Seth's absurd ideas considerably diminishing his stature as a 'noble reformer' and his ascendancy being given the form of a comic paradox.

The transformations of (2) are more complex. Youkoumian's case is fairly clear, since he is a swindler who can ingratiate himself with any ruler and survive any calamity, so his usefulness as a helper is at least doubtful. Basil's case is more difficult because narrative ellipticality deliberately makes his behaviour ambiguous. Thus, although we are shown how Basil and Youkoumian get together almost as kindred spirits (p. 98), we are deprived of the crucial talk Basil must have had with Seth somewhere between Chapters 4 and 5. If Seth obviously needs 'a man of progress and culture' (pp. 102, 115), Basil's attitude towards the 'reforms' re-mains puzzling. Since he is obviously far from stupid, the reader may legitimately ask why only at the very end of Chapter 5 does the narrator state: 'It was on that afternoon that Basil at last lost his confidence in the permanence of the One Year Plan' (p. 155). In action Basil proves a loyal helper, tactful and resourceful, as the series of joke structures showing his work at the Ministry demonstrates (pp. 121–6). Paradoxically enough, his only, yet fatal slip is caused by the civilisation he represents, namely, his 'atavistic sense of caste' and 'vexed megalomania' (p. 132). One may therefore conclude that Basil is indeed almost a model, even if somewhat erratic, helper.

The account of the reforms, (3), is continued from Chapter 1, with Seth's ideas becoming increasingly absurd and fantastic, intensifying the comedy till the middle of Chapter 6, and then turning the absurdity into pathos (when Seth frantically and symbolically continues the demolishing of the cathedral by himself, p. 184). The pathos is diminished by the comic device of the narrative assuming here the point of view of two ladies, but there can be no doubt that, totally unaware of his own absurdity, Seth is quite sincere and desperately clings to his ideals.

The multiplication of Seth's ideas also deprives the reader of sufficient signals to perceive any hierarchy of importance in the accumulated facts. Even when such a hint is provided, as in the boots affair described as being 'of greater importance than either of them [Basil and Connolly] realised' (p. 132), the consequences of such an apparently trivial matter cannot be foreseen by the characters and/or the reader. Here Waugh fully exploits the advantages of narrative omniscience.

All these manipulations radically modify (4). Seth's attempted reforms are too fantastic and incomprehensible to provoke any opposition. When it comes into being, it is caused by completely irrelevant reasons, namely, M.Ballon's desire to spite the British and his imaginary suspicions of a British plot. The whole traditional role of (4) is thus totally perverted.

Several manipulations comically transform the conflict itself. First of all, contrary to narrative principles, the emergence of the opposition and their detailed plans are all made known beforehand to the reader, Seth and to other characters. For the latter the news means a chance to escape the usual slaughter, thus producing a recurrence of the situation opening the novel. For the reader the exposure could mean some loss of suspense, unless it is accepted as another 'misleading index'.

Secondly, after a delay caused by the narrator choosing to follow the two ladies, the reader learns about the result of the rebellion only indirectly, from another comic 'guessing game', this time from snatches of conversations by various characters gathered at the British Legation.

Finally, the success of the opposition is followed by the Coronation, i.e. in the scheme proposed above, variant (5b), presented in grotesque, satiric and macabre terms. The apparently premature exposure of the opposition's plans indeed proves to have been another 'misleading index', because the ceremony unexpectedly culminates in Achon's death and the failure of the opposition. Thus, both traditional endings of the scheme are turned upside down and the whole system collapses.

Instead of following the suspended plot of Seth, the narrative concentrates on variant (5b), i.e. 'the progressive ruler's ideas being carried out by others', though modified by the convention of an adventure story (or its parody), with such typical elements as a secret mission, arduous journey, revenge on a villain, followed by the ceremonial funeral, feast, and speech. On the level of ideas Basil's speech seems particularly significant. The juxtaposition between Seth's actual life as previously shown and the idealised image of a ruler with all the numerous, traditional virtues implies a surrender of the representative of civilisation to the power of local tradition, mightier than any reality. It is also an acknowledgement of the force of an ideal which persists in the world of barbarism while in civilisation it belongs among fairy tales. In a larger context, the incongruities ridicule Basil's school-boy's dreams, the convention of adventure story and, finally, the ideological aspect of civilisation.

Yet aesthetically strongest effects are produced by the notorious episode of Basil unwittingly consuming Prudence. As a narrative device, Prudence's fate is a case of literalism, a realisation of Basil's utterance – 'I'd like to eat you', and her reply – 'So you shall, my sweet . . . anything you want' (p. 180). It exposes the mechanism by which civilisation petrifies not only language and its metaphorical possibilities, but also the very emotions such terms originally described – all the loves in the novel are deprived of feelings while observing appearances and verbal conventions.

The immediate effect seems superficially similar to that of Connolly's disclosure of Seyid's fate but the differences are more telling. First of all, the disclosure is not sudden but has the form of

Basil's suspicions being gradually confirmed. Secondly, it relies on the preceding culinary particulars of the feast, which constitute gratuitous, exaggerated details typical of black humour. Thirdly, if Connolly's disclosure in Chapter 1 is immediately blocked by an inhibitory sequence of joke structures, in Chapter 7 Basil's response is replaced by a long and appropriately grim description of the barbaric dances of the natives and the obviously symbolic beginning of the rain, as if to provoke reflections rather than inhibit them. Finally, there is a crucial difference between the signs involved: Seyid is hardly more than a name, whereas Prudence is a more fully concretised, although secondary character, a relatively innocent figure and victim of pure chance (in spite of her meaningful name).

These attributes are important both ideologically and aesthetically. If the accident happened to such a character as, e.g. Dame Mildred, her satirical presentation would partly justify it (cf. the scene of her feeding the 'doggies' and driving away hungry children – p. 157). The result would then be some kind of ironic, even if exaggerated, justice, but Waugh combines here the victim's innocence and chance, thus excluding any easy rational explanation.

The shock is largely due to the narrative codes used. One may point out various events of even more macabre nature, for instance in Greek mythology (cf. the myth of Tantalus), whose effects are by no means so intense. Thanks to the naturalistic code and Prudence's fuller concretisation Waugh diminishes the temporal distance and weakens the effects of comedy while intensifying the shock which is clearly meant to provoke reflection, not so much about barbarism, but rather about the reader's own civilisation. The examination of the latter in the novel has shown a civilisation reduced to hedonism and the mindless search for animal pleasure, superficially concentrating on manners while ignoring morals and spiritual values, indifferent towards others, seeking excitement at any price, without any awareness of the perils of regressing back into barbarism. The aesthetic value of the incident serves precisely the purpose of making this point indirectly, yet with sufficient emphasis.

Since Prudence plays no major role in the underlying scheme, it is a measure of the importance of the aesthetic effects that her fate is invariably included in plot summaries by various critics. The effects of this joke structure are more functional aesthetically and

symbolically than referentially or structurally and they are so
strong that critics feel unable to ignore them, while simultaneously
accepting the basic scheme of a reformer. The conclusion indicates
the fact that the aesthetic and structural planes do not always
coincide, as has repeatedly been noted above, when major events
in the underlying plot are ignored, suspended and replaced by
episodes irrelevant for the plot but significant on the aesthetic and
ideological planes.

As always in comic narratives, the last chapter plays a crucial
role on all the levels of the semiotic hierarchy, analogically to a
multiple punch-line in joke structures. Its first scene brings one
major revelation, namely, Sonia's refusal to hear any 'traveller's
tales', dismissed as 'far-flung stuff' (p. 232). It is not simply a
repetition of the theme of indifference, because Sonia's attitude
deprives Basil's racket of its essential purpose, namely, something
to brag about, by questioning its credibility. And since Basil's tale
constitutes such a large portion of *Black Mischief*, the novel as a
whole might be placed in the category of the 'far-flung stuff' which
loses its value by being overused. This label would question all the
previous conclusions and create one more narrative joke on
Waugh's part, deliberately baffling the reader's potentially serious
interpretations: but such a generalisation is negated by the fact that
it is not the last scene in the novel.

The remaining part of the chapter presents the final state of
Azania as a third variant of the ending: since both the 'reformer'
and the 'opposition' are defeated, victory goes to a third party,
namely, the foreigners, and Azania becomes a Joint Protectorate.
The solution changes nothing in Azania as a system – life goes on
unchanged inland and civilisation again introduces its usual share
of absurdities on the coast, comically summing up most of the
events from the previous chapters. Perhaps the most illustrative
example is the preservation of the wrecked car and building a road
around it (p. 235), ostensibly to respect property laws but in fact to
spite the French: since the whole revolt was initiated by M. Ballon,
the episode again produces a comic reversal and concludes the
so-called submerged plot of the car.[8] On a higher level, these
incidents imply the continuity of tradition, especially in several
'inherited' submerged plots (e.g. rumours about Connolly and
Mme Ballon), comically, though emphatically stressing its essentially spurious nature.

Finally, the closing image of the novel is not a joke structure at all but an obviously symbolic description: 'the soft, barely perceptible lapping of the water along the sea-wall' (p. 238). The image might seem contrary to the short and violent clash presented in the novel, but this last sentence implies the crucial factor of time which imposes a longer perspective, covering not only Seth's short-lasting reign but the whole history of attempts to 'civilise' Azania. How far this image concerns all civilisation may be a subject of far-reaching speculations, but it certainly fits Waugh's own ideas expressed elsewhere:

> Civilisation has no force of its own beyond what is given it from within. It is under constant assault and it takes most of the energies of civilised man to keep it going at all . . . Barbarism is never finally defeated. . . .[9]

THE INTEGRATIVE ASPECT OF *BLACK MISCHIEF*

To sum up the analysis, some remarks should be made about the dependent or integrative aspect of the novel, when *Black Mischief* is seen as a component of a larger whole which it simultaneously constitutes and enriches. A study of several of such higher signs, e.g. the poetics of the epoch, literary tradition or convention, would go beyond the scope of this paper, so let us concentrate on the immediately higher whole, namely Waugh's *oeuvre*, which clearly possesses the nature of a sign.[10]

Although *Black Mischief* is often seen as quite a new venture, it is by no means all that innovative. First of all, it shows a continuation of characters representing civilisation, not only of recurring types, but also ideologically significant figures. If one compares the features of 'the Bright Young People' from *Vile Bodies*, such as fanciful irresponsibility, lack or loss of ideals, authorities and roots, one will easily notice that they all recur in the representatives of the world of civilisation in *Black Mischief*. A difference may perhaps be noticed in one representative of 'the Bright Young People', Basil Seal, who has found an apparent 'direction' in his search for adventures on a much larger scale, only to discover the falsity of his schoolboy dreams and the crucial gap between ideas and reality.

Secondly, the theme of the confrontation of barbarism and civilisation was present in Waugh's fiction from the beginning. His first novel, *Decline and Fall*, opens with a scene of English aristocracy 'baying for broken glass', exposing an element of barbarism rooted in this apparently highly civilised class. A more literal clash between the two, including comic misunderstandings, lack of communication and British condescension, appears in such characters as Chokey in *Decline and Fall* and Baroness Yoshiwara in *Vile Bodies*. Finally, even the code of naturalism also appears in the previous novels in short fragments (e.g. the sports in *Decline and Fall* or the junk-yards in *Vile Bodies*).

What is really novel in *Black Mischief* is the combination of all these earlier elements and their expansion, so that the relation between barbarism and civilisation now becomes the main structural opposition of the dynamic system of the novel, the world of barbarism being consistently generated by the code of naturalism. As a result, there emerges an additional level of world-code complexes in the semiotic hierarchy and the latter is integrated vertically, as opposed to the horizontal, sequential integration in the earlier novels. It is precisely this new type of deeper semiotic integration that will be further perfected in later works.

Even more interesting is the development of the persistent theme of tradition, recurring in practically all Waugh's fiction. In the novels preceding *Black Mischief*, tradition occurred mainly as a 'missing dimension' (together with religion, positive values etc.), usually embodied in the great houses. In *Black Mischief*, tradition is examined also in the example of a barbarian country and shown as a paradoxical phenomenon, spurious and falsified, yet necessary and powerful.

Finally, in terms of aesthetic-emotional effects, *Black Mischief* seems unique among Waugh's early novels, due to the intensity of the black comic mode. It does not mean that the preceding novels lacked instances of black humour (e.g. the fates of Lord Tangent and Prendergast in *Decline and Fall*), but in *Black Mischief* it becomes a predominant mode of the whole work. It is a result of such factors as a set of variations on the theme of cannibalism, the codes of naturalism and the absurd, and the absence of lyrical passages (particularly evident in comparison with *Vile Bodies*). *Black Mischief* is a perfect combination of all these factors resulting in Waugh's finest example of black comedy before *The Loved One*.

In its immediate successor, *A Handful of Dust*, the very real achievements of *Black Mischief* are easily discernible. On the level of narrative strategy *A Handful of Dust* shows not only the same reliance on 'empty' signs and ellipticality to produce joke structures but also the same temporal parallelism of the first two chapters, which create the contrasted worlds of the Beavers and of Hetton Abbey. Both worlds are generated by means of distinct codes, thus again producing a semiotic hierarchy characterised by vertical integration (and a much larger number of world-code complexes in the later novel). The crucial event in the first half of *A Handful of Dust*, John Andrew's accident, involves essentially the same combination of an even more innocent victim, chance, foreshadowing, and a deliberate attempt to make rational explanation impossible; the other climax, Tony's delirious visions, is also turned into a peculiar summing up of most events in the novel, while the whole Brazilian section may be seen almost as a direct continuation of *Black Mischief*. In addition, there are essentially the same principles of construction which, in respect to *A Handful of Dust*, have been called 'grafting and carpentering'.[11] Finally, the later novel generally continues the same set of characters, missing dimensions, potentially expandable images, ideas and a cyclical, dynamic system.

In a broader perspective, going beyond *A Handful of Dust*, *Black Mischief* may be seen as having contributed a set of themes, techniques and ideas for several later novels, such as *Scoop* (a 'mellower' version of *Black Mischief*), *Put Out More Flags* (the 'dark' background of war, Basil Seal and a series of his exploits), *The Loved One* (black humour), some episodes in *The Sword of Honour* (e.g. Ritchie-Hook and the Dakar expedition), and, obviously, *Basil Seal Rides Again*. As a result, the position of *Black Mischief* in Waugh's *œuvre* seems very important indeed, and its contribution to the repertoire of the writer's poetics is quite considerable.

These conclusions also provide a clue to the popularity of Waugh's fiction in exotic parts of the world. It would be too rash to perceive direct parallels in the reception of his works there, because such observations might merely echo a somewhat superficial claim by P.A. Doyle, who states that *Black Mischief* 'ridicules the notions that civilisation and culture can be superimposed on an essentially barbarian country by ignoring practicality and eschewing common sense'.[12] If Waugh's novel had been limited to such a topical theme, it would have been unlikely to achieve such a universal appeal. It is precisely due to the fact that this theme is merely a pretext and a means for a much deeper examination of universal concepts of civilisation and its constituent elements of tradition, culture, values and ideals, carried out by means of complex joke structures all containing the proverbial grain of truth, that *Black Mischief* is read and appreciated in quite unexpected places. The Russian scholar quoted at the beginning provides an indirect confirmation of this conclusion when he states that Waugh's writings are 'close to those of Gogol, Saltykov-Shchedrin, Leskov, Chekhov and Bulgakov'.[13] The common features of the work of these authors, and that of Waugh, are the very things which mark their works out as being of lasting significance; stories which offer a brilliantly entertaining surface which presents popular and topical themes with a mixture of comedy and pathos, whilst gradually revealing underneath their authors' deep commitment to great humanistic and spiritual values, both as a warning, and as a source of hope.

NOTES

1. G. Andjaparidze, 'Evelyn Waugh and the Modern Satirical Novel' in *20th Century English Literature: A Soviet View* (Moscow, 1982), p. 336.
2. For a discussion of a basic model of the joke, the theoretical assumptions of its semiotic analysis, and its functions in longer narratives see my 'Towards a Poetics of Comic Narratives: Notes on the Semiotic Structure of Jokes', *Semiotica*, 1985, 53:1/3, pp. 145–163 and *Evelyn Waugh's Writings: From Joke to Comic Fiction* (Lublin, 1985).
3. A. Jolles, *Formes simples*, tr. by A. Buquet (Paris, 1972); the original appeared as *Einfache Formen* in 1929. The nine forms include: legend, saga, myth, riddle, proverb, case, memoir, tale, and joke.
4. This indicates the basic difference between the present approach and that of R.M. Davis who examined the creative process of writing these works in his *Evelyn Waugh, Writer* (Norman, Oklahoma: 1981). In this respect the present study may be regarded as a supplement to Davis's analysis.
5. All page references made in the text concern E. Waugh, *Black Mischief* (Harmondsworth, 1977). Page references are also added to denote 'scenes', i.e. narrative fragments separated by spaces, because of differences between particular editions.
6. E. Waugh's 'Open Letter', in *The Letters of Evelyn Waugh*, ed. by M. Amory (London, 1980) p. 77.

7. Cf. C. Segre, *Structures and Time. Narration, Poetry, Models*, tr. by J. Meddemen (Chicago, 1979) pp. 122–36.
8. Term after A.Pasternak-Slater, 'Waugh's *A Handful of Dust*: Right Things in Wrong Places', *Essays in Criticism*, 1982, 32:1, pp. 48–68.
9. E. Waugh, *Robbery Under Law. The Mexican Object-Lesson* (London, 1940) p. 278; cf. also R.M. Davis, op.cit., p. 56.
10. For a definition of a writer's *œuvre* as a subgenre see A. Fowler, *Kinds of Literature: An Introduction to the Theory of Genres and Modes* (Cambridge, Mass., 1982) pp. 128–9.
11. Cf. R.M. Davis, op.cit., p. 51–61.
12. Term after S. McCarthy, *The Modes of Comedy* (Hythe, Scotland 1980) Chap. 6, pp. 65–84. McCarthy uses the term pejoratively, but the approach assumed in this paper shows such a practice to be perfectly legitimate in comic fiction. Cf. the relations between 'The Incident in Azania' and 'Consequences' and *Black Mischief*, and 'The Man Who Liked Dickens'and *A Handful of Dust*.
13. P.A. Doyle: *Evelyn Waugh*, (Grand Rapids, Michigan: Eerdmans, 1969), p. 17.
14. Andjaparidze, op.cit., p. 337.

2

Imagined Space in
Brideshead Revisited

Robert M. Davis

By changing the title of his work in progress from 'A Household of the Faith' to *Brideshead Revisited: The Sacred and Profane Memories of Captain Charles Ryder*,[1] Evelyn Waugh put Ryder at the center not just of the narration but of the novel. Since, as Jeffrey Heath puts it, 'most adverse criticism really originates in a distaste for Charles Ryder',[2] any attempt to take the novel seriously will have to confront the problem of a narrator who is sometimes uncharitable and often unpleasant, who refuses to criticise his own past, and who seems unregenerate at a time when he is supposedly converted to a new way of life.

A few critics, notably Heath and William J. Cook, Jr.,[3] have pointed out distinctions between the attitudes of the youthful Charles and the narrating Ryder (an artificial but useful distinction I retain hereafter), but they tend to rely on paraphrases of his statements rather than on discerning the structure of the mind which formulates them. If we look at that mind, it seems clear that the novel deals not with Charles Ryder's changing opinions and feelings or even with his acquiring a body of doctrine, but with his conversion in the strict sense: the old, without being obliterated, is transformed into the new.[4]

The process of conversion is somewhat obscured by the novel's circular structure of Prologue, body (two books in the original English and all American versions; three in the 1960 and current English editions), and Epilogue. In chronological terms, the novel begins at Oxford in 1923 and traces Charles's friendship with Sebastian Flyte and growing involvement with his family through Sebastian's descent into alcoholism, the dispersal of the family, and Charles's becoming an architectural painter. In the final movement of the body, Charles returns to Brideshead Castle with Sebastian's sister Julia and witnesses in the death of her father the

22

power of divine grace to overwhelm merely human desires. At some point, he is converted to Roman Catholicism and begins military service in the Second World War. As the Prologue begins in early spring, 1944, he is disillusioned with the army, but his unit's transfer to Brideshead, now a campsite, revives his imagination, and after narrating the body of the novel, he exhibits in the Epilogue a new charity and serenity.

This is conventional enough in structure and simple enough in outline, and in the body of the novel Waugh distinguishes easily enough between the mature narrator and the immature actor. But the situation in the Prologue is more complex. In chronological terms, Ryder has already become a Catholic, supposedly able to see the world and its inhabitants under the aspect of eternity and in the light of charity, and clearly he does not do so. This can be regarded as a failure in characterisation, especially by readers who regard spiritual growth as instantaneous and irreversible: perhaps Waugh did not realise how unpleasant and uncharitable Ryder is. Or it can be regarded as a failure in construction: Waugh had to make Ryder seem unduly limited in order to leave room for his change in attitude in the Prologue.

Or perhaps Waugh used the Prologue to establish the fundamental ways in which Ryder sees and judges. The title, construction, and several extended passages of the novel emphasise the narrator's concern with time and memory and his habit of distinguishing between *now* and *then*. But Ryder also makes, in less obvious fashion, an equally important distinction between *here* and *there*. In fact, for most of the novel he regards space as divisible into circumscribed and mutually exclusive areas. Characteristically, he regards himself as either an outsider trying to get in or a prisoner trying to get out, and in either case he attempts to solve his problem by imagining – quite properly for a painter – an enclosed, aesthetic space.

The Prologue establishes Ryder as fixed in the here and now. Five of the first nine paragraphs begin with 'Here', another establishes the space of the lunatic asylum in contrast to the army camp, and two others contain indications of time. The tenth begins 'So, on this morning of our move, I was entirely indifferent as to our destination'.[5] In short, except for the vague war from which Ryder feels himself and his men excluded, he perceives no 'there', and except for the increasingly demoralised four years of his army service and the three months of increasing depression at the camp in which he begins his narrative, he is unable to imagine or create for the reader a 'then' either in the sense of a hoped-for future or of a remembered past. Furthermore, the scene before him has been removed from normal time and space. The army camp is poised uneasily between its past as a farm and its aborted future as a housing development. The lunatic asylum, with 'cast-iron railings and noble gates', 'trim gravel walks and pleasantly planted lawns', is more solidly established in space, but its inhabitants are 'collaborationists who had given up the unequal struggle, all doubts resolved, all duty done, the undisputed heirs-at-law of a century of progress' (4/12) and have no securer hold on past or future than do the soldiers – or Captain Charles Ryder. He has not given up the struggle, but he lacks the means to pursue it effectively. Not until the end of the Prologue, when the landscape of the as yet unnamed Brideshead reminds him that there is another possible then and there, can Ryder fully understand that he has been enclosed in a kind of 'dungeon' (17/26) and step out of it into his memories.

In the body of the novel, however, Charles characteristically seeks not liberation but enclosure as an escape from the complexity of the outside world through what Ryder images as 'that low door in the wall . . . which opened on an enclosed and enchanted garden, which was somewhere, not overlooked by any window, in the heart of that grey city' (31/39–40) and almost 300 pages and sixteen years later as 'a world of its own of peace and love and beauty; a soldier's dream in a foreign bivouac' (321–2/353). Neither is simply the pastoral refuge referred to in the title of Book I, 'Et in Arcadia Ego'. Charles may regard it this way, but Ryder sees it in a different context.

In terms of the novel as a whole, Charles's refuge is not static and timeless but a place in which he can develop properly. Ryder describes his youthful self as stunted by

> a lonely childhood and a boyhood straitened by war and over-shadowed by bereavement; to the hard bachelordom of English adolescence, the premature dignity and authority of the school system, I had added a sad and grim strain of my own. Now . . . it seems as though I was being given a brief spell of what I had never known, a happy childhood. . . .   (45/54–5)

In other words, like Ryder in the novel as a whole, Charles has to regress in order to progress, to return to an earlier stage in order to grow. His mother has died in the war; his father is apparently indifferent and certainly eccentric; and before meeting Sebastian he has only the most conventional ties to his contemporaries. He seems destined for a university career of 'entertaining the college intellectuals to mulled claret' in an overheated room, 'my mind weary with metaphysics' (29/37).

To make reparations for vomiting into the window opened to clear Charles's room and his head, Sebastian invites Charles to luncheon on what is described as 'foreign ground' (31/39), a new and exotic setting with a very different cast of characters. This experience leads Ryder to refurnish his own room and life. He does not look beyond the present, and in Chapter Two the lectures about the conduct of his life given by his stuffy cousin Jasper and the exotic Anthony Blanche resemble each other in presenting a career for him to consider. Jasper's vision of a conventional Oxford career bores him; Blanche's offer to open to him the world of the Parisian homosexual avant-garde both frightens him and offers unanswerable criticism of the charming pastoral world in which Sebastian tends a teddy-bear instead of sheep.

Even that world seems closed to Charles during the ensuing vacation. In fact, he is most an outsider during his confinement to his father's London home, full of dead relics from the past, a sarcophagus which cannot nurture. London is all around him, but the house is the only scene of dramatised or even narrated action, and Charles can only long for the ease and freedom which he imagines Sebastian enjoying in the present at Brideshead and in prospect at Venice. Unlike Ryder in the Prologue, he can at least imagine somewhere else and resent the fact that he is excluded, but he cannot grow.

When he is called to Brideshead to attend Sebastian, the house and grounds become for him a kind of postnatal womb. His drawing the fountain not only converts him to the baroque aesthetic but, in a figure apparently drawn from embryology, enables him to feel 'a whole new system of nerves alive within me' (82/94). At this point, Charles can see only visual and therefore timeless and uncomplicated beauty, but though Sebastian can wish that it could 'be like this always – always summer, always alone, the fruit always ripe and Aloysius in a good temper. . . .' (79/91), the ellipsis at the end shows his awareness that this Arcadia cannot sustain even the presence of his family.

The trip to Venice which follows this idyll indicates that Lord

Marchmain, Sebastian's father, has managed to sustain the illusion that he can maintain a private, sensual-aesthetic world isolated from social, political, and domestic demands. In his substitute for Brideshead, a rented palazzo, 'designed for the comfort of only one person, and I am that one' (98/111), with his pleasant and compliant mistress, Cara, he seems impassive and impervious. In 'the immense splendours of the place', apparently so historical that it is suspended outside time, even Sebastian becomes restive enough to remark, 'It's rather sad to think that whatever happens you and I can never possibly get involved in a war' (101/114). Only Cara seems aware of process – the love of illusion and hatred of his wife which brought Lord Marchmain to this point; the immersion in childhood which will make Sebastian unhappy; the alcoholic tendency which the son has inherited.

Sobered by her analysis and the return to his father's house, Charles can never quite recapture the pastoral gaiety of the previous months. Autumnal Oxford, no longer enchanted, shrinks to Charles's and Sebastian's rooms and a few 'Hogarthian little inns' (108/122) on side streets. Anthony Blanche may not have existed inside Charles's enchanted garden, but in leaving 'he had locked a door' (107/121), and Charles and the rest of his circle are denied even the possibility of entering the world he represented. During this period, instead of making the rapturous trip to Brideshead, culminating in a visit to the cosy nursery, Charles and Sebastian go into London society, high and low, and wind up in jail cells which excite Sebastian's claustrophobia. Back in Oxford, they are gated for the rest of the term.

When Charles does return to Brideshead, human complication outweighs aesthetic harmony. Brideshead can still nurture Charles's imagination, but none of the Flytes seem able to appreciate the beauty of the castle and grounds as a whole. On Charles's first visit, organised by Sebastian to escape the women who have invaded Oxford, Sebastian ignores the shrouded splendors of the public rooms to return to the nursery and to the love of his nanny. Later Sebastian calls 'cosy' the Painted Parlour, in which all elements become 'a single composition, the design of one illustrious hand' (77/89). Lady Marchmain has remodelled her sitting room to embody 'the intimate feminine, modern world' in opposition to 'the august, masculine atmosphere' of the rest of the house (138/154). Cordelia thinks the appalling Art Nouveau chapel beautiful. Lord Brideshead can pose aesthetic questions without any hope of understanding beauty. And near the end of the novel, Lord Marchmain, absent for twenty-five years, confines himself to the Chinese drawing-room as the setting for his death-bed.

Because Charles is an outsider, he can see more clearly than the members of the Flyte family both the aesthetic harmony of the house and the discord among its inhabitants. The family is hardly composed of the 'ravening beasts' (79/91) of Sebastian's melodramatic imagination, but instead of real contact with each other they seem to come together in a series of tableaux which represent, not embody, family life. Charles, as Sebastian's friend, is increasingly confined to particular rooms, so that he loses the sense of the house as an aesthetic whole and imaginative refuge. Sebastian is never really part of the family, and as he lapses into alcoholic distrust, he finds Charles 'No help' (168/189). When Lady Marchmain tries to bring Charles into the circle to link Sebastian to her, he resists her so strongly that he gives Sebastian money for drink and is expelled by his bewildered mother.

Leaving Brideshead, he thinks forever, he imagines that he 'was leaving part of myself behind', a part like 'material treasures' which ghosts must find to 'pay their way into the nether world'. This image introduces, almost casually, the major theme of the division of self and the consequences of that division and links that theme with the search for a *there* in which reintegration can take place. At this point, however, the low door of the earlier image is shut: 'open it now and I should find no enchanted garden'. Instead of what he thinks illusion, he promises himself that he will live 'in a world of three dimensions – with the aid of my five senses' (169/190, 191).

He is able to do so because, in temporal and spatial terms, he has been able to imagine both a future beyond an Oxford and Brideshead which had seemed timeless and a different imaginative space: Paris and a career as an artist, though in very different sexual and stylistic terms than Anthony Blanche had offered. However, though his concepts of there and then are expanded, his sojourn in Paris serves, in contrast to the General Strike, to reveal him as outside the life of his country.

The dimensions of public time and space are represented by Rex Mottram, the Canadian *arriviste* who bursts into the Flytes' world and carries Julia away from her family and her religion. Rex seems to have no past, does not in fact recognise that personal or social past has any meaning, and the space which he inhabits is defined by newspaper publicity and networks of financial, political, and sexual power. In Julia's terms, and those of the novel, Rex is 'something absolutely modern and up-to-date that only this ghastly age could produce. A tiny bit of a man pretending he was the whole' (200/223).

Sebastian seems to be crippled in another way. Estranged from his family and even from his raffish friends by his alcoholism, Sebastian drifts into North Africa and into the company of a cashiered Legionaire, unsuitable by any definition. In fact, Sebastian has recreated in Fez something like the atmosphere of Oxford or Brideshead

> in the walled city, whose streets were gentle, dusty stairways, and whose walls rose windowless on either side, closed over-head, then opened again to the stars; where the dust lay thick among the smooth paving stones and figures passed silently, robed in white, on soft slippers or hard, bare soles; where the air was scented with cloves and incense and wood smoke. . . .
>
> (211/234)

Perhaps because Charles has been replaced by Kurt, he sees only the disparity between the beauty of the setting and the scruffiness of its inhabitants and ignores what Ryder calls 'the key I lacked': Sebastian's need to care for someone else rather than simply be beautiful and charming and eccentric (215/239), and to continue doing so as a difficult vocation rather than to immure himself in static, pastoral space. And in conventional terms, Sebastian has removed himself from the family and from the kind of history represented by the General Strike which precedes this episode.

Charles, full of his newly discovered powers as an artist, is at this point able to ignore the worlds of power and of love. His painting of the Flytes' London house, soon to be destroyed, is at first so absorbing that he loses track of time, and his art helps him to fix in paint a world that has no future in a carefully circum-scribed and manageable space. In fact, his art draws upon but does not fully recognise a conception of the past which is as much emotional as historical and which, cut off from the past, cannot sustain him.

The novel's final movement opens with the realisation that the 'hours of afflatus in the human spirit, the springs of art' are linked to memory, which is life, 'for we possess nothing certainly except the past' (225/251). Ten years into his career as an architectural painter, he has lost 'the intensity and singleness and the belief that it was not all done by hand – in a word, the inspiration' (227/252). Characteristically, disillusioned by where he is, emotionally as well as physically, he seeks another *there*, Central America and Mexico, which 'should have quickened me and set me right with myself' (228/253). But the private space of art is no refuge. His wife recognises that he is unchanged emotionally; Anthony Blanche returns to point out that he is unchanged aesthetically; he admits that 'despite this isolation and this long sojourn in a new world, I remained unchanged, still a small part of myself pretending to be whole' (228–9/254).

In fact, when he returns to civilisation, there is no place for him. His New York hotel room is alternately stuffy and noisy; his cabin on the liner is crammed first with 'a litter of cellophane and silk ribbons' (236/262) and then with boring guests at a pointless cocktail party; surveying the halls and public rooms of the ship he repeats, as he had in the Prologue, 'Here' to emphasise his physical and imaginative confinement (237/263).

The discovery that Julia is a fellow passenger frees Charles's imagination much as Sebastian's incursion had freed it at Oxford – Charles explicitly identifies him as Julia's 'forerunner' (257/284) – and the view of Brideshead had freed it in the Prologue. A storm drives the other passengers to their cabins and provides space in which Charles is 'made free of her narrow loins' (261) – or, in the even stronger spatial implications of the 1960 edition, 'It was as though a deed of conveyance of her narrow loins had been drawn and sealed. I was making my first entry as the freeholder of a property I would enjoy and develop at leisure' (288).

But the storm's end closes their private world and returns Charles to Celia's world of 'Art and Fashion' (276/304), 'a day of nightmare – crowds, critics, the Clarences, a luncheon party at Margot's, ending up with half an hour's well-reasoned abuse of my pictures in a pansy bar . . .' (273/301–2). In fact, Charles almost welcomes Anthony Blanche's condemnation not only of his current paintings but of his whole artistic career, though he finds it easy to reject the sleazy refuge which is the logical result of the way of life Blanche offered him more than a decade earlier at Oxford. And with the opening concluded, Ryder is free to leave London and his wife to travel to Brideshead in Julia's company.

This time the house is full of a fair approximation of 'ravening beasts', Rex Mottram and his political and financial cronies. However, though they are in the house, they do not possess it, and on two occasions Julia and Charles are able to escape their antiphonal chatter, the second time into a night and scene invested with the glamour of myth. The space and time of the lovers, the passage seems to imply too insistently, can hold itself apart from the world of King Edward's abdication and of Hitler's threat to peace. Or, as Julia puts it, 'Rex isn't anybody at all . . . he just doesn't exist' (274/302).

The lovers can count the days when they have been apart, and Charles envisions a lifetime of days together spent in the peace which the landscape seems to promise:

> all the opposing slope was already in twilight, but the lakes below us were aflame; the light grew in strength and splendour as it neared death, spreading long shadows across the pasture, falling full on the rich stone spaces of the house, firing the panes in the windows, glowing on cornices and colonnade and dome, drawing out all the hidden sweetness of colour and scent from earth and stone and leaf, glorifying the head and golden shoulders of the woman beside me. (279/307–8)

This is a painter's view – he has in fact been doing a portrait of Julia – and the peace is static. Julia, raised in a sterner theology, means 'much more' by peace and feels 'the past and the future pressing so hard on either side that there's no room for the present at all' (279/308). Given this attitude towards time, it is hardly surprising that she reacts to the theological implications of her older brother's remark about her living in sin with an almost hysterical monologue which culminates in the vision of a wasteland outside the barred gates of heaven.

Julia seems to recover from her passion of remorse, and the lovers proceed with the divorces which will allow them to put 'life in some sort of order in a human way, before all human order comes to an end' (291/320).

The lovers' purpose is made to seem all the stronger in contrast to the report of Sebastian's fate from Cordelia, the youngest, more sensible, and most charitable member of the Flyte family. Having lost Kurt to the Nazis, Sebastian abandons Europe and returns to North Africa with the vague idea of 'escaping to the savages' (307/338) as a missionary, admitting that he needs a missionary for himself. Cordelia envisions his future as a kind of underporter attached to a monastery, alternatively drunk and pious, the suffering from the alcoholism leading, through grace, to holiness. Since Charles cannot understand this process, which Cordelia sees as universal rather than as particular to Sebastian, she sketches a consolation suitable for a painter, describing 'a beautiful place . . . by the sea – white cloisters, a bell tower, rows of green vegetables, and a monk watering them when the sun is low' (309/340).

However, even Charles has begun to feel the pressures of history and eschatology. Thinking of Sebastian as the forerunner to Julia, he reflects that 'perhaps all our loves are merely hints and symbols' and envisions life as passage through many doors and corridors in pursuit of 'the shadow which turns the corner always a pace or two ahead of us' (303/333). Earlier (226/not in 1960), shadows had been seen as counterfeit selves, to be escaped. Here they hint at a unified self toward which the 'tiny bit of a man pretending he was the whole' is destined to strive. Later, as he reflects upon Cordelia's narrative and upon what, in contrast to her beautiful sister, she represents, he formulates the image of a mountain cabin, 'everything dry and neat and warm inside', in the path of accumulating weight and the inevitable avalanche which will destroy 'the little lighted place' (310, 311/341). The setting and the solitude of the inhabitant represent a shift in Charles's vision from that of 'the joyful youth with the Teddy-bear under the flowering chestnuts' (309/340). The languor and opulence of idyllic love in high summer which characterised Arcadian Oxford and Brideshead have given way to a winter dream of limited and tightly enclosed comfort which cannot survive sun and thaw.

Charles is able to postpone full realisation of the consequences of his new vision because Lord Marchmain returns to Brideshead to try to embody in static, aesthetic terms the dream of timeless earthly bliss which the two men share. In fact, Lord Marchmain is confined, physically and imaginatively, to a single room, but he arranges it as he would a stage set or a tableau for a painting. He is quite conscious of doing so, saying to Charles when the last detail is settled, 'You might paint it . . . and call it "The Death Bed"' (318/349).

As a young man, Charles had been drawn to Lord Marchmain's Byronic panache, finding his leisurely and carefully-ordered enjoyment of sensual pleasure more attractive than his own father's reclusive antiquarianism. Now he is given the prospect of becoming not only his son-in-law but his successor at Brideshead when

Lord Marchmain decides to leave the estate not to his crabbed and scrupulous elder son, Lord Brideshead, but to Julia because she is 'so beautiful always; much, much more suitable' (321/353) and because she seems likely to live by her father's worldly values. The inheritance, Charles thinks,

> opened a prospect; the prospect one gained at the turn of the avenue, as I had first seen it with Sebastian, of the secluded valley, the lakes falling away one below the other, the old house in the foreground, the rest of the world abandoned and forgotten; a world of its own of peace and love and beauty; a soldier's dream in a foreign bivouac; such a prospect perhaps as a high pinnacle of the temple afforded after the hungry days in the desert and the jackal-haunted nights. Need I reproach myself if sometimes I was rapt in the vision? (321–2/353–4)

In purely human terms, the answer is a qualified 'No'. In religious terms, of course, Charles desires the things of the world rather than of eternity – though it might be argued that he rejects religion more because it threatens to destroy his cosmology than because it bars his possession of Julia and Brideshead.

House and woman embody Charles's last and strongest temptation because he is no longer able to imagine a *there* as refuge or alternative to his *here*. Central America has been unavailing; Europe is threatened by a war which, at the point of Ryder's narration, has ended the humanist dream which had sustained Charles at the beginning of his career; he is cut off from Sebastian and from his past. But he somehow feels that Lord Marchmain's resistance will give him not only literal but imaginative space.

That conception of space cannot sustain Lord Marchmain. In his rambling meditation on his family's past and his own present, he is driven to conceive himself imprisoned in the cellars and imagines blasting his way to freedom. At the crisis, when he is unconscious and confined to his deathbed, he cannot escape. As the priest approaches the dying man to absolve him of his sins, individualising names and details of the setting are omitted to emphasise 'the drama [that] was being played again by two men – by one man, rather, and he nearer death than life; the universal drama in which there is only one actor' (338/not in the 1960 edition). After Lord Marchmain – the proper name returns – makes the sign of the cross, Charles realises, alluding to 'the veil of the temple being rent

rom top to bottom' (339/371), that his whole imaginative world has
)een destroyed, that he will not marry Julia, and that he will never
nherit nor inhabit Brideshead.

In the Epilogue, the house and grounds have been despoiled
ınd even Charles's paintings on the panels of the garden room, his
modest contribution to the fabric of the whole, have been obliter-
ıted. However, Ryder is undismayed, in fact 'unusually cheerful'
'351/381), because the climax of Lord Marchmain's submission has
ɔnabled him to move beyond static, aesthetic considerations of a
ɔlace as refuge to a conception of process in which, under the
ıspect of eternity, value is preserved even though things and
ɔlaces are destroyed.

As a painter, Charles had 'loved buildings that grew silently
with the centuries, catching and keeping the best of each generation, while time curbed the artist's pride and the Philistine's
vulgarity, and repaired the clumsiness of the dull workman'
(226/251). As narrator, Ryder looks beyond place and time to
discover 'Something quite remote from anything the builders intended' in the flame of the appallingly-designed sanctuary lamp
which 'could not have been lit but for the builders and the tra-
gedians' (351/381). Since he had learned to see all places and all
actions in light of a larger purpose, Ryder can give up the idea of
an earthly *there* to which he can escape from *here*, can see what
seems to be past loss in light of hope, and can fit together the tiny
bits – artist, lover, soldier – into a whole, Captain Charles Ryder,
which comes together only as the novel ends.

NOTES

1. For a discussion of the manuscript and later versions of *Brideshead
   Revisited* and other Waugh novels, see my *Evelyn Waugh, Writer* (Norman: Pilgrim Books, 1981).
2. Jeffrey Heath, '*Brideshead*: The Critics and the Memorandum', *English
   Studies*, 56 (June 1975), 222.
3. Jeffrey Heath notes the general pattern in Waugh's fiction of the
   conflict between his secular imagination, which constructed 'lush
   places', and his religious impulse, which regarded mere secular freedom as a spiritual dungeon. His book, *The Picturesque Prison: Evelyn
   Waugh and His Writing* (Kingston and Montreal : McGill-Queen's University Press, 1982), also has an extended and provocative analysis of
   Brideshead Revisited. Heath sees a greater split between character and

narrator and between sacred and profane than my reading admits. William J. Cook, Jr., *Masks, Modes, and Morals: The Art of Evelyn Waugh* (Rutherford: Fairleigh Dickinson University Press, 1971). Cook makes, in Chapter Five, the interesting distinction not merely between Ryder as character, the 'then I', and as narrator, the 'now I', but between the narrator and the 'intermediate I' who functions in the body of the novel and whose reliability falls somewhere between the jejune Charles and the mature narrator. Cook's theory helps to explain Ryder's obvious limitations in the Prologue, and his discussion of levels of knowledge and reliability in the rest of the novel is valuable.

4. The best discussion of the theological implications of conversion for the novel is Thomas Prufer's 'The Death of Charm and the Advent of Grace: Waugh's *Brideshead Revisited'*, *Communio*, 10 (Fall 1983), 281–90.

5. *Brideshead Revisited* (Boston: Little, Brown, 1945), p. 6. I cite (parenthetically hereafter) first this edition because it is the closest now in print to Waugh's intention at the time of composition and second, should the passage survive Waugh's revisions, the Chapman and Hall edition of 1960. The passage quoted is from p. 14, 1960.

3

Arcadian Minutiae: Notes on *Brideshead Revisited*

Jean Louis Chevalier

Those golden times And those Arcadian scenes that Maro sings,
And Sidney, warbler of poetic prose . . .

William Cowper

'*Et in Arcadia ego*' is the motto engraved on the skull Charles Ryder
has in his room at Oxford in 1923, at the end of his first year. The
skull is part of 'All *this*' (B1.II,52),[1] a phrase of Jasper's during this
'last visit and Grand Remonstrance' (B1.II.50), that exposes his
younger cousin's life-style, the men he associates with, the line of
conduct he pursues, the luxury articles he collects. No matter how
honestly Charles is now endeavouring to give a fair account of the
scene, as also of his whole life, his recent renouncement of a world
of pomp and vanity, previous to the collapse of the war, cannot
inspire in him a dumb feeling of condonation of Jasper's irksome
ways. They still sound offensive and silly for all their bearing the
hall-mark of sanity. A few digs at the impromptu mentor cannot be
repressed, gravity is touched up with irony, and a mixed effect of
pathos and dry sarcasm is achieved in the record. It is Charles's
natural disposition and style to turn over a new leaf upon an
old one.

So it is more than suggested in Charles's narrative, by way of
introduction, that Jasper might not have been so vehement, censorious and 'resentful' had he not just 'failed to do himself justice
on the subject of Pindar's Orphism' (B1.II.50). This doctrine, its
challenge of the political, social and religious order of Ancient
Greece and its advocacy of rather a shamanistic marginality, are
immediately felt to be far too subtle for such a smug moron as
Jasper, especially if expressed in Pindar's fine lyrical visionary

poems. Furthermore, to grace Jasper's sententious dressing-down with the name of 'Grand Remonstrance' adds up to deliberately and disproportionately ridiculing him, for he is not much of a Pym. Yet he is shown to direct his reproofs with something of Pym's belief that he was exhibiting the common sense of the common man when inciting the Commons to give fair and foul warning to the King. Now, the King's extra fault was leniency to the Papists: when calling on Charles 'formally during [Charles's] first week' (B1.I.34) at Oxford, Jasper had already remarked:

> Beware of the Anglo-Catholics – they're all sodomites with unpleasant accents. In fact, steer clear of all religious groups; they do nothing but harm (B.1.I.35)

– and when discussing 'the matter' of his 'faith' or 'foible' and speaking seriously of his people being 'a mixed family religiously' (B1.IV.102), Sebastian will eventually remark:

> It's not just that [Catholics] are a clique – as a matter of fact, they're four cliques all blackguarding each other half the time – but they've got an entirely different outlook on life; everything they think important, is different from other people (B1.IV.102).

> Oh dear, it's very difficult being a Catholic (B1.IV.98).

> I wish I liked Catholics more (B1.IV.102).

The King, in addition, happened to be called Charles. Not to mention Ryder meaning Cavalier. Something like persecution is in the air on the occasion of Jasper's 'Grand Remonstrance' against the flighty charms of à la Flyte elegance and breeding which no Roundhead can ever even begin to understand. The mockery is twofold. With the obvious intent of making fun of his blockhead of a cousin, Charles, as a narrator, misappropriates and perverts the appellation of a historical event whose importance defies fun-making, and, in so doing, he – undesignedly? – crowns himself as an actor in his own tale – a freshman, a heathen, a sufferer from uninvited cousinship, but not an Arcadian in the tainted meaning of the word – with the undeserved halo of the one English king who died on the block.

From obloquy to obliquity, which deriding Ryder is the least *Easy* of them all? Not-so-young Jasper, who never was anything but oldish and pretended it hurt him as much as it hurt Charles to give him a verbal thrashing? Still-very-young Charles, whose studied and very new routine hardly allowed of its being disturbed by such obtuse expostulations? Life-beaten Charles, in this his first and last analytical narrative, when he actually scourges himself with the past, considering and telling all that was or was not said and done?

> *Que de fois seul, dans l'ombre, à minuit demeuré,*
> *J'ai souri de l'entendre, et bien souvent pleuré . . .*[2]

It is a far cry from remembering many a time and oft to recording in writing for the first and only time. Perhaps no maiden voyage can ever be recounted without the defensive protection of patronising, for fear of succumbing to mawkishness or vainglory –

> It is easy, retrospectively, to endow one's youth with a false precocity or a false innocence (B1.I.35)

– or, worse, to the severity and repudiation typical of the new convert –

> *Je vois, je sais, je crois, je suis désabusée . . .*[3]

No *ton juste* in such matters may be found waiting *in medias res* – nor indeed *sub rosa*, as demonstrated in the text – between now and once upon a time, as no such equipoise, equanimity and equidistance are attainable or indeed available. Revisiting is visiting again, not afresh. It is not an *encore*. It takes place in altogether different circumstances whose configuration it has here been the aim of the Prologue to display, and above all it takes place in a different turn of mind:

> could I have known then that I would one day be remembered with tears by a middle-aged captain of infantry? (B1.I.49)

The tears are there all right, but they only relate Charles with himself, they do not tell his tale. Although it is rather a case of the irruption of more than nostalgic sorrow –

> *Les souvenirs sont cors de chasse*[4]

– than of an addiction to visionary delectations –

J'aime le son du cor, le soir, au fond des bois[5]

– autobiographical writing spells fiction nonetheless, memoirs remain a process of re-creation, and memories work as intimations of life-as-mortal-change. For all 'those languid days at Brideshead' (B1.IV.91) and the 'gilly flowers growing below the windows which on summer days filled [Charles's room at Oxford] with fragrance' (B1.I.35), Arcadia was actually experienced and is being proffered in writing as something more than a dream or a post-adolescent fixture of youngmanhood.

Although defined peritextually as 'a souvenir of the Second War rather than of the 'twenties or of the 'thirties, with which [this novel] ostensibly deals' (Preface.10) – that is to say, as an intimate refabrication from a store of unforgettable, exquisite memories that are better left alone in the common run of existence, and even more so in wartime – Arcadia, in respect of both the spirit of the place and the tempo of the adventures, used to be the actual image and ideal reality of Wonderland –

> I was in search of love in those days, and I went full of curiosity and of the faint, unrecognised apprehension that here, at last, I should find that low door in the wall, which others, I knew, had found before me, which opened on an enclosed and enchanted garden, which was somewhere, not overlooked by any window, in the heart of that grey city (B1.I.39–40).

But the Wonderland is now paradoxically meant by narrator and novelist alike to be the mystical *terra incognita* both in *The Sacred and Profane Memories* and in 'a novel which [. . .] aims at verisimilitude' (Preface.10).

Under the auspices of verisimilitude, Charles's Arcadia does not evolve exclusively from the simplicity which, after his fall from false felicity (lived as true) into the dire perception of moral values, his memory is now capable of recapturing and accounting for as the urge to cast a slough of moroseness and misery. Instinctive in the act and studied consciously if not conscientiously in post-Arcadian days, this divestment in search of happiness did not aim at and does not achieve self-revelation in any form of pastoral academy figure or academising posture – 'lying on the roof, sunbathing' (B1.IV.100), with 'no clothes on' (B1.IV.102), is more of a factual, anecdotal snapshot than a symbolical image of mysticism and/or eroticism – but it was meant to partake of, and it now tends to revive and explain, 'a sense of liberation and peace' (B1.III.90), 'beauty [. . .] new found' (B1.IV.93), 'tranquil time' (B1.V.143) and 'the languor of Youth' (B1.IV.91).

In other words, it purports to achieve and enjoy, and call forth, the miracle of completude, the unimaginable and yet enviable reunion of the one sorry half of one's everyday self to the other unrealised half of one's entire being – recognised as the soul after other forms of restitution – a half which one gradually becomes aware of having been originally separated and estranged from, but which suddenly and hopefully grows discernible in the distance, approachable, seizable, proximate, and present. For all the sophisticated expressions of its quest and recovery, this is a simple desire, but one whose primary force would not suffice alone to sustain the verisimilitude of Charles's narrative: for Arcadia is also to be found in a species of humour, touched with sardonic fulgurations, which innervates the tale and flashes whenever it would incline towards the precipice of self-pity. Granted that Charles's general revisitation of his past is made up of a series of memories of visits and meetings, period-pieces which to him were epoch-making, the truth or, in lieu of an impossible *ton juste*, the *ton sonnant juste* of his ruminations, is sustained by a continuous alternation of pleasant or not so pleasant or quite unpleasant happenings of the visiting and meeting kind –

It was to that first visit that my heart returned on this, my latest (B1.I.29).

I date my Oxford life from my first meeting with Sebastian (B1.I.32).

[Thinking] me a suitable subject for detailed guidance, [. . .] [Jasper] called on me formally during my first week, [. . .] then he [. . .] laid down the rules of conduct which I should follow (B1.I.33–4).

I knew Sebastian by sight long before I met him (B1.I.37).

Nor, when at last we met, were the circumstances propitious (B1.I.37)

'We should not dream of being so offensive as to suggest that you never met us before.' (B.1.I.41)

Now meeting [Anthony Blanche], under the spell of Sebastian, I found myself enjoying him voraciously (B1.I.41).

'You won't have to meet them.' (B1.I.43)

'I want you to meet Nanny Hawkins. That's what we've come for.' (B1.I.44)

In the roll-call of such callings, Jasper's police raid strikes the rather robust, rugged note of a man not amused, liking to act '"like an uncle"' (B1.II.50) and speaking out with 'game-cock maturity' (B1.II.55) in the surprising hope of being heeded by a greenhorn he does not 'want to sit back and see [. . . .] making mistakes which a word in season might save [him] from' (B1.I.51). 'Looking back, now, after twenty years, there is little I would have left undone or done otherwise', Charles observes in an explanatory mood, specifying: 'I could tell him . . . I could tell him too . . .' (now) – but never telling his cousin visitor (then) what he had set his heart on, only resorting to 'what was not in fact the truth', keeping his 'secret and sure defence', feeling 'no need for these sophistries' (B1.I.55).

Sophistries imply subtle, equivocal, dubious reasoning, where to confuse is to confute. Charles's refusal to put them to such use amounts to declining battle with an irate censor of the counsels of Arcadia, whose readymade disparagements preclude intelligent conversation through clever casuistry. When he voices them at last in his narrative, they are not gambits any longer but statements of extinct truths.

In the meantime, impervious to the nicety of mutism, Jasper gives full vent to his distaste and scorn of the skull by dubbing it '_that_ peculiarly noisome object', whereupon Charles, now a diligent narrator if an apparently idle aesthete in those days, includes in his retrospective report a flat, or seemingly flat, and parenthetic description of the _corpus delicti_ –

(a human skull lately purchased from the School of Medicine, which, resting in a bowl of roses, formed, at the moment, the chief decoration of my table. It bore the motto '*Et in Arcadia ego'* inscribed on its forehead.) (B1.II.52)

As 'chief decoration', such a centrepiece serves an articulate purpose. Upon Charles's room as a place of graceful living it bestows the supreme accomplishment of

> *Là tout n'est qu'ordre et beauté,*
> *Luxe, calme et volupté*[6]

– and in so doing it creates the illusion of a second halo around Charles himself as an actual votary of the same programme. The emblematic significance of his ornamental arrangement is derived jointly and severally from the evocative power of its components, the skull, the roses and the motto. In the first place, a skull is not *a thing of beauty* but a dire reminder of mortality, loveliness passed once and for all *into nothingness, a memento mori* used alongside a crucifix to furnish a monastic cell. However, Charles's room is no cell and his present self has no use for a crucifix. Nevertheless, if the style of the symbol is altered, its meaning does not wilt: it is conjured up by the semi-pagan, semi-Marian associations of the roses. These are undeniably beautiful and offer a paradigm of transience whose relevance is drawn from their own quintessentially frail loveliness –

> *Et rose elle a vécu ce que vivent les roses,*
> *L'espace d'un matin.*[7]

For Charles, to rest a skull in a bowl of roses is to evince an exquisite sense of the ephemereality of human existence and to display poetic intelligence of mystical imagery, since roses are not merely emblems of youth and beauty, they are also procession and altar flowers. The bowl in which the skull is set to rest amounts to an altar of repose, which lends the skull a quasi-sacramental value.

To read this baroque lesson in the skull-cum-roses assemblage, no text is necessary. Yet there is one, whose aim is to make it even more conspicuous. In lieu of the Christian hope of a heaven still to be gained, its reference to Arcadia calls to mind pagan nostalgia for a bygone haven of peace, love and art, adding up to an assertion of happiness. That particular species of Arcadian happiness is not to be viewed as the exciting and consoling promise of divine bounty. It is not a recompense for the actual experience of misery, but an invitation to the instant enjoyment of delights destined to obliteration when the future is perfected. The present moment is one's only chance, not to work one's own salvation but to gratify enough of one's desire to ward off regrets through satiation –

> *Vivez, si m'en croyez, n'attendez à demain.*
> *Cueillez dès aujourd'hui les roses de la vie.*[8]

A rose is a rose is a rose . . . and more than a rose. Bliss is in the time before the rose is *sick*. Death does not spare Arcadia, it defines it – see Poussin. Life is to be lived here and now, before dusk, before dust.

This is not much of a discovery but in the circumstances Charles's text says more. Hackneyed as they may seem to the worldly-wise, such pieces of age-old wisdom are found afresh by each generation of life-experimenters, like Charles in his halcyon days. '*Et in Arcadia ego*' is his treasure-trove at the time of his first manhood and remains rather ambiguously the cherished emblematic sentence he selects to cap the corresponding section of his reflective narrative. His belated renunciation of Arcadian ethics and aesthetics does not abolish 'after twenty years' (B1.II.55) his sense of elation on first embracing them, which makes for the evocative intensity of memories in whose resurgence self-distancing is not meant to sever or to alienate but to restore a sense of continuity. The self-made Arcadian novice is *father to* the life-made Christian convert. Charles's *portrait of the artist as a young dandy* is neither without pose nor without banter, but it is not devoid of affectivity. The doggie in him, that conceited puppy learning so friskily how to run with the hounds and nobs, does not obliterate the motherless dogie, a more vulnerable probationer than he cares to remember and explain at length.

This is perhaps especially perceptible in non-committal comments where jeering sparkles as a matter of course, a matter of discourse, not as an admission of self-pity or self-love. Such a one is:

> 'Yes,' I said, glad to be clear of the charge. 'I had to pay cash for the skull.' (B1.II.52)

The direct implication in this rejoinder is that the other obvious but parenthetically detailed pieces of 'evidence of profligacy' in his room –

> '*that* [. . .]?' (the box of a hundred cabinet Partagas on the sideboard) 'or *those*?' (a dozen frivolous, new books on the table) 'or *those*?' (a Lalique decanter and glasses) (B1.II.52)

– have not been paid for, cash or otherwise. Yet they are far more honest possessions. For all their being *de luxe* amenities for the Epicure, they are straight, usual and used in a normal way – for smoking, reading and drinking – respectable, commendable, manly occupations most of them, Bracknellwise. Were it not for the skull, Jasper could hardly vilify them at one fell swoop. Only '*that*' skull spells misuse. It has been misappropriated and is now diverted from its other than devotional accepted purpose. The School of Medicine, a scientific institution, not a firm of Beaveresque decorators, will provide skulls for the anatomical study of man, not for the inscription of professions of faith, the supine comforts of beds of roses and the unholy delectations of young gentlemen. This is why skulls must be paid for in ready money. They are meant for serious entreprise, not self-indulgence, that crime of the voluptuary.

Not a major crime, taking it by and large, but a distinctly offensive and/or ludicrously naive misdemeanour, capable of crosscurrents of interpretation. First and foremost, in spite of its *Nevermore* implications, or because of them, a skull cannot be obtained on the never-never: consequently, it clears its owner of the charge of debt on its very own head. Charles's relief at not being at fault precisely and only about that most questionable of his many curios, is childish and droll. The comedy lies in the narrative conveying offhandedly that under the attitudinizer there is still a green youngster to be found skulking, all too eager to exonerate himself from the more venial aspect of his dissipation. Furthermore, not to mention the error in taste which Jasper as the representative of standard values finds so repellent, his introducing the theme of (non)settlement of accounts as the crowning disgrace of a skull foreshadows with dramatic fun the two rules which will prove to apply to the profane doings and sacred undoing of Charles's life, and to act as the base of his memories. They sound like wisecracks – crime does not pay – crime must be paid for – but are laws that reign supreme in the course of existence, *in articulo mortis,* and on the Day of Judgment. For the time being, the skull-in-a-bowl-of-roses Arcadian *mise en scène* is only a solecism, but one that is liable to moulder. *There is a canker in the rose.* Charles the neophyte cannot see it, if only because the finger of scorn pointing at this admirable creation of his is Jasper's. But age, somehow or other, has jasperised reminiscing Charles, who catches himself using its impurity as a patch or, better still, a beauty spot, enhancing all that can and does remain pure in his memories.

Not that he led an exactly pure life – he never claims his new ways and new friends were what is called pure, and there is a good deal of criticism implied or apparent in what he tells and how he tells it – but there is still a sense in which Arcadia was pure: he is not searching after what he did but what he felt; he is not trying to apologise for what he cultivated but to report what happened to him. It may well have been trite as a studied affectation, but it was sincere, and so is its present unaffected and affecting study. If self-pity were the pass-word between 'I was in search of love in those days' (B1.I.39) and '"I don't want to make it easier for you [. . .]. I hope your heart may break; but I do understand"' (B3.V.373), the whole proposition of recollection would be noisome and obnoxious. But these and many more remarks are rather agonising admissions of solitude.

> *Soyez la bienvenue, Solitude, ma mère . . .*
> *Solitude, ma mère, redites-moi ma vie*[9]

are words Charles might now accept as his own, but could not have considered when Arcadia showed its first signs of promise.

Arcadia is a fine counter-symbol of solitude, a utopian antidote which would sublimate solitude by calling for friendship and recognition, fellow beings and fellow feelings seeming as vital in life as from beyond the grave. As it is, a professed Arcadian, yearning for the freedom of the 'enclosed and enchanted garden' at the age of taking flight, ranks himself amongst the awkward squad that cannot cope with the demands of life, not in the heavenly host of the privileged few, but on the pitiable list of bruised escapists, life's casualties. Had it been only the double decor of Oxford and Brideshead, Arcadia would indeed be a side issue, a blind alley. But Arcadia is also love, and its presumedly profane actors, Sebastian first and foremost, and later Julia –

> *Ambo florentes aetatibus, Arcades ambo,*
> *Et cantare pares, et respondere parati*[10]

– are the forerunners of the sacred storm. The enchantment may have been a mirage, a harmonious mirage of lovable places and adorable people, but Charles cannot be denied the right to look upon and into his past and, even on realising that it was a mirage, to remember how it used to be his first semblance of an ideal reality, from whose account his memories are now trying to bring out a second, more meaningful reality, upon which to build, when all is said is done, an infinite reality, the truth which, after his tale is told, he calls 'a small red flame' (Epilogue.381). Only then can he speak of 'the fierce little human tragedy in which I played a role' and of 'something none of us thought about at the time' (Epilogue.380–1). But at the beginning of his Flyte days he is still innocent of knowledge; when the tragedy starts, he can still believe it to be a fairy play in whose performance he may exchange solitude for election. Illusion is at the core, but the mirage is sincere –

> *Et tout le grand ciel bleu n'emplirait pas mon coeur.*[11]

Conversely, what Charles, by dint of hard reflexive work and self-examination, realises in the forties is that neither in the twenties nor in the thirties was he ever a real Arcadian. A *fides Achates* and a Peeping Tom by turns, his fate was not to belong, but to wish to belong, and to belong askew.

> *Quomodo sedet sola civitas.* Vanity of Vanities. All is vanity. And yet that is not the last word (Epilogue.380)

– he asserts at the end of his narrative, when it is into another Garden that, repenting, he would beg for admission. Because it was an epitaph, '*Et in Arcadia ego*' were his first words and he chose them for a prospective motto. Because it is an epitaph, '*Et in Arcadia ego*' are not his last words and he chooses them for a retrospective cartouche. To '*put off the old man*', to '*put on the new man*', to '*lie not one to another*',[12] he must, if only to discard it, reinarcadianise *the multitudinous seas* of solitude of his youth and, to disenchant it, disclose it in the narration. He is not a renegade Narcissus, he is not an indulgent charlatan, he is not an exhibitionist flaunting his emotions, but he had not become impervious to *those golden times and those Arcadian scenes* that were his Waste Land: for the wilderness to be tangible, its marvellous temptations must be revived as they are revisited. Arcadia is intact but not quite equal to itself in memories and narrative, because one thing, one soul, has moved on – one ego.

Charles's ego is a central character in his Arcadian days, and a major *dramatis persona* in his post-Arcadian memories, whose place in either cast it is not easy to assess. Charles never was a candidate for the part of hero or juvenile lead, but he did not confine himself to the office of confidant and/or understudy which he was sometimes commissioned to hold in a certain way and whose duties he carried out otherwise. His was a half instinctive, half purposive part, now supporting, now sidestepping, instinct and purpose alternately directing him. In spite of his insistence on being now almost an old fogey – so emphatic an insistence that it has been taxed with posturing by those deaf to the accents of distress – 'now in my sere and lawless state' (Prologue.17), 'homeless, childless, middle-aged, loveless' (Epilogue.380), 'always awake and fretful an hour before reveille' (Prologue.13), 'aghast to realise that something within me, long sickening, had quietly died' (Prologue.14) – and also of his disowning of the young man he used to be, Charles, as a narrator, does not turn traitor to his ego that was. When sketching out a self-portrait 'at the age when my eyes were dry to all save poetry', to explain how and why 'Hooper was no romantic', he conjures up 'across the intervening years' (Prologue.17) the unquiet image of a torn personality admitting of several interpretations –

> *Vêtu de probité candide et de lin blanc*[13]

> *Un pauvre enfant vêtu de noir,*
> *Qui me ressemblait comme un frère*[14]

If there is any appositeness in the evocation of these familiar figures from cultural lore, it lies in the opposition of colours not being read as a substitution but as a complementarity of symbols. Be his clothing perceived as white or black, in either dress there is no break of continuity between the substance and the shadow of

Charles's ego, nor are they mutually exclusive. But they have been estranged, and their accidental reunion is painful:

> on the instant, [. . .] an immense silence followed, empty at first, but gradually [. . .] full of a multitude of sweet and natural and long forgotten sounds: for he had spoken a name that was so familiar to me, a conjuror's name of such ancient powers, that, at its mere sound, the phantoms of those haunted late years began to take flight.
> Outside the hut I stood bemused (Prologue.24).

This might be an overture to Romantic lamentations of the full-organ, bleeding-heart variety, in whose lavishness lies a healing virtue –

> *S'il fallait maintenant parler de ma souffrance,*
> *Je ne sais trop quel nom elle devrait porter,*
> *Si c'est amour, folie, orgueil, expérience,*
> *Ni si personne au monde en pourrait profiter.*
> *Je veux bien toutefois t'en raconter l'histoire,*
> *Puisque nous voilà seuls, assis près du foyer.*
> *Prends cette lyre, approche, et laisse ma mémoire*
> *Au son de tes accords doucement s'éveiller . . .*
>
> *Et quand je pense aux lieux où j'ai risqué ma vie,*
> *J'y crois voir à ma place un visage étranger . . .*
>
> *Il est doux de pleurer, il est doux de sourire*
> *Au souvenir des maux qu'on pourrait oublier . . .*
>
> *N'en parlons plus . . . – je ne prévoyais pas*
>   *Où me conduisait la Fortune.*
> *Sans doute alors la colère des dieux*
>   *Avait besoin d'une victime;*
> *Car elle m'a puni comme d'un crime*
>   *D'avoir essayé d'être heureux.*[15]

This is not Charles's style, but, were it not for God, it would have been his state of mind. To have found God is to give Fortune, *outrageous fortune*, the name of Providence and, without making it easier to deal with all of one's memories –

Comforter, where, where is your comforting?[16]

– it removes the need for a Mentor or a Muse to warn that
although such effusions will eventually generate their own sating
and sedative, they are a form of detrimental addiction, and their
course must be diverted towards more restorative evocations –

> *L'image d'un doux souvenir*
> *Vient de s'offrir à ta pensée.*
> *Sur la trace qu'il a laissée*
> *Pourquoi crains-tu de revenir?*
> *Est-ce faire un récit fidèle*
> *Que de renier ses beaux jours?*
> *Si ta fortune fut cruelle,*
> *Jeune homme, fais du moins comme elle,*
> *Souris à tes premiers amours.*[17]

The question is not about Arcadia being *'doux souvenir'*, *'beaux
jours'* and *'premiers amours'*: the answer is obvious – but whether
The Sacred and Profane Memories of Captain Charles Ryder are *'un récit
fidèle'* in the making of which the narrator does not 'deny' his past,
and his mood eventually turns from 'dread' to 'smiling': the
answer is not so obvious but may be worked out from the assumption that the transition from dread to smiling is achieved in re-
fraining from 'denial'. Denial spells dread. The faithful tale of cruel
fortune brings out smile and appeasement. In the course of a
Romantic destiny, the *'pauvre enfant vêtu de noir'* keeps reappearing
as *'un jeune homme vêtu de noir'*, *'un étranger vêtu de noir'*, *'un convive
vêtu de noir'* *'un orphelin vêtu de noir'*, *'un malheureux vêtu de noir'*,
always looking like a brother – *'étrange vision'* – *'ange ou démon'* –
'ombre amie' – before it is understood to be *'la Solitude'*.[18] Such a
naming is cold comfort but a truth, at the very least, is achieved. To
read Arcadia as a mirage inverting solitude into companionship is
to master one more truth. *Truth has a quiet breast.* Hence the
possibility of smiling as one goes –

> *Cet homme marchait pur loin des sentiers obliques*[19]

– a disposition and direction *devoutly to be wished*, that 'a small red
flame – [. . .] there I found it this morning, burning anew among
the old stones' (Epilogue.381) might kindle –

I quickened my pace and reached the hut which served us for
our ante-room.
'You're looking unusually cheerful today,' said the second-in-
command.   (Epilogue.381)

These are the last words in the narrative of a man whom the
'sentiers obliques' of his memories have led, along the ramifications
of *primrose paths* to and from Arcadia, towards an 'ante-room', in a
seemingly 'unusually cheerful' mood. Several lessons may be read
in such a conclusion: that an ante-room is not a dead-end but a
temporary stage, a promising place, a waiting-room likely to open
on what will be the real room, a hopeful purgatory instead of a
hopeless hell: that unusual cheerfulness occurs after the unbur-
dening of one's conscience, in the expectation and desire of absolu-
tion, together with a sense of liberation: that whoever is in charge
here below is no more than second-in-command: that Charles has
now come clean.

These things – the beauty, the memory of our own past – are
good images of what we really desire: but if they are mistaken
for the thing itself they turn into dumb idols, breaking the hearts
of their worshippers. For they are not the thing itself: they are
only the scent of a flower we have not found, the echo of a tune
we have not heard, news from a country we have never visited.[20]

To reach this vision of his past and rate it at its true value
without loading it with disgrace and degrading himself, it has been
necessary for Charles to go over that stretch of Wonder- and
Waste- Land which he still calls Arcadia, and to conduct his
searching examination in an acutely penitent though not
indiscriminately abhorrent mood. This allows for his new intelligence and disillusioned awareness of Arcadia as 'not the thing
itself', and for the paradox of his having nonetheless, at one time,
really 'found' the 'flower', 'heard' the 'tune' and 'visited' that
'country' of illusion.
There is still much to be accounted for in that paradox, in how
Charles tells the story of his adventures in Arcadia, and how soon,
but not immediately, 'good images' fail to meet 'what we really
desire'. The manner of his tale lies in an infinity of space images,
and its matter amounts to his loss of innocence.
'Et in Arcadia ego' is a phrase that, as a motto as well as a title,

emphasises localisation, situation, position, place – also area, expanse, stretch, territory, domain – and bounds, limits, confines – and again motion, movement, moves within and without, etc. Indeed, to read the Book of Arcadia while bearing this in mind is to go from spatial similes to spatial metaphors, almost all of them admitting of all-embracing, symbolical interpretation:

'I have been here before,' I said; 'I have been here before;' [. . .] and though I had been there so often, in many moods, it was to that first visit that my heart returned on this, my latest. (B1.I.29) – That day, too, I had come not knowing my destination. (29) – In her spacious and quiet streets, men walked and talked as they had done in Newman's days. (29) – the bells rang out high and clear over her gables and cupolas. (29) – It was this cloistral hush which [. . .] carried [our laughter] over the intervening clamour. (29) – Here [. . .] came a rabble of womankind, [. . .] sightseeing and pleasure seeking, [. . .] pushed in punts about the river, herded in droves to the college barges. (29) – Echoes of the intruders penetrated every corner. (30) – The front quad, where I lived. (30) – the don who lived above me. (30) – a printed notice proclaimed this outrage [Ladies' Cloakroom] [. . .] not six inches from my oak. (30) – 'Will you be lunching in?' (30) – 'It all came in with the men back from the war.' (30) – 'And there's some even goes dancing with the town at the Masonic.' (30) – Sebastian entered. (31) – 'You're to come away at once, out of danger.' (31) – 'Where are we going?' (31) – Beyond the gate, beyond the winter garden. (31) – we escaped collision with a clergyman [. . .] pedalling quietly down the wrong side of High Street, crossed Carfax, passed the station, and were soon in open country on the Botley Road; open country was easily reached in those days. (31) – 'The women are still doing whatever they do to themselves before they come down.' (31) – 'We're away.' (31) – [Hardcastle] thought he was coming with us.' (32) – At Swindon we turned off the main road. (32) – Sebastian [. . .] turned the car into a cart-track and stopped. (32) – The fumes of the sweet, golden wine seemed to lift us a finger's breath above the turf and hold us suspended. (32) – 'Just the place to bury a crock of gold,' said Sebastian. 'I should like to bury something precious in every place where I have been happy and then, when I was old and ugly and miserable, I could come back and dig it up and remember.' (32) – I date my Oxford life from my first meeting with Sebastian. (32) – We were in different colleges and came from different schools. I might well [. . .] never have met him, but for the chance of his getting drunk one evening in my college and my having ground-floor rooms in the front quadrangle. (32–33) – when I first came up. (33) – 'nowhere in the world' (33) – 'it all comes out of capital'. (33) – 'before I was going up, your cousin Alfred rode over to Boughton especially to give me a piece of advice.' (33) – Jasper [. . .] had come within appreciable distance of a rowing blue; he was [. . .] a considerable person in college. He called on me [. . .] and stayed to tea [. . .]; he covered most subjects (34) – 'You want either a first or a fourth. There is no value in anything between.' (34) – 'Go to a London tailor [. . .]. Join the Carlton now [. . .]. If you want to run for the Union [. . .] make you reputation *outside* first [. . .]. Keep clear of Boar's Hill. [. . .] Steer clear of all the religious groups [. . .]. Change your rooms.' (34–5) – 'Before you know where you are.' (35) – I do not know that I ever, consciously, followed any of his advice (35) – there were gilly flowers growing below the windows. (35) – the dates marking one's stature on the edge of the door (35) – *A Shropshire Lad* [. . .] *Sinister Street, South Wind.* (36) – my earliest friends fitted well in that background; they were [. . .] a small circle of college intellectuals, who maintained a middle course of culture [. . .]. It was by this circle that I found myself adopted during my first term. (36) – At Sebastian's approach these grey figures seemed quietly to fade into the landscape and vanish. (36) – my eyes were opened. (37) – His eccentricities of behaviour [. . .] seemed to know no bounds. (37) – My first sight of him was in the door of Germer's. (37) – 'the Earl of Brideshead went down last term.' (37) – there appeared at my window. (38) – His friends bore him to the gate. (38) – 'It wasn't one of my party. It was someone from out of college.' (38) – when I returned. (39) – lunching out. (39) – I went there uncertainly, for it was foreign ground and there was a [. . .] warning voice in my ear which [. . .] told me it was seemly to hold back. (39) – that low door in the wall [. . .] which opened on an enclosed and enchanted garden. (40) – 'I put myself unreservedly in the hands of Dolbear and Goodall.' (40) – cards of invitations from London hostesses (40) – The party assembled. There were three Etonian freshmen, mild, elegant, detached young men who had all been to a dance in London [. . .]. Each as he came into the room. (40) – 'I

couldn't get away before,' (41) – wholly exotic. (41) – he had
been pointed out to me often in the streets. (40) – '*I who have sat
by Thebes below the wall And walked among the l-l-lowest of the
dead* . . .' (41) – stepping lightly into the room (42) – 'Home they
brought the warrior dead' (42) – 'Where do you lurk? I shall
come down to your burrow and ch-chivvy you out like an old
st-t-toat.' (42) – 'I must go to the Botanical Gardens [. . .] I don't
know where I should be without the Botanical Gardens' (42) –
When [. . .] I returned to my rooms, [. . .] I turned [the screen]
face to the wall. (42) – an obscure refuge. (42) – I was lying beside
him in the shade of the high elms. (43) – We drove on [. . .] We
drove on and in the early afternoon came to our destination. (43)
– 'What a place to live in!' (43) – I felt [. . .] an ominous chill at
the words he used – not 'that is my home,' but 'it's where my
family live.' (43) – 'Don't worry, they're all away. [. . .] They're
in London.' (43) – We drove round the front into a side court –
Everything's shut up. We'd better go in this way' – and entered
through the [. . .] passages of the servants' quarters – 'I want
you to meet Nanny Hawkins. That's what we've come for' – and
climbed [. . .] stairs, followed more passages [. . .], through
passages [. . .], passing the wells of many minor staircases
[. . .], up a final staircase, gated at the head. (44) – Sebastian's
nanny was seated at the open window; the fountain lay before
her. (44) – Sebastian introduced us. (44) – 'Julia's here for the
day. [. . .] you going to see his Lordship in Italy, and the rest on
visits. [. . .] what they always want to go to London for [. . .].
(44) – 'The lovely daughter that Lady Marchmain is bringing out
this season.' (45) – the collection of small presents which had
been brought home to her. (46) – 'The new [girl] is just up from
the village [. . .] she's coming along nicely.' (46) – But Sebastian
said we had to go. (46) – 'It's all shut up.' (46) – Sebastian
unbarred one [shutter]. (47) – His mood had changed since
[. . .] we had turned the corner of the drive. (47) – The whole
interior had been gutted, elaborately refurnished and redecor-
ated. (47) – 'Now, if you've seen enough, we'll go.' (48) – 'An
aunt kept an eye on me for a time but my father drove her
abroad.' (48) – '[My mother] went to Serbia with the Red Cross.
My father [. . .] just lives alone in London with no friends.' (49)
– 'There are lots of us. Look them up in Debrett.' (49) – The
further we drove from Brideshead, the more he seemed to cast
off his uneasiness. (49) – 'We'll get to Godstow in time for

dinner, drink at the Trout, leave Hardcastle's motor-car and walk back by the river.' (49) – The sun was behind us as we drove, so that we seemed to be in pursuit of our own shadows. (49)

Page after page, the other four chapters of Book One, not to mention the other two Books, would yield a comparable succession of telltale images, of which it seems more symptomatic to quote the whole unsorted load of one chapter rather than to highlight a choice selection from the entire narrative. Worthy of note are the degree of intentionality and the range of styles in the use of these images, the variety of speakers using them, and the ground plan and frontiers they trace out. All the characters in the chapter – Charles, Sebastian, Jasper, Anthony Blanche, Nanny Hawkins, and one society news columnist – in direct or reported speech – and the narrator in his descriptions and assessments – express themselves in terms of space, either without, so to speak, giving a thought to the clichés they use, or conversely choosing them for their full, if hackneyed, figurative value, or else dropping them in the conversation to give it peculiar piquancy or disturbing ambiguity, or even making them obviously focal, while in the narrative their rich, symbolical significance is conveyed in carefully controlled, dramatically situated, finely polished sentences. The phrases may be colloquial, slangish, polite, non-committal, witty, ironical, felicitous, or simply neutral, they all have a comparable, conscious or unconscious effect, and eventually set off an extensive chain reaction of entrances and exits, admissions and evictions, membership and quarantine, havens and haunts, cocoons and imagos – genuine or engineered, sham or dreamt, festering or pure.

Arcadia is all this, in itself as well as in relation to the satellite states that spatial references map out. Oxford is an enchanting city, tranquil and magnificent. Brideshead is an enchanted castle, paradisiac and maleficent. London is sombrely bright, a magnetic place of endless variety. The countryside is idyllic. Charles's father is under a curse and cannot share anything with anybody. Jasper's course is marked out with do's and dont's. Nanny Hawkins sits an immovable vigil over ceaseless comings and goings. Anthony Blanche has explored all sorts of worlds. Julia is coming out. A new maid is coming along. Oxford etiquette is lunching out, getting away, joining, keeping clear, and many other modes of motion, lurking included. Eights Week is the time of female infestation.

Some men are detached. Some have been to the wars. Some dance with the town. Colleges have obscure refuges. Circles adopt you. The Union wants to know what you look like outside. Abroad is a place of death, and exile, and exotic dubiousness. No wonder Charles is confused.

Enter Sebastian, archangelic, and all that was hazy or out of the straight takes shape and sense. What shape? What sense? Images abound, a majority of them creating again spatio-temporal perspective projections –

> I sometimes wonder whether, had it not been for Sebastian, I might have trodden the same path as Collins round the cultural water wheel. [. . .] It is conceivable, but not, I believe, likely, for the hot spring of anarchy rose from depths where was no solid earth, and burst into the sunlight – a rainbow in its cooling vapours – with a power the rocks could not repress.
>
> In the event, the Easter vacation formed a short stretch of level road in the precipitous descent of which Jasper warned me. Descent or ascent?

> > (B1.II.54)

Arcadia is indeed short-lived, but the unequalled intensity of the experience lasts you a life-time –

> the more ancient lore which I acquired that term will be with me in one shape or other to my last hour

> > (B1.II.55)

– upsetting all of Jasper's 'broad outline' (B1.II.53) and confirming all of his prognostications and prejudices. Even Charles's father, at his most sinisterly 'gleeful', resorts to topological imagery to define the other side of Arcadia, and rather stupendously hits on the very *antipathies* of Wonderland –

> 'On the rocks? In Queer Street? [. . .] Your grandfather once said to me, "Live within your means [. . .]."'
>
> 'Your cousin Melchior [. . .] got in a very queer street. *He* went to Australia.' [. . .]
>
> 'You're very welcome, my dear boy [. . .]. Stay as long as you find it convenient [. . .]. Your cousin Melchior worked his pass-

age to Australia *before the mast.'* (Snuffle) 'What, I wonder, is
"before the mast"?'

(B1.III. 75–6)

So far, so bad. 'Oh, *la fatigue du Nord!'* (B1.II.60), as Anthony
Blanche puts it during his own Grand Remonstrance, 'a warning
against charm', or Sebastian painted from the life –

> 'Narcissus, with one pustule – he never did anything wrong;
> never *quite*; at least he never got punished. Perhaps he was just
> being charming through the grille [in the confessional] – in a
> kind of way, exquisite – that little bundle of charms – there is
> really no mystery about him except how he came to be born of
> such a *very sinister* family – Do you ever feel there is something a
> *teeny* bit gruesome about Sebastian? No? Perhaps I imagine it – at
> times he seems a little insipid – With that very murky back-
> ground, what could he do except set up being simple and
> charming, particularly as he isn't very well endowed in the Top
> Storey. We couldn't claim *that* for him, could we, much as we
> love him? – when dear Sebastian speaks it is like a little sphere of
> soap sud drifting off the end of an old clay pipe, anywhere, full
> of rainbow light for a second, and then – phut! – vanished, with
> nothing left at all, nothing.'

(B1.II.61–7)

Even if Anthony Blanche's aim is not primarily to disparage
Sebastian but to encourage 'that very rare thing, An Artist', that
Charles hides 'behind [his] cold, English, phlegmatic exterior'
(B1.II.62), Sebastian is here smashed to smithereens and even the
iridescent image of the rainbow is used against him. The injury to
his character is beyond recall; the effect on Charles may not be
immediate, but from now on he will catch himself in the act of
studying the behaviour of his friend and considering his own
motives. Which is what most of his memories and his narrative of
them amounts to.

The fall of Sebastian is another story. For all his being thought of
as the Spirit of Arcadia and the Master of its Revels, he may well
never have been in Arcadia –

> *Le coeur d'un homme vierge est un vase profond.*
> *Lorsque la première eau qu'on y verse est impure,*

> La mer y passerait sans laver la souillure,
> Car l'abîme est immense et la tache est au fond[21]

– nor have been a real influence on Charles –

Because to influence a person is to give him one's soul[22]

– but only a mirror, perfect at first, then tarnished, where Charles reads and passes through his own mirage – a looking-glass.

> Tell me where is *Arcadia* bred?
> Or in the heart or in the head?
> How begot, how nourished? –
> Reply, reply.

We are born, so to speak, provisionally, somewhere; it is only gradually that we shape *within ourselves* the place of our origin, in order to be born there after the event, in a more final way every day.[23]

Descent or ascent? It seems to me that I grew younger daily with each adult habit that I acquired. I had lived a lonely childhood and a boyhood straitened by war and overshadowed by bereavement; to the hard bachelordom of English adolescence, the premature dignity and authority of the school system, I had added a sad and grim strain of my own. Now, that summer term with Sebastian, it seemed as though I was being given a brief spell of what I had never known, a happy childhood, and though its toys were silk shirts and liqueurs and cigars and its naughtiness high in the catalogue of grave sins, there was something of nursery freshness about us that fell little short of the joy of innocence.

(B1.II.54–5)

For Charles, not to include Sebastian in what is probably his most sincere vindication of Arcadia would be an act of autobiographical infidelity as well as a breach of friendship. It is to Sebastian that he owes the *finest hour* of Arcadia and, in accord with the facts, he naturally writes: 'with Sebastian', 'about us'. What these prepositions serve to mark, however, is a mere relation of propinquity and kinship; they stress rather than make up for the absence of the first person plural, the only form capable of conveying more than circumstantial association. In both active and passive voice, the dramatic subject is I – 'I grew younger . . . I acquired . . . I was given . . .' – complemented by 'a brief spell of what I had never known, a happy childhood' and 'something of nursery freshness that fell little short of the joy of innocence'.

An honest self-portrait is extremely rare because a man who has reached the degree of self-conciousness presupposed by the desire to paint his own portrait has almost always developed an ego-consciousness which paints himself painting himself, and introduces artificial highlights and dramatic shadows. As an autobiographer, Boswell is almost alone in his honesty.

I determined, if the Cyprian Fury should seize me, to participate my amorous flame with a genteel girl.

Stendhal would never have dared write such a sentence. He would have said to himself: 'Phrases like *Cyprian Fury* and *amorous flame* are clichés; I must put down in plain words exactly what I mean.' But he would have been wrong, for the Self thinks in clichés and euphemisms, not in the style of the Code Napoléon.[24]

'Happy childhood' and 'joy of innocence' may be 'clichés' that Charles 'dared write', but Arcadia he does not use euphemistically. What is to Sebastian an anguished distraction and relief from an unendurable reality that only Christ, not Bacchus, shall ultimately help him to meet, is to Charles an acquisition and a gain.

Arcadia is Sebastian's stasis, his refusal to grow up – *'Être adulte c'est être seul'*[25] – his regression and cover protection. He is a Peter Pan. Far be it from anyone to pass censure on Sebastian for his misfortune – Charles himself 'remained censorious [. . .] although Collins, who read Freud, had a number of technical devices to cover everything' only for as long as he did not become friends with 'the most conspicuous man of his year' (B1.I.37) – and charm is not such a sickening commodity as some would like one to believe, especially when it is powerless to mask maladjustment.

But in regard to Charles Arcadia is quite another matter, not a stasis but a stage in his development –

> *Si la vie est un passage,*
> *Sur ce passage*
> *Au moins semons des fleurs*[26]

– an occasion to make up for the unjust deprivation of a child's rights and outplay adolescent rancour and frustration – a positive means of adult adjustment.

Not that Arcadia renders Charles immune to concurrent and ulterior offences, errors, faults and sins, whose catalogue his narrative does not hold back, but it does not seem as if Arcadia ought to be listed among them.

Not that Arcadia is Grace, but it does seem as if in his connection with Arcadia Charles were basically evincing something of serendipity.

NOTES

1. References are given to the 1964 Chapman and Hall edition. After textual quotations, book, chapter and page are indicated between brackets.
2. Vigny, *Poèmes antiques et modernes*, 'Le Cor':

   > How many times, standing in the shades of midnight,
   > I smiled on hearing it, and oftentimes I wept . . .

3. Corneille, *Polyeucte*:

   I see, know and believe, and I am undeceived.

4. Apollinaire, *Alcools*, 'Le Cor':

   Memories are hunting horns.

5. Vigny, Le Cor:

   I like the sound of the horn, at dusk, in the heart of the woods.

6. Baudelaire, *Les Fleurs du mal*, 'L'Invitation au voyage':

   > There, all is but order and beauty,
   > Luxury, calm and voluptuous delight.

7. Malherbe, *Poésies*, 'Consolation à M. Du Périer, gentilhomme d'Aix-en-Provence, sur la mort de sa fille':

> And a rose, she lived as long as roses live,
> The space of a morn.

8. Ronsard, *Sonnets pour Hélène*:

> Live, if you believe me, do not wait the morrow,
> Pluck this very day the roses of life.

9. Milosz, *Symphonies*, 'Symphonie de septembre':

> Be welcome, Solitude, my mother . . .
> Solitude, my mother, tell me my life again.

10. Virgil, *The Bucolics*:

> Both in the bloom of youth, Arcadians both,
> Equally skilled in song and ready to exchange responses.

11. Hugo, *La Légende des siècles*, 'Aymerillot':

And all the blue sky could not fill up my heart.

12. *Colossians*, III, 9–10.
13. Hugo, *La Légende des siècles*, 'Booz endormi':

Dressed in candid probity and white linen.

14. Musset, *Poésies nouvelles*, 'La Nuit de décembre':

> A poor child dressed in black,
> As like me as a brother.

15. Musset, *Poésies nouvelles*, 'La Nuit d'octobre' (The Poet):

> If I now had to speak of my suffering,
> I know not what name it should be given,
> Whether it be love, madness, pride, or experience
> Nor if by its telling anyone might profit.
> Yet I would like to tell you my story
> Since we sit alone by the fire.
> Take this lyre, draw near, and let my memory
> Be gently stirred by your strains . . .
>
> And when I think of the places where I risked my life
> I think I see a stranger's face instead of my own . . .

> Sweet it is to cry, sweet it is to smile
> On remembering pains that one might forget . . .

> No more talk of that . . . – I did not foresee
> Whither Fortune would lead me.
> No doubt the wrath of the gods
> Was then in need of a victim;
> For it punished me as for a crime
> Because I tried to be happy.

16. Hopkins, 'No worst there is none . . .'
17. Musset, 'La Nuit d'octobre' (The Muse):

> The image of a sweet memory
> Has offered itself to your thoughts.
> On the traces it has left
> Why do you fear to return?
> Is it a faithful tale
> That which denies its happy days?
> If your fortune proved cruel,
> Young man, you must act as it
> did,
> And smile to your first loves.

18. Musset, 'La Nuit de décembre': a youth . . . a stranger . . . a table companion . . . an orphan . . . a wretch dressed in black – strange vision – angel or demon – friendly shade – Solitude.
19. Hugo, 'Booz endormi':

This man walked in purity far from devious paths.

20. C.S. Lewis – quoted by the Right Rev. Richard Holloway, 'Faith and Reason: The poet of longing and the lost boy', *The Independent*, 10 March 1990.
21. Musset, *Premières poésies*, 'La Coupe et les lèvres':

> A virgin man's heart is a deep vase.
> When the first water poured into it is impure,
> The whole sea would not wash the taint,
> For the chasm is immense and the stain lies in its depths.

22. Wilde, *The Picture of Dorian Gray*, ch. II.
23. Rilke, *Letters from Milan*, 23 January 1923.
24. Auden, *The Dyer's Hand and other Essays*, quoted by Justin Wintle and Richard Kevin, *The Penguin Concise Dictionary of Biographical Quotation*.
25. Jean Rostand, *Pensées d'un biologiste*:

To be grown up is to be alone.

26. Moncrif (François Augustin Paradis de):

> If life is but a passage,
> On that passage
> Let us at least strew flowers.

4

Evelyn Waugh and Vatican Divorce

Donat Gallagher

Over the last two years several friends rung to tell me that Evelyn Waugh's first wife had been on television and revealed that the Vatican's annulment of the Waugh marriage was a sham. Waugh had persuaded her to testify to the Roman Catholic marriage court, falsely, that before marrying they had decided they would 'never have children' – and it was this untruth that won the case.

It was a surprise to learn that so private a person as the Hon. Mrs Nightingale had consented to be interviewed on the BBC. Nevertheless on my remote tropic shore I could only believe what was told me until a transcript arrived of Nicholas Shakespeare's Arena programme 'The Waugh Trilogy'.[1] This clearly demonstrated that my friends had become over-excited by a still photograph of Mrs Nightingale accompanied by a disembodied voice (Pt 2, p. 22) quoting from a letter written by Mrs Nightingale to Dr Martin Stannard, Waugh's second-last biographer.[2] Such is the power of television! Perhaps. But that power is no more awesome than the proverbial tyranny of fashionable opinion. 'Everyone' has always 'known' that Waugh's annulment was somehow fishy. Mrs Nightingale's letter to Dr Stannard has not, therefore, been welcomed as an interesting piece of evidence to be evaluated. Instead it has been uncritically accepted and made the starting point of a train of conjectures, which have in turn mysteriously assumed the status of fact.

Mrs Nightingale writes that Waugh 'told me to say that I had refused to have children . . . I had not refused to have children, but we had agreed to wait . . .' (Stannard, p. 352). Dr Stannard then leaps into the dark and asserts, confidently, that if Waugh had admitted this truth to the marriage court it 'would have been damning evidence against the granting of an annulment' (p. 353). Mr Shakespeare amplifies Mrs Nightingale's statement, surrounds it with Dr Stannard's and his own speculations, and broadcasts the lot as a cut-and-dried documented certainty:

> In 1936, Waugh's marriage was finally annulled. The Vatican Court's decision hinged on the testimony of his first wife, Evelyn Gardner. He persuaded her to testify that they had married on the understanding they would never have children. This was not true. (Pt 2, p. 22)

And now Mr Humphrey Carpenter, Waugh's latest biographer, repeats accusation and speculation. He refrains, however, from saying that Waugh tried to persuade his former wife to testify untruthfully. Instead he has Mrs Nightingale merely 'surprised' to learn that Waugh intended to testify to the untruth that they 'never wanted children'.[3]

It is embarrassing to cast doubt on the memory of a transparently candid participant in the events. But there are good reasons for not accepting in full Mrs Nightingale's recollection that Waugh asked her to tell the court that she had 'refused to have children'. And there are compelling reasons for not accepting Dr Stannard's speculation, repeated by Shakespeare and Carpenter, that the court granted the decree of nullity on the basis of false evidence to this effect. In the first place the documentary record[4] shows that the evidence presented to the court in 1935 harmonises completely with the facts outlined in Mrs Nightingale's recent letter. Neither Mrs Nightingale, nor Waugh, nor any of the four witnesses told the court that Mrs Nightingale had 'refused to have children', or that the couple had decided they would 'never have children'. On the contrary all unambiguously said that the couple had decided to postpone consideration of children until income and health permitted. Furthermore the argument put to the court concerning the *temporary* exclusion of children was quickly dismissed. The successful argument was that the couple had entered marriage on the understanding, expressed before several witnesses, that if difficulties arose they would divorce. The basis on which the nullity decree was granted had, therefore, nothing to do with a decision, real or invented, 'never to have children'. It had everything to do with the stated determination of the couple to dissolve the marriage should need arise.

In the interests of accurate Waugh biography this matter deserves to be cleared up. Fortunately the bare facts of the case – the

grounds on which the annulment was sought, the evidence of the
two Evelyns and the principal witnesses, the relevant law and its
application, and the judges' decisions – are ascertainable from the
Roman Rota's published report of the case.[5] But these bare facts,
and later criticisms of the annulment, become intelligible only in
their legal-historical context. Waugh's early articles espousing first
abolition of civil marriage in favour of a license to produce children, then 'companionate marriage',[6] throw helpful light on his
own and contemporary attitudes towards marriage and divorce.
But the point at issue in this discussion is whether or not Waugh
obtained his annulment by fraud. The current allegations of fraud
arguably owe much to folklore about 'Vatican divorce', which in
turn owes much to the contention, and to the atmosphere of deceit
and conspiracy, that enveloped civil divorce in the 1920s and
1930s. A preliminary comment on these matters is called for.

During the last three decades Western marriage has taken a form
recently described as 'completely unprecedented in the history of
human procreative behaviour'.[7] Contraception, consensual unions,
abortion, plummeting births and soaring illegitimacies have played
their part, but the major element in the evolution has been easier,
cheaper and (more or less) no-fault divorce. Waugh's divorce and
annulment took place during decades when more liberal laws were
still being aggressively promoted by divorce law reformers and
fiercely resisted by the Christian religions and the courts. Bitter
controversy, raging from pulpit and platform, in parliament and in
the press, lent the subject a prominence unimaginable today.

On the personal level civil divorce was still likely to be shaming
and ruinous. Proof of a 'matrimonial offence' was required, and
attempts to prove an offence in court led, until 1926, to completely
uninhibited reporting, and after that to most unwelcome publicity.
To avoid all this, the husband usually 'acted like a gentleman',
which meant that he provided spurious evidence of infidelity – in
collusion with the other party – for an uncontested action. Evelyn
Waugh's *A Handful of Dust*[8] makes comedy out of Tony Last's
going to Brighton with a professional partner who renders the
evidence of 'adultery' worthless by taking along the Awful Child of
Popular Fiction. More realistically, A.P. Herbert's *Holy Deadlock*
turns John Adam's experience into tragedy. Cheated by the agency
that supplies his partner, hounded by the Law for conspiracy,
pauperised by lawyers' fees, Adam is left penniless and without
hope of remarriage. He exemplifies Herbert's point that divorce in

the 1930s was characterised by 'perjury, conspiracy, elaborate deceit and humbug'.[9]

Roman decrees of nullity in the 1920s and 1930s also attracted notoriety, particularly when the parties were socially prominent and had been through the divorce courts. But they generated hostility for other reasons as well. Like all Christian bodies the Catholic Church opposed the trend towards more freely available divorce, only more intransigently. And it boasted that where other churches 'failed hopelessly' to safeguard Christian marriage, Rome 'firmly defended' it:

> She [the Roman Catholic Church] stands apart from the laxity of other Churches because she . . . knows by divine wisdom what is the right attitude . . . and makes her stand where others give way. Her prohibition of divorce safeguards . . . the married; prevents thoughtless marriages and easy separations; protects women . . . and benefits the children . . . by securing for them a permanent home and continuous education. Divorce is bad for society, for individual morality, and for human life in its totality.[10]

Such breathtaking assurance meant that the Catholic Church's own proceedings would be jealously scrutinised, and widespread attacks were in fact made on annulments granted to the rich and famous. One such annulment, which will be discussed below, was granted to the inventor-tycoon and intimate of kings, Guglielmo Marconi. But the most celebrated annulment followed the collapse of the marriage of the Duke of Marlborough and the awesomely rich Consuelo Vanderbilt. The publicity following this so-called 'Marlborough case' imprinted upon English minds – quite unfairly as I shall argue – an indelible association between annulments and privilege, and the cynical conviction that 'You can buy anything in Rome'.

In 1895 Mrs Vanderbilt learned that her seventeen-year-old daughter, Consuelo, had become 'unsuitably' engaged. The socially ambitious mother took Consuelo away to Europe. There they met the highly eligible Duke of Marlborough, and Mrs Vanderbilt invited him to the United States. After two weeks at Newport the Duke proposed to the beautiful young heiress. Consuelo passionately rejected the proposal, but next morning found her engagement announced in the Press. The Duke then left for Canada. Until the wedding Mrs Vanderbilt subjected her daughter to threats and intimidation falling not far short of physical violence. An imperious woman, Mrs Vanderbilt later explained: 'I have always exercised an absolute influence over my daughter . . . I did not beg her . . . I commanded her to marry the Duke . . . she was completely upset . . . I overbore her opposition as the mere caprice of an inexperienced girl.' Although two children were born to the marriage, it was unhappy from the start. In 1905 the couple formally separated. In 1920 they divorced and each remarried, Consuelo to a Catholic. In 1925, in order to regularise her new marriage in the eyes of the Catholic Church, Consuelo applied to the Diocese of Southwark for the annulment of her marriage to Marlborough, and in February 1926 Southwark gave a favourable verdict on the grounds of duress and fear. The Roman Rota confirmed Southwark's decision in July 1926.[11] The Duke became a Catholic in February 1927.[12]

On the evidence presented, the decree of nullity appears justified. The line between persuasion and coercion was so clearly crossed that an English ecclesiastical lawyer writing to *The Times* as a 'Protestant and a barrister with some experience of the Divorce Court', and specifically to criticise the Roman Catholic system of impediments and annulments, said: 'I have read the reports of many of these nullity trials in "Acta S. Sedis" and "Analecta Juris Pontifici" and . . . the decision appears to me fair and justified by the evidence . . . I might refer to a similar case where the petitioner was neither a duchess nor a millionaire and obtained a decree of nullity on the ground of parental pressure . . .'[13]

Nevertheless, when news of the annulment broke in mid-November 1926 there was uproar. *The Times* received so many letters over the following month that it twice apologised for printing only a selection. It also ran an editorial and a translation of the Roman Rota's decision.[14] From the viewpoint of the present it is piquant that many correspondents attacked the Roman system of impediments and annulments as even more likely than divorce to undermine marriage. Others were shocked that Catholic law granted a decree of nullity whenever an impediment was proved – regardless of guilt, innocence, or circumstance – thus seeming to anticipate no-fault divorce. Criticism in the popular and sectarian presses was more earthy, and mostly fantastic, but it is worth discussing because elements in it, writ large, still seem to shape perceptions of the Waugh case. These were misapprehensions about facts, costs, access, and honesty.

Facts: Grotesque misinformation about the Marlborough case was widely circulated. For example, although Consuelo and Marlborough had separated in 1905, divorced in 1920, and quickly remarried new partners; and although the annulment had been sought by Consuelo six years *after* the divorce in 1926; and although Marlborough became a Catholic in 1927, one year later again; nevertheless it was widely accepted, and stated in print long after the event, that, 'After being refused a civil divorce the Duke of Marlborough became a Catholic and secured one from the Pope'. Even *The Times* editorial 'So-Called Marriage' implicitly accused the Catholic Church of conniving at the break-up of a long happy marriage. Understandably the Duke's solicitors complained that 'numerous false statements have been published about our client' and 'authoritatively stated that the application for the annulment was made by Mme Balsan'.[15]

Costs: A popular error, no doubt arising from the association of annulments with millionaires, is that annulments were exorbitantly expensive – indeed, Waugh grizzled about the expense of his. The cost of an annulment in the 1930s cannot be reliably reckoned because, once a case had gone to Rome, two kinds of fees could be involved, those levied by the courts, and those charged by lawyers in private practice. Court costs were dirt cheap, and were scaled down or remitted in cases of hardship. Southwark charged Consuelo Vanderbilt £8 10s Od for proceedings that involved three judges and two court officials sitting several times over three months; and the Roman Rota charged her £40 for proceedings which involved sittings over six months. However, the fees of private lawyers varied, as they do in all jurisdictions, with the status of the lawyer and the difficulty of the work – although it is inconceivable that the Roman advocates were as avaricious as Australian lawyers are today. When Waugh complained about the 'ridiculous fees charged by the Vatican lawyers',[16] we may assume that he was denouncing Roman advocates in private practice and that the fees reflected the complexity of his case. While extravagant in his pleasures, Waugh was canny about business. And he had been spoiled by E.S.P. Haynes, the solicitor and patron of writers who handled his divorce in 1930: 'He gave me far more in oysters and hock during its transaction', Waugh wrote, 'than he charged me in fees'.[17]

Access: The best source of information in English about the way in which the Catholic marriage courts operated is the *Canon Law*

Digest, a compilation of case reports intended for English-speaking students of canon law.[18] It holds surprises for anyone who thinks that these courts deal only with the problems of Continental princesses. Non-European cases abound. A Moslem villager with four wives on converting to Christianity may keep only one. He becomes entangled in the complex web of laws governing his choice of the one wife . . . Or an African village girl, married according to local custom, seeks a decree of nullity on the grounds that her consent was forced. The case goes from her diocese to Rome; it is lost there, goes back to Africa and back to Rome – the girl finally wins. Nor do many European and North American petitioners turn out to be illustrious. A typical case involves a father in the French provinces bullying his daughter into marrying one of his old cronies, whom the daughter describes in her petition as 'an atheist doctor with venereal disease'. Like Consuelo Vanderbilt, the daughter demonstrates duress and fear. A Voltaire would find much to mock in the Rota's legalism, but he would admit that it fell indifferently on humble and great.

Honesty: While it is demonstrable that common folk had access to the Catholic marriage courts at reasonable cost, this is not inconsistent with the courts being open to influence by the rich. In intention the Catholic courts exclude improper pressure by working principally on sworn written evidence, and in the 1930s they were reluctant to accept evidence when there had been even an *opportunity* for 'suggestion, collusion or subornation'. Then again two courts in different regions must concur before a decree of nullity becomes final, the second court conducting, not an 'appeal' in the usual sense, but a full re-hearing. But no set of procedures, in whatever jurisdiction, can entirely eliminate fraud nor the inevitable advantages of the rich, powerful, clever, or pretty. Ultimately the integrity of any system rests on the probity of those operating it. Of course from time to time a dynastic, political, or personal need to marry a Catholic in the Catholic Church has resulted in deception by the parties, or in a convenient decision by a court. But there is no evidence I know of to justify a belief that the Roman courts were, or are, so corrupt that any particular annulment, e.g. Waugh's, can be presumed dubious. The principal judge in the Waugh case before the Rota was William Heard, an Englishman of unshakable reputation.

The relevant facts of the Waugh case are these. On 17 June 1928 Evelyn Waugh and Evelyn Gardner married, somewhat recklessly, in an Anglican church. Both were twenty-four years old and both were members, at least nominally, of the Church of England. Since He-Evelyn (as he was amusingly called) was middle-class, dissipated, jobless, and apparently without prospects; and since She-Evelyn had been briefly engaged in the recent past to three unsuitable men; She-Evelyn's aristocratic mother, Lady Burghclere, exerted herself to prevent the marriage, enlisting the aid of anyone who might help.[19] Inevitably, serious discussions took place before the marriage between the Evelyns, and between each of them and their friends and families. The content of these discussions will be crucial to the case for an annulment.

On 9 July 1929, little more than one year later, She-Evelyn wrote to Waugh to say that she had fallen in love with another man, John Heygate. After a fortnight's uneasy reconciliation and a sequence of events that has only recently been clarified, She-Evelyn went to live with Heygate.[20] On 9 September 1929 Waugh began divorce proceedings. Uncontested, they were completed on 1 August 1930. Two months later, on 29 September 1930, Waugh became a Roman Catholic, 'taking for granted' the consequence that while his wife lived he could not re-marry.[21] Later he learned in a discussion of the still topical Marlborough case that his own marriage might be null.[22] Sometime in 1933 he therefore began proceedings in the Diocese of Westminster. The case was heard in five sittings during October and November of 1933. Two years later, on 28 June 1935, after what the Roman Rota was to call '*non laudabiles moras*' ('reprehensible delays')[23] in arriving at a decision, the Westminster court handed down a favourable judgement.[23] In the light of the length of these proceedings (six to nine months would have been more normal) Martin D'Arcy's statement that 'apparently the case was straightforward, so that the court quickly decided on the nullity of his first marriage' is wrong.[24] As in all such cases, a second hearing was mandatory. But Westminster delayed eight months before forwarding the papers to Rome.[25] Eventually the Rota gave its decision for nullity on 4 July 1936.

The law involved in this annulment is easy enough to outline – if difficult to apply. As do most systems of civil law, canon law stipulates certain impediments to marriage, e.g. lack of marriageable age, prohibited relationships, and no real consent. If an impediment is present at the time a marriage is celebrated, a true marriage does not take place. And if the union is later challenged, what follows in either civil or ecclesiastical law is, not divorce, but a decree of nullity. The decree of nullity declares that no marriage ever existed.

'No real consent', the impediment Waugh claimed, is known in civil as well as Church law. It can arise from such obvious causes as duress, fraud, or mistaken identity. It can also arise from failure to consent to one of the essential elements of marriage. Thus a civil 'marriage of convenience', where there has been a prior agreement not to cohabit and to divorce as soon as possible after the marriage, can be declared null in some jurisdictions. Up to this point canon law and the civil law run more or less parallel. But beyond this point the two systems diverge because each defines matrimonial consent in its own way. In common law, marriage is 'the union of a man and a woman to the exclusion of all others voluntarily entered into for life': it therefore contains three essential elements, viz. voluntary union; an expectation that the union will last for life; and one man and one woman exclusively. Canon law defines matrimonial consent more specifically and adds an essential element, viz. the right to procreative acts:

> Matrimonial consent is an act of the will by which each party gives and accepts a perpetual and exclusive right to the end that acts may be performed that are in themselves apt for the generation of children. (Canon 1081.2)

Matrimonial consent in canon law must therefore embrace four essential elements, viz. voluntary union; an intention that the union will last for life; an exclusive relationship between one man and one woman; and exchange of the right to procreative (not merely sexual) acts. If any of these elements is excluded, by a positive act of the will, matrimonial consent will be 'defective' and the marriage will be null. A simple conviction that divorce is permissible, or a simple resolution to use birth control, does not of itself override consent to marriage as permanent and procreative. For the question of nullity to arise, the essential element must be *excluded*, and it must be excluded by a 'positive act of the will'. Further, this 'act of will' must be so clearly expressed in 'the external forum', i.e. in writing or in speech before witnesses, that it can be proved in court.

As for procedure, canon law presumes any existing marriage to be valid. In Waugh's day the presumption of the law was always difficult to overcome, and in certain cases (such as the *temporary* exclusion of children) almost impossible. The burden of proof fell on the petitioner. Furthermore, while the testimony of the parties was required, it could not of itself provide proof of nullity. Documentary evidence or the sworn testimony of witnesses was essential.

The Waugh case is reported in '*Decisio* XLVIII' of the *Sacrae Romanae Rotae Decisiones . . . 1936*,[26] the Rota's official record of its proceedings. The 'Decisio' is divided into numbered sections.

Section 1 summarises the facts of the marriage, the divorce, and the first ecclesiastical hearing. It then sets out the grounds on which Waugh claimed nullity: viz. (a) the couple entered marriage having made an agreement [*eo tamen pacto*] that the union could be dissolved at the wish of either party, and (b) 'children were to be entirely excluded [*omnis prolis generatio excluderetur*] for an indefinite period [*ad tempus indeterminatum*]'.

Section 2 clarifies the law, as it applies to the case at hand, regarding the exclusion of indissolubility or permanence. A feature of Waugh's case was that both parties had believed in, and Waugh had publicly advocated, 'modern' divorce. 'It does not follow', say the judges, 'that a marriage is null simply because the parties believe that it can be dissolved'. In short there is no necessary connection between opinions (including opinions expressed in print) and choices made in life. Going further, the judges argued that belief in divorce would make nullity not more, but *less*, likely. Since nullity requires that one or both parties exclude permanence by a 'positive act of the will', a conviction that the civil law excludes permanence from all marriages will remove the motive for willing to exclude it from this one.[27] Further, before an 'act of will' excluding permanence can be made, it must be provoked by some occasion. The occasion will probably cause the 'act of will' to be manifested in writing or in speech, and therefore provable in court.

Sections 4–7 summarise the evidence given by the parties and witnesses, viz. both Evelyns, Alec Waugh, Lady Alathea Fry (She-Evelyn's sister), Sir Geoffrey Fry (Lady Alathea's husband), and Lady Pansy Lamb (friend of both Evelyns). Both Evelyns described themselves as nominal Anglicans (at best), to whom the church wedding was a 'conventional formality', and to whom the words of the ceremony 'meant nothing'. Alec Waugh explained that in the milieu in which the couple lived, marriage was regarded as a contract that could be dissolved in accordance with civil law, while Sir Geoffrey made the possibly more accurate point that they did not regard divorce as the breaking of a contract at all.

Alec Waugh went further to explain that the couple before and after their marriage believed in the ideas recently put forward by Judge Ben B. Lindsey in *Companionate Marriage*.[28] The truth is that He-Evelyn had written articles in 1929 and 1930 espousing two somewhat different views. 'Let the Marriage Ceremony Mean Something', which in part reflected the opinions of Bertrand Russel, advocated 'abolishing the civil marriage contract altogether' and replacing it with 'a licence for the producing of a child'.[29] 'Tell the Truth about Marriage' advocated views close to those of Judge Lindsey. *Companionate Marriage* opens: 'Companionate Marriage is legal marriage, with legalised Birth Control [when Lindsey was writing, birth control was still prohibited in many American states], and with the right to divorce by mutual consent for childless couples, usually without payment of alimony' (p. v). In addition Lindsey preached the necessity for instructions in the art of sex, argued that sexual freedom for the young would prevent over-emphasis on sex to the detriment of other more important aspects of life, and supported monogamous marriage as the ideal. Waugh's 'Tell the Truth about Marriage' also argues for 'a system of legal marriage . . . dissoluble . . . by mutual consent'; for teaching 'fully about birth control'; and for teaching 'children the biology and hygiene of sex'. Waugh also supported monogamy as the ideal (as did Lindsey) and contended that the 'only way in which people can now be impressed with the unimportance of sex in its narrow sense and the importance of marriage in its widest sense . . . is by allowing the widest possible freedom to young people'.[29]

As has been pointed out, these theoretical beliefs were not, in the view of the judges, a motive for the couple to exclude permanence by an 'act of will' from their own marriage, and were probably a disincentive. An occasion to provoke an 'act of will' was required, as was its external manifestation.

The occasion for willing to exclude permanence, and for doing so externally, arose from the serious worry expressed about the marriage by Lady Alathea Fry and by Lady Pansy Pakenham (later Lady Pansy Lamb). Their worry, as was said earlier, was understandable. Waugh was dissolute, penniless, jobless, and, despite the publication of *Rossetti* in April 1928, apparently without prospects. No one in April 1928 could have reliably foretold the success of *Decline and Fall* in October. Nor did Evelyn Gardner appear an inspired judge of character, since she had a recent record of three unsuitable engagements. We now know that Evelyn Gardner's family worked actively to prevent the marriage by persuading Lance Sieveking at the BBC to turn down Waugh's application for a job. Geoffrey Fry, She-Evelyn's brother-in-law, and, as private secretary to the then Prime Minister, Stanley Baldwin, an influential figure, wrote to Sieveking on behalf of the family.[30] His wife Alathea told the court repeatedly: 'We [my sister and I] had many discussions during the period of engagement . . . When they [the two Evelyns] were still engaged I had long discussions with my sister about what they would do if the marriage was not happy'. Such discussions provided the occasion for the couple to make explicit their intention to divorce should the marriage turn out badly, and to do so before witnesses.

The central issue on which the case turned was the nature of the compact or agreement that had existed between the couple in regard to divorce. During the proceedings this issue narrowed to whether or not there had existed before marriage what in French[31] was termed '*un arrangement définitif*' (which I transliterate as a 'definitive arrangement'). The existence of such an arrangement would imply that permanence had been excluded from the marriage by a 'positive act of the will'. Alathea Fry stated: 'My sister said explicitly that if her marriage was not happy, divorce would be the solution, and she would make use of it if the occasion arose'. A judge then asked: 'Was there a definitive arrangement between them on this matter?' Lady Alathea replied: 'That depends on the meaning of the words "definitive arrangement". If "definitive arrangement" implies a formal contract, I cannot commit myself to such a precise statement, but if "definitive arrangement" means that there would be divorce if the marriage was not happy, I believe that I can state this . . . my sister definitively revealed her intention of divorcing if the marriage was not happy'.

Lady Pansy Lamb's evidence went further than this. 'They came to an agreement [*s'accordèrent*] in my presence', she said,

> that, if the marriage was not happy, they would not be bound by it, and Miss Evelyn said to me that she had no intention of remaining married if the marriage did not turn out well [*si le*

mariage ne réussissait pas]. The arrangement was not a written contract but a mutual agreement, each accepting divorce as a definitive solution to possible misfortune.

The Westminster judges did not fully accept this evidence because it seemed to say 'more than the parties said themselves'.

Indeed, the two Evelyns' evidence was less precise than Lady Pansy's. She-Evelyn: 'I do not believe that there was a definitive arrangement. It was a verbal arrangement. I believe that probably, almost certainly, Lady Pansy Lamb was present when we discussed the matter'. Waugh gave similar evidence, ruling out any form of 'explicit contract': 'There was no explicit contract, although when we were engaged each of us was aware of what the other was thinking. We were in full agreement on the matter'. The judges of the Roman Rota were not satisfied with Waugh's statement, and they asked for clarification of the phrase, 'there was no explicit contract' [*Il n'y eut aucun contrat explicite*]. Waugh replied:

When I used the word 'explicit' I was using it loosely. I intended to say that there was no formal and official expression of intention, on the one hand to divorce, on the other hand to accede to divorce, but we discussed the matter fully and often. It was not a simple exchange of ideas between us, but was a true agreement [*Non era per niente un semplice scambio di idee fra di noi, ma era un vero legame . . .*].

Waugh then went on, though not without a touch of irony, to 'confirm the truth of the response given by Lady Pansy Lamb. The occasion was shortly before our marriage . . . Lady Pansy took our marriage a little more seriously than we took it ourselves . . .'. The Rota dismissed the reservations of the Westminster court.

In the light of all the evidence concerning exclusion of indissolubility presented by each party and the four witnesses, the judges concluded:

It is established beyond doubt on the evidence that the parties excluded the indissolubility of the bond of marriage by a specific act of the will. (Section 5)

In summary, and in plain terms, the evidence reveals two young people cheerfully determined on an imprudent marriage but nagged by anxious friends and family to be sensible. As 'modern' believers in 'scientific' birth-control and divorce by mutual consent, the couple reassure their advisors that they will not have children until they can afford them, and that if the marriage goes wrong they will divorce. The more earnestly friends and family press the point, the more explicit become the couple's statements that they will divorce if things turn out badly, and the more clearly formulated becomes their intention. Reverting to legal terminology, the discussions with friends and family became the 'occasion' for one or both of the Evelyns to make an 'act of will', including within their plans divorce in certain circumstances. Thus they made the option of divorce, and therefore impermanence, part of their matrimonial consent. Spoken, witnessed, and proved in court, this limitation of consent rendered it 'defective' and invalidated the marriage.

The argument regarding temporary exclusion of children was decisively rejected by the Rota because it did not nearly meet the required standard of proof. As set out in Section 3, Roman Catholic law views a marriage as invalid if the right to beget children [*ius ad prolem*] is *excluded* by one or both parties, either temporarily or permanently. But a marriage is not considered invalid if one or both parties intend merely to *violate* that right, e.g. by using birth control. The distinction between 'excluding' and 'violating' the right, as the Rota recognised, was tenuous ['*non est facile discernere*']. Consequently the court worked on presumptions. If children were to be avoided permanently, the presumption was that the right had been 'excluded'. But if children had been merely postponed, the presumption was that the right had been merely 'violated'. Overturning the latter presumption and proving that the right had been 'excluded' normally required evidence equivalent to a written contract ['*facilius admittenda est si habeatur pactum formale*'].

The evidence regarding temporary exclusion of children is set out in Sections 8 and 9. That of both Evelyns tended to show that the right had been excluded (though temporarily). But the evidence of the witnesses – on which in law the case depended – fell far short of demonstrating the point.

In the hearing at Westminster Waugh said: 'The arrangement was that, for the moment, there would be no children, but that when financial considerations made it possible, the matter would be reopened and examined anew'. The judges asked: 'Did you grant the right to normal relation?' Waugh's reply: 'Never [*Jamais de la vie*]! The point discussed before marriage was the definitive exclusion of matrimonial rights'. In this context 'matrimonial rights' means the right to acts 'apt for the generation of children' (Canon 1081.2). The Rota judges repeated the question posed by their Westminster colleagues and Waugh replied: 'My intention was not to have children for the time being [*per allora*], leaving open the possibility of discussing the question again later . . .'.

She-Evelyn gave very precise evidence.

> We agreed to exclude children until we judged that we were rich enough; then there was concern about my health. . . . We did not say definitively that we would ever have children. The only definitive arrangement was that we would not have children. . . . I would have held to the arrangement of not having normal relations [i.e. sexual relations without birth control] if my husband had asked to have them.

Whether or not Mrs Nightingale was being more loyal than frank in 1935 only she can say. But her last words very effectively indicated exclusion of right.

In law the decision could not rest on the testimony of the parties, but only on that of the witnesses. They, however, had little to offer. Sir Geoffrey Fry: 'There was no room in their little flat for children. And I suppose that in accordance with the ideas of their circle there was an agreement not to have children'. Alec Waugh: 'Such an agreement was predictable considering the way in which our family discussed the matter'. The female witnesses were somewhat better informed. Lady Alathea: 'She [Evelyn] told me definitively that they intended not to have children until they were rich enough. There was a definitive arrangement between them about this matter'. Lady Pansy testified in the same sense.

On this evidence the judges were not able to conclude, with certainty, that the alleged 'definitive arrangement' (the quotation marks are on the report) to postpone children rendered matrimonial consent defective. Since the case had in view temporary exclusion, the presumption of the law favoured the validity of the marriage. The argument based on temporary exclusion of children was therefore dismissed.

To return to Dr Stannard, Mr Shakespeare, Mr Carpenter and Mrs Nightingale's letter.

The Roman Rota's published report of the Waugh case differs fundamentally from the account popularised by Stannard, Shakespeare, and Carpenter in two ways. And the first difference occurs in an area where the Court's record must surely be held more authoritative than personal recollections.

The three biographers differ from the Rota about the ground(s) upon which the annulment was sought. All three assert that the successful ground was the permanent exclusion of children from the marriage. For Waugh 'to admit', says Stannard, that he and his wife had merely 'agreed to wait' to have children 'would have been damning evidence against the granting of an annulment' (p. 353). Carpenter repeats Stannard (p. 250). Shakespeare is as wrong as he is clear: 'The Vatican Court's decision hinged on the testimony of his [Waugh's] first wife, Evelyn Gardner. He [Waugh] persuaded her to testify that they had married on the understanding that they would never have children. This was not true' (p. 22). But the Rota does not record any argument being put to the court regarding the permanent exclusion of children. On the contrary, as demonstrated above, it records only an argument regarding temporary exclusion, which was put by both Evelyns and every witness, and which was dismissed (Sections 1, 3, 8–9). Clearly the marriage was not declared invalid because the couple decided 'never' to have children – they made no such claim; nor because of temporary exclusion – the court threw the argument out. The annulment was granted because the couple by a positive act of the will excluded permanence from their marriage, i.e. they came to an arrangement, sufficiently definite to modify matrimonial consent, that if the marriage turned out badly they would divorce (Sections 1, 2, 4–7, 10).

The second major difference between the trinity of recent biographers and the official record concerns the truthfulness of the witnesses and Waugh's alleged attempt to 'nobble' them. Stannard claims that Waugh tried to persuade his former wife to testify untruthfully that she had 'refused to have children' (p. 352). Shakespeare claims that Waugh 'persuaded her [She-Evelyn] to testify that they had married on the understanding they would never have children. This was not true' (p. 22). Stannard also claims that Waugh 'primed' Lady Pansy Lamb to say that 'the couple had wanted to remain childless' (p. 353). Further, Stannard, Shakespeare, and Carpenter all assert or imply that the two Evelyns and the witnesses did in fact present this false evidence to the court. Finally each claims that the false evidence determined the successful outcome of the case.

As the statements Waugh is alleged to have persuaded She-Evelyn and Lady Pansy to make differ radically from the statements they actually made to the court, where permanent exclusion was never mentioned; and since the evidence actually presented agrees completely with the information contained in Mrs Nightingale's letter to Dr Stannard – 'I had not refused to have children, but we had agreed to wait until we had an income that did not depend sometimes on others' (pp. 352–3); it is not easy to see what place 'nobbling' or 'priming' might have had in the annulment process.

Perhaps one might reconstruct events by taking distant hints from the correspondence of Guglielmo Marconi, who won a borderline annulment after a heavy campaign of lobbying.[32] Marconi, the Italian-Irish but non-Catholic inventor of radio, married Beatrice O'Brien, daughter of the Irish-Protestant Baron Inchiquin, in the Church of England. As Beatrice was young and ingenuous, her rural-aristocratic family was worried by the inventor-tycoon's age and 'foreignness', but eventually agreed to the marriage on condition that divorce would follow 'in the unfortunate event of things not turning out happily' (p. 254). Some years later Beatrice and Guglielmo divorced. Later still, in 1925, Guglielmo, wishing to marry a Catholic, sought an annulment of his marriage to Beatrice on the grounds that there had been a prior '*understanding* or *agreement* to divorce in the event of our marriage not being a happy one' (p. 256). With characteristic energy he embarked on a campaign to secure the annulment. This is reflected in the letters he wrote to Beatrice. The correspondence can be construed as compromising, and, when relations with Marconi had become embittered by quarrels over money, Beatrice thought to use it against him (p. 269). Alertly read, however, the letters reveal, not an attempt to suborn, but a determined campaign to collect favourable witnesses, to explain what would be required of them, and to make sure they understood what aspects of the truth to emphasise. The marriage was annulled in April 1927.

Waugh lacked Marconi's wealth and influence, and, I imagine, the shameless persistence to visit witnesses and write them long letters of instruction – followed by reminders. We have been told that Waugh sought to persuade Mrs Nightingale to give untrue evidence. But the evidence Mrs Nightingale presented to the court corresponds exactly with what we now know to be the truth.

Furthermore Waugh met his former wife only once, at lunch, immediately before the hearing. Serious 'nobbling' would require that all witnesses be coached well in advance to ensure that all told the same untrue story. The worst one can assume about Waugh, on the available facts, is that he explained to his witnesses – all friends to whom Roman Catholic matrimonial law would have seemed bizarre – what the annulment procedures were, what a witness would be required to do, and what sort of questions would be asked; and that the 'explanations' merged into 'coaching'. But the likelihood of 'coaching' having happened is small, since the Rota judges found the testimony of the witnesses regarding temporary exclusion of children 'vague' (*Testes autem vago modo loquuntur*) and quite useless for Waugh's case (Section 9). If there was 'coaching' of the kind alleged by the biographers, it had no discernible effect on the evidence.

Martin D'Arcy, S.J., Christopher Sykes, Auberon Waugh, and others have written of the Waugh annulment as 'simple'. As Sykes puts it, '. . . everyone consulted agreed that this case was simple' (p. 132), and '. . . a declaration of nullity would be allowed without difficulty' (p. 124). It may be that Waugh's case was simpler than some others of the same kind. But the kind of case was essentially complex and unpredictable. In such matters even the facts are likely to be ambiguous, and motives and intentions are inevitably mixed. Experienced canon lawyers – among whom one does not automatically number literary Jesuits – treated these cases warily. A standard canon law text book of the 1950s warned:

> It cannot be too carefully noted that the application of this principle to concrete cases is always extremely difficult. Cases do not come into the matrimonial court neatly labeled . . . 'condition contrary to the substance of marriage'. They come in a jumble of confused and conflicting testimony . . . The case which we chose for illustration was classed in opposite categories by successive decisions of the Rota, and finally the marriage was upheld . . .[33]

Reading a variety of cases confirms this pessimistic view and suggests that Waugh was moderately lucky to gain his decree of nullity. When the Rota, with world-wide jurisdiction, heard on average only fifty marriage cases each year and granted twenty annulments, no case was cut-and-dried. A single letter expressing life-long fidelity, a discrepancy in evidence, a different set of judges – any one of the many perils of going to law – could have led to a different result.

Conceptually there is nothing 'simple' about an annulment granted because a loving couple has married after agreeing to divorce in the event of the marriage failing. On the contrary it pushes the meaning of 'no real consent' as far as it will reasonably go. Of all the grounds for annulment, it can most plausibly – if mistakenly[34] – be equated to divorce, as is evident from the comment of a divorce law reformer: 'Under this system how much easier . . . to get what amounts to divorce by mutual consent than under our own rather liberal divorce laws' (Lindsey, p. 183). The same reformer viewed this ground for annulment as evidence of the Church of Rome's 'wisdom, shrewdness, psychological penetration' (p. 184).

If the Catholic Church had reason to wince at such praise, Dr Stannard might find in it reason to ponder. As a biographer Stannard believes it was impossible for the two Evelyns to have expected 'a long and happy life together' and simultaneously to have been agreed on divorce in the event of unhappiness. This was possible, he says, only 'in Catholic terms' (p. 155). In other words he implies that Waugh's annulment had no basis in human experience and was therefore a Catholic legal fiction. Most people today, however, happily accept that this double intention can, and does, occur. Certainly no advocate of divorce law reform ever regarded as paradoxical a loving couple's keeping open a line of retreat in divorce. In fact many argued that the right to divorce 'would best insure the success and permanence of the marriage' (Lindsey, p. vii).

As regards Waugh's individual state of mind before marriage, I find Dr Stannard not entirely convincing. In one place he writes of Waugh's 'longing for permanent commitment' and being 'passionately devoted' (p. 155), but soon after endorses Mrs Nightingale's description of him as neither 'warm' nor 'affectionate' (p. 185). Furthermore Mrs Nightingale has confirmed to Dr Stannard that there was an element of 'let's see how it goes' in Waugh's proposal of marriage, and that she 'never forgot it' (p. 146).[35] As I read Waugh's mind, he was sufficiently insouciant, defiant, and theoretically committed to divorce by mutual consent, as well as loving, to make possible the co-existence of a desire for permanence with a conditional intention to divorce in the event of failure. The Rota's decision to accept evidence to this effect seems to me justified both in terms of common human experience and in terms of what we know about Waugh.

Waugh's annulment was granted in the 1930s when a civil divorce commonly entailed collusion and perjury, and when controversy over marriage and divorce – to which Waugh contributed – was at its height. Vatican annulments were caught up in this agitation, and were also the target of bitter sectarian attacks. The cynicism regarding annulments which then emerged still lends colour to allegations, no matter how ill-founded, of bought or otherwise dishonest decisions. Demonstrably the ground on which the Waugh annulment was applied for, and granted, was not that asserted by Stannard, Shakespeare, and Carpenter. Furthermore, the judgement in favour of invalidity was plainly reasonable in terms of the relevant law and in terms of the evidence presented to the court. Nor was the evidence tendered by Waugh, Mrs Nightingale and the four witnesses, as has been alleged, false – it corresponds precisely with the facts presented in Mrs Nightingale's letter to Dr Stannard. It is unlikely that Waugh attempted to persuade the witnesses to lie. Finally, the information presented to the court harmonises with what we know about Waugh's life and his state of mind before marriage. Since the 1930s 'Vatican divorce' has been enveloped in folklore, and now a trinity of biographers is enveloping the Waugh annulment – albeit innocently – in myth. It is time to say quite clearly that they are wrong.

NOTES

1. Nicholas Shakespeare, writer and narrator. 'The Waugh Trilogy': Pt 1, 'Bright Young Thing'; Pt 2, 'Mayfair and the Jungle'; Pt 3, 'An Englishman's Home'. First broadcast 18, 19, 20 April 1987. BBC, Arena. I quote from the post-production script.
2. An excerpt from Mrs Nightingale's letter to Stannard appears in Martin Stannard, *Evelyn Waugh: The Early Years 1903–1939* (London: Dent, 1986) pp. 352–3.
3. Humphrey Carpenter, *The Brideshead Generation: Evelyn Waugh and His Friends* (London: Weidenfeld and Nicolson, 1989) p. 250. No authority for this statement is cited.
4. 'Decisio XLVII', *Sacrae Romanae Rotae Decisiones seu Sententiae quae prodierunt anno 1936*, cura eiusdem S. Tribunalis editae [*The*

Decisions . . . of the Holy Roman Rota . . . 1936], Vol. XXVII (Vatican City: Typis Polyglottis Vaticanis, 1944), pp. 444–50. Each of the statements made here on the authority of Rota's report of the Waugh case is fully discussed later in the article.

5. See Note 4.
6. Evelyn Waugh, 'Let the Marriage Ceremony Mean Something', *Daily Mail*, 8 Oct. 1929, p. 12; 'Tell the Truth about Marriage', *John Bull*, 23 Aug. 1930, p. 7. Rpt. in *Essays, Articles and Reviews of Evelyn Waugh*, ed. Donat Gallagher (London: Methuen, 1983), pp. 94–5.
7. Peter Laslett, 'Marriage's Ups and Downs' (rev. of *Putting Asunder: A History of Divorce in Western Society*), *Times Literary Supplement*, 4–10 Aug. 1989, p. 843.
8. Evelyn Waugh, *A Handful of Dust* (London: Chapman and Hall, 1934).
9. A.P. Herbert, *Holy Deadlock* (London: Methuen, 1934; Penguin, 1955), p. 10.
10. Rev. Dr Rumble, *Radio Replies*, 2nd Series (Sydney: Missionaries of the Sacred Heart, 1952), p. 234. First published in 1934.
11. This account is based on the summary of the Roman Rota's proceedings published in *The Times*, 8 Dec. 1926, p. 15d. The annulment has been extensively debated. An Episcopalian clergyman claimed that neither he nor the celebrant had detected any 'hint . . . [of] compulsion' on the wedding day (*Times*, 18 Nov. 1926, p. 14f). Mrs Belmont (previously Vanderbilt), despite her evidence to the Rota, was later reported in some newspapers as having denied that she had compelled her daughter to marry.
12. 'The Duke of Marlborough', *The Times*, 2 Feb. 1927, p. 15e.
13. Sir William Geary, 'The Vatican and Divorce', *The Times*, 19 Nov. 1926, p. 10d.
14. Thirty letters, mostly under the titles 'The Vatican and Divorce', appeared 16 Nov.–13 Dec. 1926; editorial, 'So-Called Marriage', 18 Nov. 1926, p. 15d; Rota's decision, 'The Marlborough Annulment: Grounds for Decision', 8 Dec. 1926, p. 15d.
15. Lewis and Lewis, 'The Duke of Marlborough', *The Times*, 27 Nov. 1926, p. 13d.
16. Quoted in John St John, *To the War with Waugh* (London: Leo Cooper, 1974), p. 15.
17. 'Lesson of the Master', *Sunday Times*, 27 May 1956, p. 8a. Rpt. in *Essays, Articles and Reviews*, pp. 515–18.
18. T.L. Bouscaren, compiler, *Canon Law Digest: Officially Published Documents Affecting the Code of Canon Law*, vols 1 and 2 with annual supplements (Milwaukee: Bruce, 1934–7).
19. Evelyn Gardner's brother-in-law, Geoffrey Fry, who was Private Secretary to the then Prime Minister, Stanley Baldwin, wrote to Lance Sieveking at the BBC on behalf of the Gardner family when Waugh was being considered for a job. Although Sieveking believed Waugh 'obviously well qualified', Fry asked him 'not to get [Waugh] a job' because Waugh wanted to marry Evelyn Gardner, 'a plan that did not

commend itself to the family' (see extract from Sieveking's unpublished autobiography in Frederick L. Beaty, 'Evelyn Waugh and Lance Sieveking: New Light on Waugh's relations with the BBC', *Papers on Language and Literature*, 25, No. 2 (Spring 1989), 188. Lady Burghclere visited Waugh's Oxford tutor and later warned her daughter against 'vodka and absinthe . . . Sodom and Gomorrah' (see Jacqueline McDonnell, 'The Tatler's Role in Waugh's Downfall', *Times Higher Educational Supplement*, 23 June 1989, p. 16). Evelyn Gardner's engagements and her attitude towards the Waugh marriage, and the events leading up to the marriage, are well covered by Stannard, pp. 134–55 and Carpenter, pp. 178–80.

20. See Stannard, pp. 183–4; McDonnell, 'The Tatler's Role in Waugh's Downfall', Carpenter, pp. 191–7.
21. Martin D'Arcy, S.J., 'The Religion of Evelyn Waugh', in David Pryce-Jones, ed., *Evelyn Waugh and His World* (London: Weidenfeld and Nicolson, 1973), p. 74.
22. Christopher Sykes, *Evelyn Waugh: A Biography* (London: Collins, 1975,) pp. 123–4, 132.
23. 'Decision XLVII', p. 445.
24. 'The Religion of Evelyn Waugh', p. 74.
25. Sykes, who was given a great deal of reliable information about the Westminster proceedings, complains that the papers were sent to Rome only after Archbishop Hinsley succeeded Cardinal Bourne in March 1936, i.e. eight months after 28 June 1935 when Westminster decreed nullity (p. 162). Sykes presents Waugh's annulment as a legally 'simple' case that was prolonged into a 'drawn-out ordeal' by this delay, and blames the 'indolence' of the President of the Court and the 'inefficiency' of the Diocese of Westminster (pp. 160–3). The Rota on the other hand censured the eighteen-month delay in the Westminster hearings, which Sykes tolerantly accepts. The kind of annulment Waugh sought was essentially complex, and, following the adverse publicity accorded the Marconi case, controversial. I therefore suspect that the delay was partly caused by official hesitation.
26. See Note 4.
27. The judges in Waugh's case took the narrow view of this matter. In a similar case the judges held that 'where a person's views on marriage are such as to make it unlikely that he or she would contemplate an indissoluble union, these may be considered by the court as evidence bearing on the actual intention of the person contracting marriage'. *Canon Law Digest*, p. 318.
28. Judge Ben B. Lindsey and Wainwright Evans, *The Companionate Marriage*, with an Introduction by the Hon. Mrs Bertrand Russell (London: Brentano's Ltd., 1928).
29. See Note 6.
30. See Note 19.
31. Evidence given to the first hearing at Westminster is printed in French. Evidence presented directly to the re-hearing before the Rota

is published in Italian. The body of the report is printed in Latin. English could not be used for the evidence because it was not then recognised by the court as an official language.

32. The following account is based on Degna Marconi, _My Father, Marconi_ (London: Frederick Muller, 1962), pp. 149–63 (marriage), pp. 242–63 (annulment), pp. 269ff (use of correspondence against Marconi).

33. T.L. Bouscaren and A.C. Ellis, _Canon Law: A Text and Commentary_, 2nd rev. ed (Milwaukee: Bruce, 1951), p. 560.

34. Lindsey was uninformed about annulment procedures: 'Agree when you marry . . . that you will quit by mutual consent if you can't make a go of it, and apparently you can . . . convert that marriage into an "annulment" by mutual consent merely by making known to the Rota the existence of such an agreement' (p. 183). This ignores the arduous legal process required. More importantly it ignores the questions put to couples planning to marry in the Roman Catholic Church, which made it very unlikely that they could later claim an annulment on this ground. The Waugh and Marconi annulments were assisted by the fact that the applicants were nominal Christians who married like-minded partners in a Church of England for sentimental rather than religious reasons. That the Rota granted only twenty annulments per year indicates how rigidly the marriage laws were administered.

35. Michael Davie, ed. _The Diaries of Evelyn Waugh_ (London: Weidenfeld and Nicolson, 1976), p. 305: 'When Waugh proposed . . . he suggested that they should get married "and see how it goes"'. It was a fatal phrase, for it gave Evelyn Gardner the sense that Waugh was not wholly committed to the alliance. Nor perhaps was she . . .'. In speaking to Stannard, Mrs Nightingale confirmed that Waugh used 'words to that effect' (p. 146).

5

Evelyn Waugh and the BBC

Winnifred M. Bogaards

Evelyn Waugh emerged as a writer in the same year the BBC came of age as a public broadcasting authority. Over the next four decades both grew in influence and reputation. While their mutual concern for literature ensured a continuous interconnection throughout this period, there was never the slightest agreement in their social philosophies. Though the BBC changed radically after World War II, Waugh disapproved of what it was before the conflict as much as what it became after the peace. Although he worked very hard to change his own position in the social hierarchy operative in Britain when he came of age in the twenties, throughout his life Waugh wished for as little change as possible in the structure itself. The BBC, on the other hand, was from its inception consciously designed as a force to create social change and became, perhaps half-consciously, a mirror reflecting it. The interdependence of and the antagonisms between Waugh and the Corporation illustrate in a limited context larger forces at work in British society in this century.

In the 1920s two new means of communication, the cinema and the wireless, transformed mass entertainment and home life. The BBC began regular broadcasting in November 1922. By March 1923, 125,000 people had received licences; by the end of 1924 that number topped one million; by 1931 one family in three had a wireless set (Branson, 233). The increase in numbers was made possible by rapid decreases in prices through the decade. In 1923, when the average earnings of a skilled industrial worker were £3 6s, sets costing between £25 and £35 were affordable only for the middle class, with the result that many working people built their own crystal sets at home. By 1925, however, the price had dropped to under £10 and by 1930 the wireless, technically much improved, was, like the car, an unexceptional part of everyday life bringing urban and especially rural areas into daily contact with a larger world (Branson, 234–5).

In 1927 the original British Broadcasting Company, formed by the manufacturers of the receiving sets and licensed by the Post Office to build broadcasting stations and transmit programmes, was transformed into the British Broadcasting Corporation, an independent, publicly appointed body with which the manufacturers no longer had any connection (Branson, 233). Most influential in formulating its social role was its first Director-General, John Reith, a deeply religious man. Reith was convinced that broadcasting must be conducted 'as a Public Service, with definite standards . . . not . . . used for entertainment purposes alone . . . [It] should bring into the greatest number of homes . . . all that is best in every department of human knowledge, endeavour and achievement . . . The preservation of a high moral tone is obviously of paramount importance' (Mowat, 242). It must also be impartial. At the time of the General Strike in 1926 Reith cancelled the broadcast of the Archbishop of Canterbury appealing for a settlement out of his fear that this broadcast might be made an excuse by Winston Churchill for commandeering the BBC as an instrument of government propaganda (Mowat, 320).

A typical weekday's broadcasting included around three or four hours of music, ranging from classical to popular; an hour of readings from or talks about classical and serious contemporary literature; a half-hour for each of children and sports programmes; two twenty-five minute weather and news broadcasts; and two or three hours of current affairs. On Sundays no programmes interfered with morning church services; the afternoon was devoted to classical music, with perhaps a half-hour of scenes from Shakespeare; the evening included church services of two different denominations and 'The Week's Good Cause', more classical music and one weather and news programme (Branson, 236–7).

In 1964 social historian Harry Hopkins mockingly described the BBC of the interwar years as 'an almost perfect embodiment of the old authoritarian culture: truth and beauty handed down, with due care and befitting gravity, from the Portland Place Olympus' (226). While this statement is not false, it carefully ignores the fact that precisely the same statement could be made about the public school-university system of formal education found in Britain during this period (and later), except that the latter was very expensive and therefore available only to the middle and upper classes, and on average inferior in both breadth and depth in the areas of music, current affairs and literature (unless one is speaking of the university specialists in these fields) to the education provided free by the BBC. In addition to the regular programming, adult educational talks, first broadcast in the autumn of 1924, became a regular feature of the Corporation in 1927 when R.S. Lambert, who had served as a tutor for the Workers Educational Association, joined the BBC specifically to establish them. The Hadow Report of 1928 recommended the setting up of formal or informal 'listening groups' to discuss these programmes and over a thousand had been created by the winter of 1930–31 (Briggs, II, 218–21). The BBC was the Open University of the interwar period. Before World War I an intelligent lower-class man like E.M. Forster's Leonard Bast in *Howard's End* (1910) was doomed to frustration because he could never afford a decent education and rarely a single concert ticket. After 1922 he had only to turn a dial. Oddly, Forster and other members of the Bloomsbury group, who shared Reith's belief that society could be changed for the better by raising the cultural level of the lower classes, and who lectured for the Workers Educational Association, did not become broadcasters, although Forster and Desmond MacCarthy gave their time freely to the discussion of policies for the fledgeling Talks Department (Briggs, II, 127).

By his own account in his aptly named autobiography, *A Little Learning*, Waugh was a very badly educated graduate of an average public school and Oxford when, on 30 August 1924, he returned home to find his father had bought 'a horrible wireless apparatus' (*Diaries*, 176). Four days later he describes his 'father's new electrical machine' as a 'tiresome toy' (*Diaries*, 179). On 15 September he relishes a friend's joke 'that cancer is caused by wireless' (*Diaries*, 179). On 23 November 1925, when the boys at the school where he was teaching were allowed to listen to a concert on the wireless, the experience 'confirmed me in my detestation of the invention' (*Diaries*, 235). The aversion was indeed lifelong.

Radio offered little that would have pleased young Evelyn Waugh in the aimless, frequently drunken, always impoverished and generally depressed years after he left Oxford in 1924 with a poor third until he found his literary vocation in 1927, or later. Serious music lovers were the listeners best served by the BBC; because he was tone deaf (and in later life totally deaf in one ear), music was an art form he could never appreciate. Because radio was an aural medium, it could not cater to his one strong interest, the visual arts. The BBC's religious programming had little appeal to the young Waugh, who had lost his inherited Church of England faith at public school, and even less to the older Waugh, who became a devout convert to Catholicism in 1930. While his father and brother Alec were, like so many other Englishmen, enthusiastic cricketers who could enjoy radio commentaries on this and other sports, Evelyn had not the slightest interest in athletic activities. He knew nothing of science and had no mechanical skills so could not join the many amateurs who loved building and tinkering with their sets even when they had little interest in the programme received. Current affairs and news programming would have bored a young man whose diaries of the twenties reveal, with one exception, not the slightest interest in the larger world around him. He did force himself to notice the General Strike (250) but followed the crisis in the newspapers (251) rather than on the wireless (and of course supported the government side, volunteering as a special constable). While literature certainly interested him, he wanted to read books not listen to them being read.

On 21 February 1927, the year the BBC became a Public Corporation, Waugh, having been sacked from his most recent job as a schoolmaster, announced in his diary that 'the time had arrived to set about being a man of letters' (281). He kept that promise almost immediately by getting a trial position as a journalist with the *Daily Express* and having a story accepted for publication. By July he had settled down to work on his biography of Rossetti, which was published in April of 1928. Waugh may have detested the wireless and banned it from his personal life, but from the beginning he realised the importance of publicity in advancing his professional career (Stannard, 216–17). The fact that he wrote to Lance Sieveking of the BBC, proposing a talk on Rossetti for the artist's May 12 centenary, a month after his book's publication (it was not accepted), is his tacit admission that this medium was now a firmly established and powerful force shaping public opinion.[1]

As Frederick L. Beaty has recently revealed, he also attempted to get employment with the BBC in order to finance his marriage to Evelyn Gardner. He had a previously unknown interview with Lancelot Sieveking for that purpose sometime between his proposal on 12 December 1927 (*Diaries*, 284, 294–5) and their elopement on 27 June 1928 (Beaty, 189). Sieveking's unpublished 'Autobiography' reveals that Geoffrey Fry, husband of Evelyn

Gardner's sister, first sent him a note asking that he get Waugh a job, then another asking him to go through the motions at the interview but not to employ him because he was not acceptable to Gardner's family.[2] Ironically, John Heygate, the lover who would wreck this brief marriage in the summer of 1929, was at the time employed as a news editor at the BBC (Stannard, 183).

Despite these inauspicious beginnings, the relationship between Waugh and the Corporation lasted for the rest of his life and followed a fairly consistent pattern for those next thirty-five years. When Waugh needed publicity or money, he approached the BBC, but most often the BBC approached him, an indication of his reputation as an important writer and of the Corporation's policy of bringing to its listeners the best of contemporary literature. When projects floundered the cause was most often the Corporation's inability to meet his demands for extraordinarily high fees.

By 1930 the publication of *Decline and Fall* (1928) and *Vile Bodies* (1930) had raised Waugh from poverty and obscurity to a position of fame and fortune he never relinquished. When the average wage in Britain was £260 a year and the entire world was suffering from economic depression, Waugh was making £2500 a year (*Diaries*, 20 May 1930, 309) and spending every penny of it in order to keep a place in the fashionable, titled and wealthy circles he now frequented (Stannard, 215).

In May 1930 the BBC paid Waugh 20 guineas for dramatising John Buchan's *Thirty-Nine Steps* (22 May 1930 contract, CFI); two months later they wanted him to come in for a voice test (7 July 1930 letter, TFI) but he replied there would be little point if they found his 'avarice insupportable' and since he was getting £20 for writing a thousand words, he expected £25 for speaking a thousand (undated 8 or 9 July 1930 letter, TFI). The price was too high (LF reply of 10 July 1930, TFI). Two years later they paid him 25 guineas, more than they paid anyone else, for an 1800 word talk 'To An Old Man' in the series 'To An Unnamed Listener' with an additional 15-guinea fee for printing the talk in the *Radio Times* (J.R. Ackerley, letters of 9 and 11 August, 5 and 27 September 1932, TFI). Although his trip to the Arctic forced him to decline (undated c. 9 July 1934 letter to Ackerley, TFI) an offer to take a satirical part in the new series of talks, 'Speeches that Never Happened' (Ackerley letter of 4 July 1934, TFI), monetary considerations again cancelled his participation in the series 'Among the British Islanders'. The BBC wanted Waugh to write dialogue in which the chief character would be a Martian anthropologist collecting notes on Great Britain 'since you have often written on the strange habits of British tourists' (JSAS letter of 23 October 1934, TFI). They offered 15 guineas, which Waugh rejected in one of many concise and witty cards to or about the Corporation: 'B.B.C.L.S.D.N.B.G' (4 November 1934 card to Peters, *Letters*, 92). Waugh wanted an unacceptable 30 guineas for the dialogue (letter to A.D. Peters, 12 November 1934, TFI).

On the other hand, when Waugh needed publicity for his collection of short stories, *Mr. Loveday's Little Outing*, he approached the Corporation (30 June 1937 letter from Peters, TFI) and they broadcast 'Bella Fleace Gave a Party' (National Service, 29 August 1937) and 'On Guard' (West Regional Service, 18 March 1938). Waugh's regular appearances on the BBC from 1936 may be attributed to his pressing need for money to finance his marriage to the aristocratic Laura Herbert on 17 April 1937 (Stannard, Chapter 13). An extract from *Decline and Fall* was broadcast on the Empire service on 16 July 1936. In 1937 he made a five minute appeal for St Joseph's Nursing Home on 'The Week's Good Cause' (National Service, 29 August) and talked with Victor Bridges for half an hour in the series 'Readers and Reading' (West Regional Service, 16 November). In 1938 extracts from his travel books were read on the National Service series 'The Englishman Abroad' (7 June) and he gave a fifteen-minute talk in the West Regional Series 'Up to London' (21 June).

The Thirties were good years for both Waugh and the Corporation, bringing them both popular success and critical acclaim. Both expanded their horizons, though with different aims. In December 1932 the BBC began the Empire Service, whose English-language broadcasts were principally designed to keep British expatriates in touch with the mother country.[3] Waugh left behind him the narrow, insular little world described in his diaries of the twenties to become a world traveller and foreign correspondent in places as diverse as Spitzbergen, Ethiopia, British Guiana and Mexico. His travel books of the period seek to inform British readers about these exotic locales while such satiric novels as *Black Mischief* (1932) and *A Handful of Dust* (1934) counterpoint savagery abroad with savagery at home.

Despite his regular and lucrative appearances on the medium, Waugh still took pride in not listening to the wireless. He wrote in his diary for 23 August 1939: 'am maintaining our record as being the only English family to eschew the radio throughout the crisis' (437), and forced his dinner guest Lady Diana Cooper to go to her car to catch the news bulletins (*Letters*, 125; *Diaries*, 29 June 1939). After he joined the Royal Marines in December 1939, his letters to his wife record his ongoing battle against the machine. The mess had only two rooms, one with a ping-pong table, the other with a wireless; 'the noise is overwhelming' (15 January 1940, *Letters*, 134). As soon as he got on the mess committee he began 'trying to suppress the wireless, ping-pong table & other, rare recreations of my juniors' (23? January 1940, *Letters*, 136) but without success. Ten months later he complains that 'in the mess the wireless plays ceaselessly' (16 November 1941, *Letters*, 157).

And, he might have realised, inevitably. Despite Waugh's aversion, in a world of air raids and paper shortages, radio was the most important and reliable means of entertainment, education, propaganda and communication. 'The reassuring voice of the BBC reached out across the oceans and the jungles and the deserts' (Hopkins, 22). It played the vital role of making 'genuine contact with the mass of ordinary people', lightening the boredom of war workers and soldiers such as those in Waugh's mess, binding home and war fronts in a common camaraderie (Hopkins, 227). Fortunately Reith had already resigned as Director General in 1938 because there was no room in the new world created by the war for his approach to programming, or for announcers who wore dinner jackets at the microphone 'to establish the proper tone' as they had done since 1925 (Hopkins, 226). In 1941 the first British soap opera, 'Front Line Family', went on the air and lively popular entertainers like comedian Tommy Handley on ITMA ('It's That Man Again') cheered both beleaguered civilians and war-weary servicemen (Hopkins, 227).

The BBC now encountered so formidable a demand for information from soldiers who had their first opportunity for education through its programmes that 'it was driven to devise for the Forces Programme a new type of radio feature at first entitled "Any Questions" but soon rechristened "The Brains Trust"' (Hopkins, 21) on which Professor C.E.M. Joad was a regular member, and gained a national reputation as a sage answering listeners' questions. Waugh took part in one of these programmes on 2 April 1942. In his diaries Waugh savaged the two regular members of the panel (Commander Campbell was 'vulgar, insincere, conceited'; Joad 'goatlike, libidinous, garrulous') and the format ('the questions the panel had to answer were too general to allow proper discussion within our limits') (Leave: Wednesday 1 April-Saturday 11 April 1942, 520). He reported to his agent Peters that when the Brains Trust people were 'smugly saying that anyone ought to be paid equal wages with soldiers . . . I suggested that we made a start by each accepting 1/3 for his afternoon's work. They were aghast but ashamed to dissent so I left them with that decision but the certainty in my mind that they would rat as soon as my back was turned.' If they ratted (as they did) he promised to 'give the press the full story with details and I hope to do something to discredit Joad (which is greatly in the national interest)' (4? April 1942, *Letters*, 159), a promise he kept in an interview in the *Daily Sketch* reported in the *Evening Standard*.

Despite his total disgust with this experience of popular education, Waugh appeared on a version of the programme a second time, solely because he wanted to insult Lord Rothermere. Many people organised private versions of the popular programme during the war for charitable or entertainment purposes,[4] among them Waugh's friend Ann O'Neill (later Lady Rothermere). He accepted an invitation to take part in her 'Brains Trust' so that he could then refuse the dinner she and Rothermere usually gave afterward, citing his distaste for Rothermere's refusal to serve wine to his guests as his reason. As he admitted in his diary, 'my malice has undone me' (written on Thursday 30 December 1943, 556); there was no dinner afterwards and he was forced to take part in an event which was even 'more painful than I expected. Bill Astor shone in a horrible sort of way. Two seedy socialists, the editors of *New Statesman* and *Evening Standard*, were outstandingly bad. Hugh Sherwood cocky. I was sulky and cross, the audience very unintelligent' (*Diaries*, written on 31 January 1944, 557). Three months later he described these efforts to educate the masses to his friend Lady Dorothy Lygon in equally scathing terms (23 March 1944, *Letters*, 181–2).

At this time Waugh secured three months' leave to begin writing *Brideshead Revisited* (1945) a novel which, together with the later war trilogy *Sword of Honour* (1952–61), expresses his disillusionment with the war and the changes it brought to British society. Like Charles Ryder in the novel, Waugh had at Oxford and later escaped from a middle class home he considered dull and shabbygenteel (Stannard, 91, 93, 97, 102, 111, 447) into a moneyed, upper class circle of often riotous, luxury-loving Bright Young Things through talent, wit and spurts of hard work. Conversion to Catholicism in 1930 had given him a sense of permanent spiritual values which sustained him both in the face of his first wife's adultery and as he racketed alone through the pleasure palaces of high society. The annulment of his first marriage enabled him to marry again, happily, into a Catholic branch of the same aristocratic family. His new wife's grandmother generously bought the couple the fine country house Piers Court as a wedding present at a price (£3550) which Waugh could ill have afforded himself (Stannard, 439, 441, 444, 449). Just as he had attained everything he wanted, the war changed everything. For nearly a decade he had been able to indulge his taste for fine food and drink, fashionable clothing, first-class travel. Now he found himself, like Ryder, in a sensually deprived world where all luxuries were rationed or non-existent. Like Ryder he mourned the great country house, symbol of his chosen values, first encountered in all its glory in the twenties, desecrated at war's end by an invasion of lower-class Hoopers.

The election of a socialist government in 1945 radically changed the old power structure, continuing the heavy wartime taxation of the class with which he had allied himself in order to provide basic services and to build red-brick universities for those who had never before had such opportunities. The self-made country squire from the middle class had no sympathy for other bright young men from the lower classes who were seeking their room at the top, especially when their paths were being smoothed at his expense. A 1952 letter to Nancy Mitford is representative of his views: 'I make £10,000 a year, which used to be thought quite a lot, I live like a mouse in shabby-genteel circumstances, I keep no women or horses or yachts, yet I am bankrupt, simply by the politicians buying votes with my money' (14 January, *Letters*, 365). In *Scott-King's Modern Europe* (1947) and *Love Among the Ruins* (1953) he describes a new society in which boring uniformity, bureaucracy and an absence of beauty are the dominant characteristics.

There is no evidence that Waugh saw any connection between the excellent free education the BBC had been offering those who could not afford a formal one in the interwar period and the demands for social change after World War II, but that connection undoubtedly exists. There is no evidence that he shared the view of the former head of talks for BBC-TV, and later BBC research historian, Leonard Miall that the solidly Labour Forces vote which

brought the socialists to power was largely attributable to the
education in current affairs provided by the Army Bureau of
Current Affairs and wartime BBC broadcasts such as the 'Brains
Trust' he so much despised.[5] He simply saw the Corporation as
part of the enemy camp.

While Waugh fought in the decades after the war to turn back
the clock, the BBC, under the guidance of its new Director-
General, Mr W.J. Haley, formerly Joint Managing Director of the
Manchester Guardian and the *Manchester Evening News* (Briggs, III,
552), sought to make itself a medium reflecting the new Britain.
With considerable diplomacy he created a compromise of three
quite different programmes for the three large social classes, giving
each a name which tactfully avoided the slightest reference to
class: the 'Light Programme' for Waugh's Hoopers, the 'Home
Service' for the middle class and the 'Third Programme' for the
cultural elite (Hopkins, 227). The old 'Empire Service' became the
'Overseas Service' with such external services as the Arabic, Far
Eastern, African and Latin American broadcasting in foreign languages with the aim of representing British culture to colonial and
ex-colonial peoples.[6]

The BBC conducted 'Listener Research' to find out what would
please those who tuned into the Light Programme which, by 1949,
had captured almost two-thirds of all BBC listeners (Hopkins, 227).
The answer was undemanding music, panel games, request and quiz
programmes, fifteen-minute 'real-life' serials and comedy shows
(Hopkins, 228). The BBC staff quintupled in size in the postwar
period in order to provide this new 'pop radio' (Hopkins, 231).

On 23 June 1947 Waugh recorded in his diary the amazing news
that he had purchased a wireless set. 'Sir Max Beerbohm had made
me think that the Third Programme might interest us, particularly
when we are in Ireland. I have listened attentively to all programmes and nothing will confirm me more in my resolution to
emigrate' (681). His views of the Light Programme and its deleterious effects on the nation were neatly summed up in a letter to John
Betjeman just after the wartime comedian Tommy Handley ('It's
That Man Again') died in 1949: 'BBC jauntiness of the Tom (Glad
he's dead) Handley sort was infecting aesthetics & pushing it
below the surface into popular underworld' (18 January, *Letters*,
296). His own work for the Corporation was almost always broadcast on the Third Programme. It followed almost the same pattern
found in the Thirties. Usually the BBC approached him with

suggested projects after which his demands for extraordinarily high fees were either accepted or the projects shelved. Often he was difficult and demanding as he had not been before the war; however, when it suited him to approach the Corporation, he was courteous and cooperative.

According to Sykes (345), postwar relations between Waugh and the BBC began very badly when they sent an emissary who offended him to ask him to introduce the usual 'World Round-up' programme before the sovereign's Christmas broadcast in 1945; he angrily refused and the insult was never forgotten. Sykes refers to the emissary only as 'Kurtweiler', the nickname Waugh gave him, but in *The Master Eccentric: The Journals of Rayner Heppenstall*, Heppenstall reveals that he was not only the emissary but an admirer of Waugh's writing who had suggested him for this programme (239). Heppenstall angrily denies Sykes's representation of Kurtweiler as 'a disappointed novelist, a deeply class-conscious man . . . who regarded Evelyn's work as decidedly inferior to his own' (238–40) and wonders why Sykes never asked him for his account of this occasion (242). Although the BBC files provide no objective evidence about Heppenstall's behaviour, they do prove Sykes wrong about the date, which was 1946, and suggest that Waugh behaved at least as badly as he claimed Heppenstall had done. Waugh's desire to escape rationing and other deprivations of postwar British life led him to give serious consideration to this proposal that he be the 'leading Christian writer' who would travel to various European capitals for three weeks to prepare a narrative to accompany broadcasts of Christmas music from the Christian cities of Europe (Rayner Heppenstall, letter of 25 October, Waugh's reply of 28 October 1946, SFI). The project was ultimately dropped because Waugh demanded his fees and expenses in foreign currencies, but Heppenstall's internal memo on his meetings with Waugh make clear how obnoxious Waugh had been ('Mr. Waugh repeatedly pointed out to me that he was "used to living luxuriously"') and how much his behaviour had been resented: 'My personal impression of his voice in conversation is that it is a little pompous and unattractive . . . My personal opinion is that Mr. Waugh is sufficiently interested in the amenities of the tour proposed to do a thoroughly competent job of reportage on the places suggested, but that his self interest is sufficiently marked to prevent an inspired occasion' (Heppenstall to D[irector of]F[eatures], 4 November 1946, SFI).

In June 1947, the year Waugh published widely his responses to Hollywood and Forest Lawn Cemetery, the BBC wanted to get him for their 'Books and Authors' programme to talk about Hollywood or anything else he fancied (Arthur Calder-Marshall, letter of 6 June 1947, TFI), but their fee of 12 guineas was not sufficient (12 June 1947, *Letters*, 253). However, Harman Grisewood, then Director of Talks, was particularly anxious to get a recording of Waugh reading from his article 'Half in Love with Easeful Death: An Examination of Californian Burial Customs', published in the *Tablet*, and also to make a permanent processed recording for Archives (Eileen Malony letter to Head of West Regional Programmes, 18 February 1948, TFI). Eight months later he succeeded by increasing the fee to £25 for the first and subsequent broadcasts, with a further £17 for overseas repetitions and a personal recording fee of 15 guineas for the first broadcast, with 75 per cent for repeats at home and 50 per cent for those overseas, the fees to go to a Catholic charity (BBC contract, 13 February 1948, TFI).

Grisewood's staff, who had to execute this commission, were much less pleased than he with the prospect. Eileen Malony of Home Talks, London, wrote to the Head of West Regional Programmes:

> I am afraid circumstances compel me to wish on to you a baby of a particularly tiresome nature . . . As you will see from the attached correspondence Mr. Waugh's attitude towards this proposition is not exactly co-operative . . . I suggest you put your best-natured, most patient and long-suffering Talks producer on to the job as these qualities will be required in a very high degree. (18 February 1948).

In the spring of 1948 the BBC investigated the possibility of getting Waugh to dramatise *Scott-King* and *The Loved One* (Val Gielgud to H. Dickinson, 23 April 1948, SFI). Waugh thought it was too early to do *The Loved One* but wanted to collaborate on the script for *Scott-King* with someone from the Corporation (Dickinson to Gielgud, 12 May 1948, SFI). Nothing came of this suggestion at the time or in 1952 when Waugh consented to a proposed BBC production of *Scott-King* to be dramatised by Lance Sieveking (Davis, *Catalogue* E736; Beaty, 192).

In the summer of 1948 Waugh's close friend Christopher Sykes joined the advisory board of the Third Programme but neither of his first two proposals for Waugh programmes reached the air. He suggested a semi-dramatised version of *Work Suspended* (Sykes to Waugh, 1 June 1948, SFI) to which Waugh agreed (internal memo of 7 June, SFI) but the Corporation decided the work could not be easily or effectively adapted (Stephen Potter internal memo, 14 July, SFI). On 16 July 1948 Sykes asked Waugh to do a talk on Georges Bernanos, who had just died (TFI). Waugh replied that he could not accept because '*je ne parle pas ni comprens la langues des grenouilles*' (undated postcard postmarked 19 July, TFI). A year later he refused an offer from the Schools Broadcasting Department to give a short talk on his impressions of Abyssinia (John Hunter Blair letter of 27 June 1949, TFI) with a postcard on which he had written the single word 'No' (undated; postmarked 29 June, TFI). P.H. Newby of the Talks Department was equally unsuccessful in 1950 when he asked Waugh for an unpublished short story and to be part of a conversation with a 'sympathetic friend' about his work (3 July 1950, TFI). Waugh replied the latter proposition was not 'practicable, because I never mention my writing to my friends' and the former impossible because 'an unpublished short story will cost you a great deal more than you can afford' (5 July 1950, TFI; *Letters*, 330).

In 1951, however, at Sykes's insistence (Sykes, 346), Waugh offered to do a critical talk on the 100 best books as selected for the Festival of Britain (Sykes's letter to Ronald Boswell, 15 February 1951, TFI). They accepted enthusiastically (Boswell telegram to Sykes, 15 February, TFI) and subsequently agreed to a fee of 50 guineas for a twenty-minute talk plus Waugh's first-class expenses for travel to London (Boswell to John Montgomery of A.D. Peters, 24 April, TFI). They were equally pleased with Waugh's suggestion that he examine the exhibits from the point of view of progress and give the talk the title 'A Progressive Game' (Waugh postcard to Ronald Lewin, 25 April; Lewin's reply of 3 May, TFI).

Perhaps hoping to take advantage of these unusually amicable overtures, Ronald Lewin proposed in May that Waugh comment on a series of six talks by Bertrand Russell on 'Living in an Atomic Age' (4 May, TFI), but Waugh declined in a letter of 6 May (TFI) worth quoting for its expression of his uncompromising religious views:

It is nice of you to suggest my answering Lord Russell but I am not the man for it. He is to me as Fr. Copplestone is to him. I am

no trained philosopher. I do know enough, however, to realise
that there is no such thing as a general Christian philosophy
common to all the 'Churches' in this country.

There may here & there (I think in Cornwall) be survivals of
orthodox Calvinism – mad, bad and dangerous to know, but at
least coherent & consistent. Apart from that there is simply
Catholic philosophy. The other 'Churches' make sense so far as
they borrow from it.

The unusually smooth negotiations over 'A Progressive Game'
took a less happy turn when Waugh sent in his script. Lewin told
him, 'you have not done either yourself or, perhaps, the exhibition
justice'. He complained that Waugh had misrepresented the
judges by saying they had chosen the hundred 'best writers' when
they made it clear they had selected 'a hundred representative
writers' (10 May, TFI). Although Waugh told Sykes privately, 'I
don't want to take a course in "creative writing" from this nonen-
tity', (Sykes, 347), he agreed with surprising alacrity that he had
misrepresented the judges' aims and made further changes (undated postcard received 14 May, TFI), but Lewin was still not
happy (internal memo of 15 May, TFI) nor were the producers to
whom he showed the script (internal memo of 17 May, TFI). The
talk was, however, broadcast on 17 May with the result that the
Director of the National Book League complained that the opening
sentences were 'damaging to the interests of the League'. Waugh
agreed to revise them (John Montgomery of A.D. Peters to Lewin,
24 May, TFI) before the text appeared in the *Listener* of 31 May
(872–3). It is clear from this correspondence that Waugh made
more than the 'few alterations' Sykes mentions in his account of
the episode (Sykes, 346–7).
    Waugh may also have been more than usually co-operative
about 'A Progressive Game' because he wanted to use the BBC to
provide exposure for and a defence of his novel *Helena*, a critical
failure when it was published in 1950. Even before it was finished
Waugh regarded this novel as a work of art which would nevertheless please no one else. 'My *Helena* is a great masterpiece. How
it will flop', he wrote Nancy Mitford (16 November 1949, *Letters*,
313). According to Sykes (344), he and Third Programme Director
Harman Grisewood had to battle hard from January 1951 onwards
to get the BBC to agree to a dramatisation of the second part of the

novel in a first-class production by Sykes ultimately broadcast on 16 December.[7] In October Waugh wrote Grisewood that he wanted 'to preach' on the wireless the day before the novel was broadcast in order 'to explain to listeners the point of the story which the reviews missed. Expense no object' (undated, c. 24 October post-card, TFI), a plan which was accepted. Waugh suspended his distaste for the wireless long enough to listen to the dramatisation and wrote Miss Flora Robson, the actress who played Helena, warm praise of her performance.[8]

In his biography (344–5) Sykes attributes the antipathy to Waugh which he discovered at the BBC during the fight for *Helena* to the fact that

> a larger proportion of those responsible for the literary part of its output were men of talent who had not fulfilled earlier promise. They were naturally envious of one whose gifts, in their own estimation, were in no way above their own, but who, never-theless, had hit the jackpot. Most of such people were extremely class-conscious and thus repelled by his extreme conservatism, and his openly expressed contempt for the age of the common man . . . When Evelyn offered the BBC *Helena*, the novel by him that they most despised, these people instinctively obstructed its chance of success.

The next sentence in Sykes's text begins, 'Evelyn had never been at pains to be on good terms with the BBC', but Sykes makes no connection between this well-documented fact and the antipathy Waugh encountered in the Corporation, nor does he reveal here what is clearly stated in his letters to Waugh, that, with some few exceptions, he shared his friend's low opinion of the BBC staff. Harman Grisewood agrees with Sykes's estimate of the jealousy and envy of Waugh present at the Corporation,[9] but Sykes clearly overstates his case. If a jealous wish to suppress Waugh consumed the larger part of the BBC's literary staff, it is difficult to under-stand why they sought contributions from him several times a year from 1932 until his death.

Harman Grisewood provides a more accurate (and amusing) recollection of Waugh and his relationship with the Corporation:

> E.W.'s antipathies were not always easy to account for – and they sometimes included an element of satire and exaggeration,

to amuse both himself and whomever he was talking to. If he found the person took him quite seriously without humour E.W. would 'pile it on' in order to shock and to make the person feel awkward. This was a sort of punishment for being insensitive to The Waugh Idiom, made fashionable if not invented by Maurice Bowra and the membership of what was called 'The Hypocrites Club.' John Sutro, Osbert Lancaster, C. Sykes were among those who understood this not very widespread idiom – and oh yes the Lygon girls and N. Mitford and Cyril Connolly. It was a small circle – Oxford based – and part of the idiom was scorn or pretended scorn for anything or any person outside the circle.

The BBC was exactly the sort of institution which attracted EW's disdain – popular, serious, endeavouring to improve the taste of the working class and still coloured by a Scottish Calvinist puritanism stamped upon it by Lord Reith. It was vaguely left-wing because the 'left' were at that time associated with Improvements for the working class. All this was deeply antipathetic to EW. I rather doubt if he would ever have agreed to broadcast if it were not for the efforts of Christopher Sykes whom EW recognised as part of the circle referred to above and myself. C.S. was rather loosely attached to the BBC and so was more tolerated by EW than I who was pretty well a foundation member! And therefore came in for the full treatment of scorn. When he left my office one day to go home with me to have a drink he noticed I wore no hat. 'I suppose you are too poor,' he said 'to get yourself a hat. I expect they pay you a pittance.' I knew the idiom and didn't bother about the remark. BUT next day – to my surprise – and very characteristic of EW this is – there arrived from Locks in St James' St a very beautiful grey bowler – as a present – and as a humiliation.[10]

Additionally, the BBC Third Programme had, before Grisewood's tenure as Controller, a strong element of the Bloomsbury circle which Waugh detested for its G.E. Moore-King's College, Cambridge-Apostles Society belief that the cultured elite had a responsibility to bring enlightenment to the masses, although Grisewood notes that its members 'held themselves aloof from the BBC's paternalistic outlook upon the lower classes'. He recalls that when he was in charge of the Third Programme, Harold Nicolson, a marginal member of the Bloomsbury world, popular broadcaster and BBC Governor, told him 'it was my DUTY to join the Labour

Party so as to convey to the "underprivileged" what benefits we had received from our upbringing. . . . I thought Harold's advice bizarre in the extreme – not as to his aim for improvement but as to the necessity of joining the Labour Party to achieve it'.

While he was controller, Grisewood was conscious of the influence of his predecessor, George Barnes

> who was a devout Kingsman, a follower of Keynes and of the 'Apostles.' He made me understand the exclusivity of Kings College – and took me to stay there and to meet the dons. His mother was a Strachey – Lytton S. was one of his 'heroes.' Bloomsbury was to a great extent Cambridge-based and in London continued that style of exclusivity – very different from my University. George told me that his circle at Cambridge (Kings-based) regarded Oxford as 'worldly.' I was quite unprepared for this accusation – and later thought of it as evidence of a 'superior person' outlook – which I thought regrettable and a weakness.
>
> E.M. Forster, a great friend of my predecessor, scolded me when I became the Controller for arranging a series of concerts of light classical music including a good deal of 18th century 'entertainment' music. He called on the then Director General to complain that Grisewood was vulgarising the Third Programme. I asked Forster to lunch – where he was quite amiable but deeply suspicious of me – rightly guessing that I thought his Kings College coterie outlook was too limited and 'superior person' to be suitable to the BBC's aim for the Third Programme.
>
> I remember saying to George when I was his assistant that it was time we heard more Aristotle and less Plato. . . .[11]

As early as 1952, Sykes and other of Waugh's close friends noted that he was 'becoming more arrogant, more quarrelsome, and indulged his horrible delight in needling on sensitive spots more freely than usual' (Sykes, 352) but no noticeable change is evident in his relationship with the BBC in this period. In December 1952 the North America Service asked Waugh to be one of the British speakers on a Columbia Broadcasting System program 'This I Believe', statements of personal conviction from successful men and women in various fields (J. Keith Kyle letter of 31 December, TFI), but when he found the fee was only 8 guineas (Mrs K.M. Kirwan, letter of 23 January 1953, TFI), he sent one of his famous printed postcards: 'Mr. Evelyn Waugh greatly regrets that he cannot do what you so kindly suggest' (undated, postmarked 24 January, TFI). He did, however, accept 15 guineas to be interviewed by Stephen Black on the Overseas Service 'London Calling Asia' in the series 'Personal Call', broadcast on 29 September, Waugh stipulating that it was not to be transmitted on the United Kingdom or North American services (Hugh Burnett letter of 16 July, Waugh postcard reply of 17 July, Burnett letter of 22 July 1953, TFI).

In April 1953 Waugh was certainly arrogant and obnoxious (but no more than he had been earlier) in his response to the BBC's request to adapt his stories 'An Englishman's Home' and 'Excursion in Reality'. A staffer reported 'The eccentric gentleman told Lance Sieveking that there were no actors or actresses good enough to interpret his works, and that consequently he would never allow any of them to be dramatised; and he has apparently not even replied to his agent's request for permission. I am afraid, therefore, that we must put the project on one side until after his demise' (Charles Lefeaux memo to Mary Hope Allan, 17 April 1953, TFI). One gets the strong feeling that the writer hopes this event will take place soon!

By contrast, all of his negotiations with the Corporation from June to November were conducted with the utmost courtesy. Ludovic Kennedy, an acquaintance of Waugh's and husband of the admired ballerina Moira Shearer, who had just become editor of 'First Reading', a new literary magazine on the Third Programme, received an immediate and charming reply (17 September, SFI) to his 16 September request for a new Waugh short story. Waugh had no story but offered him a pre-publication extract from *Officers and Gentlemen* (1955), the account of Guy's visit to the Highland laird (undated postcard, misdated c. 1948 by the BBC, SFI), which Kennedy eagerly accepted (22 September, SFI) and which Waugh told Nancy Mitford she could hear on 25 October (22 October 1953, *Letters*, 412).[12] He was cordial and co-operative in all the correspondence leading to his now famous interview on 'Frankly Speaking', broadcast 16 November. Although he claimed a fee of 40 guineas and exceptionally high expenses of £18 18s 6d (John Montgomery of A.D. Peters to Ronald Boswell, 14 September, Boswell's reply of 15 September, TFI), he offered to provide the three interviewers (Stephen Black, Charles Wilmot and Jack Davies) who came to his home with the 'best luncheon I can and charge you only for the ingredients' (9 September, TFI). He expressed his sincere gratitude when given a chance to repeat and improve the original recording (letter to Weltman, 21 October, TFI).

The response to the interview was varied. One listener, identifying herself only as 'State Registered Nurse' wrote the BBC:

> My congratulations (and sympathy) to you gentlemen upon the handling of this very difficult human(?). I think he is a *horror*. We need *cheering up*. We are miserably contending with the high cost of living – who was responsible for presenting us with this *additional* misery? There is something about Roman Catholics that makes me *shudder*. I am quite sure that somewhere, sometime, they burnt me at the stake (postcard, 16 November, TFI).

Waugh's friends, like Sykes, were delighted, feeling 'Evelyn scored throughout. It was a triumph for him' (Sykes, 356). The BBC people were equally pleased, believing the broadcast 'hit exactly the right note and achieved what I have always regarded to be the programme's objectives, i.e., to present the listener with a clear picture of the real character of the interviewee' (Pat Dixon to D.F. Boyd, 18 November, TFI). Waugh himself wrote Nancy Mitford, 'They tried to make a fool of me & I don't believe they succeeded' (11 December, *Letters*, 415) but Sykes (356) says Waugh looked on the occasion as an 'ugly humiliation'.

There is evidence to support both opinions about Waugh's reaction in the record of his trip to Ceylon in February 1954. On the boat he experienced a period of madness in the form of taunting, condemning voices coming out of the air and the lamps (letters to Laura Waugh of 3, 8, 12, 16 and 18 February, *Letters*, 418–21) brought on by his injudicious mixing of large doses of chloral, bromide and alcohol, to which Sykes attributes his obnoxious behaviour from 1952 to this voyage. He was quickly cured once the cause was discovered and wrote an almost literal account of the experience in his 1957 'conversation piece' *The Ordeal of Gilbert Pinfold*.

One of the two events which take over Pinfold's mind during his shipboard delusions is the BBC interview, described in some detail before his voyage. 'Angel', the chief of the three interviewers, poses questions which 'were civil enough in form but Mr Pinfold thought he could detect an underlying malice' (15). Listening to the broadcast on the cook's wireless, Pinfold repeats Waugh's comment to Nancy Mitford, 'They tried to make an ass of me. . . . I don't believe they succeeded' (16) but on board ship the BBC plays a significant part in bringing the varied voices mocking and persecuting him; on the Third Programme a literary critic condemns his fiction (67–8) and on a Light Programme a populist poet laughingly reads his badly-written letters to a studio audience. After days of such visitations Pinfold decides that Angel, the BBC interviewer, is responsible (146–7). Angel then begins a constant interrogation, similar to the interview, addressing him familiarly as 'Gilbert'. When Waugh first responded to the 'Frankly Speaking' proposal he had insisted there be no 'bandying about of Christian names and so forth, of the kind which deeply shocks me in some of the performances I have sometimes begun to hear' (letter to J. Weltman, 2 September 1953, TFI; *Letters*, 409). Pinfold's sensitivity about proper forms of address also echoes another Waugh controversy with the Corporation which occurred just before he began writing *Pinfold* in the summer of 1955. Waugh was incensed that he was referred to as 'Waugh' and not 'Mr Waugh' on the BBC programme 'The Critics' and wrote to Harman Grisewood to complain. Grisewood replied, 'No reprimand would alter the practice you complain of – it is part of the change [in social custom] that has already come about'.[13] Unsatisfied, Waugh told Sykes he had 'reported him [Grisewood] & them to the Director General' Sir Ian Jacob (15 July, *Letters*, 445), who wrote Waugh supporting Grisewood but adding, with exquisite tact, 'that great commanders and other illustrious persons were referred to in writing by a simple surname'.[14] The last comment on the BBC-Waugh-Pinfold conflict came from Stephen Black, the interviewer who was the model for Angel, asking if, in the circumstances, Waugh would send him an autographed copy of the novel.[15] There is no record of Waugh's reply.

Shortly before the 'Frankly Speaking' interview was broadcast, Waugh was being difficult again. When F. Leon Shepley, Head of the South European Service, asked him to be part of a series of profiles of British people outstanding in their fields to be broadcast for the Italian Service (5 November 1953, CFI), Waugh replied that he found it 'difficult to believe that a profile of myself, however rosy, would calm the anti-English frenzy of the Italian people' but said he would give information if Shepley sent 'a young man with three five pound notes in his hand to the Hyde Park Hotel' (7 November 1953, CFI; *Letters*, 412–13). On 10 November the Copyright department wrote to Waugh saying that they could offer no more than 10 guineas, to which Waugh replied by telephone that he wanted the money in notes; a cheque was no good. When they couldn't oblige he rang off (CFI). Shepley expressed his regret with a wit worthy of his adversary: 'We shall probably fill the gap with a profile of the average English tax-payer' (10 November, CFI).

There were far more failures than successes in the BBC's efforts to get Waugh on the air from this time until his death in 1966. Understandably, he turned down a request to be on the revived 'Brains Trust' with two other authors which arrived while he was still recovering from his Pinfold experience (Hugh Burnett to Waugh, 25 February; Waugh's undated reply postmarked 1 March 1954, TFI). A year later, when asked to be part of a series for the General Overseas Service in which leading British novelists discussed their approaches to the novel (Kay Fuller, 17 March 1955, TFI), he replied, 'My fee for conversation is one guinea a minute and expenses. For the "preliminary sorting out of ideas" there will be a charge of 10/6 a minute' (undated postcard postmarked 18 March, TFI). As he well knew, this fee was far beyond the budget available (Fuller, 21 March, TFI). A 'Mr Waugh greatly regrets' card (undated, postmarked 16 September 1955, TFI) was his reply to a request for anecdotes on the anniversary of the opening of the Cafe Royal (Sasha Moorsom, 15 September, TFI). He apparently did not even bother to reply to 1956 requests to be part of a series of talks by novelists about novels they failed to complete (R.E. Keen, 6 April, TFI) or part of a panel discussing some of the points raised in his 'Noblesse Oblige' exchange with Nancy Mitford (Christopher Rowland, 18 May, TFI).

From 1956 onward he was in declining health and spirits, preoccupied from 1957 with the time-consuming task of writing the official biography of his close friend Monsignor Ronald Knox (1959). In 1958, the year he ignored a request that he join other novelists who had adventures behind the lines during the war in a discussion of their experiences (P.H. Newby, 15 May, TFI), he wrote to John McDougall of Chapman and Hall, 'I decided on reflection that I had only a year or two ahead in which I was capable of original work and I shouldn't waste that time in hack work' (18 April, *Letters*, 507). On 25 August 1960 (TFI) his agent told Anthony Derville of the 'Woman's Hour' that Waugh had too many other commitments to consider being a guest on the programme (23 August, TFI). After this date he used enormous fees as his means of escape: £100 (18 February 1961, TFI) to take part in a programme on the techniques and ethics of interviewing (R.E. Keen, 16 February 1961, TFI); £100 plus £10 expenses (31 July 1961, TFI) for a short interview about *Unconditional Surrender* (Kay Fuller, 27 July and 23 August 1961, TFI), 100 guineas (13 September 1961, TFI) for a conversation between two men who have drawn on their military experience in their fiction (Anthony Thwaite to Waugh, 11 September; Clyde Logan to John Montgomery, 20 and 21 September 1961, TFI).

With three exceptions, the BBC successes in this period consisted in getting Waugh's agreement to have others adapt his novels for radio. Barbara Bray wrote Waugh on 26 March 1954 (SFI) proposing these adaptations after consulting Sykes who wanted to do them. Waugh agreed to discuss the matter with Sykes (27 March, SFI). On 19 July (SFI) Bray was preparing clearance for *Put Out More Flags*, with Waugh and Sykes as co-adaptors. On 27 July (SFI) she was making plans for a co-production of *Work Suspended*. On 23 August 1954 Waugh decreed that no one but Christopher Sykes was to adapt his novels for the BBC (Davis, *Catalogue* E862; Beaty 192–3) and on 15 March 1955, for a fee of £500, he granted the Corporation permission to dramatise *Put Out More Flags* and *Brideshead*, provided Sykes would write the scripts and cast the parts (27 April internal memo, SFI; Davis, *Catalogue* E878; Beaty 193). On 1 June 1955 (SFI) Donald McWhinnie thanks H[ead of] F[eatures] for making Sykes available to do the adaptations of these two novels, the former slated for broadcast on 24 September (undated memo, SFI). For unknown reasons, Sieveking rather than Sykes adapted *Brideshead* in a programme transmitted 9 April 1956 on the Home Service (Barbara Bray to John Montgomery, 14 March 1956, SFI; Beaty, 193). Beaty quotes a letter of 23 April 1956 from Waugh to Sieveking in which Waugh tells him, 'I hear on all sides that your adaptation was ingenious' (Beaty 194). Probably this success explains why Sieveking was also granted permission to dramatise *Decline and Fall* (Home Service, 29 August 1960; Beaty, 196) and *Scoop* (Home Service, 18 November 1963; Beaty 197), but no explanatory records exist in the BBC Written Archives. *The Ordeal of Gilbert Pinfold* was proposed for adaptation by Michael Bakewell on 18 September 1959. A memo of 31 March 1960 indicates the script by Bakewell is set to go, Waugh to have final approval, for a fee of £250. Waugh did approve the script (Davis, *Catalogue* E1150) and the broadcast was aired 7 June 1960 on the Third Programme (Programme Index).

The Archives do reveal that negotiations for *Scoop* had begun seven years earlier with the report that the BBC could not get broadcast rights under the terms of a film contract (19 June and 30 July 1956, SFI). On 29 November 1956 (SFI), Waugh's agent wrote to Bray that *Scoop* was now available because the film option had expired and Waugh was agreeable if Sykes did the adaptation. Sykes must not have been available because a script by Felix Felton was rejected by McWhinnie on 5 December 1956 (SFI). On 22 January 1957 (SFI) the Copyright Department warned that film negotiations for *Scoop* were likely on again, their sale to Rank confirmed on 25 March (John Montgomery to Bray, SFI). After that the Archives are silent.

On 18 November 1959 (SFI) Hugh Burnett wrote Waugh inviting him to appear on the television interview programme 'Face to Face', the interviewer to be John Freeman. It is a measure of Waugh's reputation that he was sought for a programme which had already included Edith Sitwell, Bertrand Russell, Nubar Gulbenkian, Adlai Stevenson and Carl Jung. Later Waugh would tell Nancy Mitford, 'Last week I was driven by poverty to the humiliating experience of appearing on television' (21 June 1960, *Letters*, 545), but Leonard Miall recalls the circumstances of his acceptance rather differently. Waugh did not want to appear on television but rather than refusing outright, took his usual high financial stand with the Corporation, telling Burnett on the telephone that the BBC could not afford his fee. Burnett then asked what the fee was. Waugh, perhaps remembering that he had told his agent in 1947: 'price for television £50 in a false beard. With the naked face £250' (12 June, *Letters*, 253), named the latter sum. Although the regular fee was £100, Burnett accepted immediately, to Waugh's surprise and consternation. When Burnett requested an increase in his programme budget from Miall, the latter told him to send Waugh a 'nice letter' and to make sure that his contract took all rights in the programme in return for his exceptional fee (Michael Johnston to John Montgomery, 30 May 1960, TVWC). Since other interviewees were also compensated for overseas sales, Waugh was left happy in the belief that he had scored financially against the Corporation when in fact he received less than any of the other guests on the programme.[16]

Having been so neatly outmanoeuvred in the negotiations, Waugh was no doubt doubly determined to triumph on the programme itself. Christopher Sykes (407) describes his performance as

> well thought out and brilliantly executed. . . . At the end of the interview Mr Freeman asked a question that, with a less skilled opponent, would have been a deadly thrust. He said something of this kind: 'How is it, Mr Waugh, that, with your strong views on the right to privacy, you consent to appear on this programme in the view of millions?' Gently smiling, Evelyn replied: 'For the same reason that you do. I need the money.'

Hugh Burnett himself wrote Waugh (28 June 1960, TVWC) praising his 'bearing, fortitude and skill. I gather parties were held in London to celebrate the occasion of Mr Waugh's appearance on the television screens'. No Archives records exist for his far less controversial 1964 'Monitor' TV interview with Elizabeth Jane Howard (16 February) to which he agreed without fuss for a fee of £300 (Davis, E 1331 and 1134), probably because it provided publicity for his forthcoming (September 1964) autobiography.

Waugh's last two radio broadcasts were given to help literary colleagues, with Sykes acting in both cases as the intermediary with the Corporation. Sykes recalls (404–6, 410–13) that Waugh's determination to give a talk which would clear P.G. Wodehouse of wartime charges of treason resulting from broadcasts he did for the Germans and celebrate his eightieth birthday was fraught with difficulties. Many at the BBC resented Waugh's earlier complaints about being referred to as 'Waugh' rather than 'Mr Waugh', and his recent appearance on 'Face to Face'. Others still believed in Wodehouse's guilt despite Sykes's researchers in Corporation files which showed that the BBC, attempting unsuccessfully to maintain Reith's avoidance of government intervention, had opposed the Ministry of Information's insistence that the 1941 denunciation of Wodehouse be broadcast on the subsequently proven grounds that his recordings were wholly innocuous. In 1953 Waugh had written the editor of the *Daily Mail*, 'Now that Mr Wodehouse has at last published the true facts of the case, it would be seemly if the BBC invited the originator of this war-time attack [Waugh's longtime adversary, Duff Cooper] to make an apology to one of the most brilliant of living English stylists' (24 November, *Letters*, 414). After considerable preliminary work by Sykes, Waugh approached the BBC on 24 September 1960 (TFI) proposing a talk which would in effect constitute the apology he had suggested earlier. Sykes also stresses the umbrage of those who felt the proposal had not gone through the usual channels as being responsible for the efforts 'to relegate the talk to part of an insignificant and little-heard programme' but the Archives correspondence emphasises a fear of libel he does not mention. When they gave Waugh a copy of the original attack by 'Cassandra' of the *Daily Mirror* (W.N. Connor), they asked that Waugh inform Connor of his plans (28 September 1960, TFI). Since the matter was a delicate one, the approval of the then Director General, H. Carleton Greene, was requested and given (23 December 1960, TFI). The BBC wanted a half-hour talk by Waugh because the potentially libellous Cassandra broadcast would not then be the centrepiece (Marriott to H.F. and Sykes, 12 January 1961, TFI). On 4 March 1961 Waugh wrote to both the Director General (TFI) and Sykes (*Letters*, 562) of his displeasure at fitting the talk 'into a space called "the World of Books." It should be a STUNT with a place of its own' to emphasise that '"Here for the first time in its history the BBC is making an *amende* for ancient injustice inflicted on a great artist by a low politician."' When they received the script, they consulted their legal advisors (L.P.R. Roche, 29 May 1961, TFI) who advised the risks of libel were slight (L.P.R. Roche, 30 May 1961, TFI) and the talk went ahead, at the usual time for 'World of Books' but as a special feature on the Home Service (a nice compromise), 15 July 1961.

No records exist in the BBC Archives about Waugh's final broadcast, a memorial to his old friend the historical novelist Alfred Duggan, but Sykes's account (441–2) stresses how smoothly the negotiations he instigated at Waugh's request and the actual recording session went. The broadcast on 2 July 1964 brought to a quiet close a relationship of thirty-seven often tumultuous years.

NOTES

1. Good Friday 1928, Talks File I, BBC Written Archives, Reading. All future references to these archives will be given in the text abbreviated to TFI, SFI (Scriptwriter File I), CFI (Copyright File I), and TVWC (TV Waugh Clump). I am indebted to Auberon Waugh for permission to quote from this and all subsequent letters from Evelyn Waugh, and to

the BBC for all material in their copyright. Particular thanks are due to Miss Caroline Cornish of the Archives Staff for her assistance.

2. Beaty, 188–9, quoting from the corrected master copy, pt.3, ch. 3: 54 of the manuscript in the Sieveking Collection of the Lilly Library at Indiana University.

3. Interview with Leonard Miall, BBC Washington Correspondent 1945–53, Head of Television Talks 1954–62 and BBC Research Historian, 1975–84.

4. Letter from Leonard Miall, 9 September 1989.

5. Interview with Leonard Miall, 31 July 1989.

6. Interview with Leonard Miall, 31 July 1989.

7. The BBC Archives contain no record of this battle which is, however, described in Sykes's letters to Waugh in the personal collection of Auberon Waugh, catalogued by Alan Bell. The relevant letters are dated 14 November 1950 and, in 1951, 9 March, 22 April, 7 May, 27 July, 16 and 22 August, 4, 8, 14, 17, 19, 22, 29 and 31 October, 25 November, and 1 December. I am indebted to Mark Sykes for permission to refer to these letters.

8. I am indebted to Mark Amory who gained Auberon Waugh's permission to give me a copy of this unpublished letter.

9. Letter to the author, 12 September 1989.

10. Letter to the author, 19 July 1989.

11. Letter to the author, 25 July 1989.

12. No records pertaining to this broadcast are in the BBC Written Archives.

13. Letter of 12 July 1955 in the Auberon Waugh Papers catalogued by Alan Bell. I am grateful to Mr Grisewood for permission to quote from this letter.

14. 19 July 1955 in the Auberon Waugh Papers catalogued by Alan Bell.

15. 5 April 1958 in the Auberon Waugh Papers catalogued by Alan Bell.

16. Interview with Leonard Miall, 31 July 1989.

REFERENCES

Beaty, Frederick L., 'Evelyn Waugh and Lance Sieveking: New Light on Waugh's Relations with the BBC', *Papers on Language and Literature*, 25, 2 (Spring 1989), 186–200.

Branson, Noreen, *Britain in the Nineteen Twenties* (Minneapolis, Minn.: University of Minnesota Press, 1976).

Briggs, Asa, *The History of Broadcasting in the United Kingdom*, 3 vols (London: Oxford University Press, 1965).

Davis, Robert Murray, *A Catalogue of the Evelyn Waugh Collection at the Humanities Research Centre, The University of Texas at Austin* (Troy, N.Y.: Whitston, 1981).

Heppenstall, Rayner, *The Master Eccentric: The Journals of Rayner Heppenstall, 1969–1981*, ed. Jonathan Goodman (London: Allison and Busby, 1986).

Hopkins, Harry, *The New Look: A Social History of the Forties and Fifties in Britain* (Boston: Houghton Mifflin, 1964).

Mowat, Charles Loch, *Britain Between the Wars: 1918–1940* (Chicago: University of Chicago Press, 1955).

Stannard, Mark, *Evelyn Waugh: The Early Years 1903–1939* (London: Paladin, 1986).

Sykes, Christopher, *Evelyn Waugh. A Biography* (Boston: Little Brown, 1975).

Waugh, Evelyn, 'Brains Trust Asked to Take Soldiers' Pay', *Daily Sketch*, 8 April 1942, p. 3. Reported in 'No Army Pay for Brains Trust – Yet', *Evening Standard*, 8 April 1942, p. 3.

Waugh, Evelyn, *The Diaries of Evelyn Waugh*, ed. Michael Davie (Boston: Little Brown, 1976).

Waugh, Evelyn, 'Half in Love with Easeful Death: An Examination of Californian Burial Customs', *Tablet*, 190 (18 October 1947), 246–8.

Waugh, Evelyn, *The Letters of Evelyn Waugh*, ed. Mark Amory (London: Penguin, 1980).

Waugh, Evelyn, *The Ordeal of Gilbert Pinfold* (London: Chapman and Hall, 1957).

6

Evelyn Waugh and Humour

Alain Blayac

Humour, English humour, has always been a subject of interest (and puzzlement) for the French who have always had the utmost difficulties in understanding their neighbours, hence the number of French essays devoted to the analysis and explanation of the concept. Across the Channel, the notion strikes deep roots in the British collective unconscious. Born of the medical 'theory of humours', it still prevailed during the Renaissance. Initiated by Hippocrates, theorised by Galien, it referred to the four fluids of the human body: blood, phlegm, yellow bile and black bile. Physical diseases, as well as mental and moral temperaments, were the result of the relationship of one humour to another. When the humours were in balance, an ideal temperament prevailed, genial or melancholy according to the circumstances. This explains how the word 'humour' came to mean disposition, then mood or characterised peculiarity, like folly or affectation.

In literature, even though Chaucer and Shakespeare had amply drawn upon the subject, it was Ben Jonson who created the 'Comedy of Humours', depicting characters whose behaviour was determined by a single trait or humour. The Prologue to *Every Man Out of His Humour* gives the first definition of both 'humour' and 'humorist'.

Asper: *Why humour, as 'tis ens, we thus define it*
To be a quality of air, or water,
And in itself holds these two properties,
Moisture and fluxure: as, for demonstration,
Pour water on this floor, 'twill wet and run:

Likewise the air, forced through a horn or trumpet,
Flows instantly away, and leaves behind

A Kind of dew; and hence we do conclude,
 That whatsoe'er hath fluxure and humidity,
  As wanting power to contain itself,
Is humour. So in every human body,
 The choler, melancholy, phlegm and blood,
  By reason that they flow continually,
 In some one part, and are not continent,
 Receive the name of humours. Now thus far
  It may, by metaphor, apply itself
Unto the general disposition:
 As when some one peculiar quality
 Doth so possess a man, that it doth draw
  All his affects, his spirits, and his powers,
  In their confluctions, all to run one way,
 This may be truly said to be a humour.

Cordatus: *[. . .] now if an idiot*
 Have but an apish or fantastic strain,
It is his humour.

Asper: *Well, I will scourge those apes,*
 And to these courteous eyes oppose a mirror,
  As large as is the stage whereon we act;
  Where they shall see the time's deformity
 Anatomised in every nerve, and sinew,
  With constant courage, and contempt or fear [. . .]
Now gentlemen, I go
 To turn an actor, and a humorist,
Where, ere I do resume my present person,
 We hope to make the circles of your eyes
  Flow with distilled laughter . . .[2]

The comedy of humours has its characters, eccentrics, maniacs, lunatics, swindlers, victims, and its themes of eccentricity, whims and fancies, madness. It creates 'humour', what is laughable, whose creator is the 'humorist'. Since then, and up till today, humour has developed and endured in Britain and its arts. In the last thirty years, considerable progress has been made towards the definition of humour. An article dating back to the eighteenth century[3] suggests that the English are animated by a natural, original vein called 'humour'. According to it, everyone in England offers some bizarre slant of mind, some original humour. In the course of time, the term became the expression of a collective mood which the English relish and cultivate. Unlike the Cartesian French, who turned their backs on sentiment and the concrete to move towards concept and the abstract, the English leaned towards humour, which they linked with the particular and the ephemeral; in the process they initiated a literary climate which could only flourish in a people born of the union of the Anglo-Saxon heart and the Anglo-Norman mind.[4]

Michel Serres's latest book, *Le Contrat naturel*,[5] opens on a description of a painting by Goya: two men brandishing cudgels are fighting on quicksands. Intent on their duel, they forget that they have already sunk knee-deep in the mud. Each motion, each gesture they make contribute to their being gradually buried together. Their aggressivity determines the rhythm of their sinking and the time of their interment. Such blindness to the surrounding world is by no means new or incredible; the trouble is that it is pregnant with catastrophic consequences. As such, the painting could perfectly illustrate the lesson of Evelyn Waugh's fiction, if, that is, a dash of humour were added to the Spanish artist's tragic manner.

Indeed Waugh may be considered as a typical representative of the British dual nature, even in the very reductive clichés about his life which see him first as a young scapegrace iconoclast, later as a bitter ageing hypochondriac. In this essay, we shall take as a starting point the (today widely-held) hypothesis that Waugh is a genuine moralist and satirist, who draws on all the forms of humour to propound in an oblique manner the moral, religious and philosophical principles which he advocates for the saving of the individual and society.

What is humour? Before attempting to answer the question, let us suggest that it is high time the reading public, and indeed the critics, realised that humour and humorists must not be made light of, Evelyn Waugh no less than others. To be humorous about humour amounts to confusing the object and the instrument of the study. Let us also remember that the notion is increasingly arduous to grasp; everybody discusses and defines it in more or less overlapping or contradictory ways, when it should be strictly circumscribed so as to avoid commonplaces or overgeneralisations.

Historically, French, unlike most other languages, split its vocabulary into *'humeur'* and *'humour'*, hinting at a new awareness of the phenomenon seen as a rational reaction and, for such as knew a little philology, suggesting its emotional and affective roots. Seen from a different perspective, an essay on Evelyn Waugh, whose Britishness is both ingrained and peerless, cannot but make the distinction between English and American humours. L.W. Kline[6] believed the latter resulted from the conflict between a sense of inner freedom and external societal pressures: thus American humour acts as a safety-valve. Today in the USA one encounters a growing temptation to reduce 'humor' to an aesthetic of the absurd and the nonsensical which is by no means the case in Britain. In his own study, Escarpit presents the 'British sense of humour as an aesthetic form of the self-consciousness', in other words as a national reflex of discretion and decency, concurrently individual and collective (transposed in Waugh's writings to the point of becoming the mask behind which the satirist lurks and chastises through laughter), whereas in the USA, he regards the word as indicating a national reflex of indiscretion or indecency. Two last capital distinctions must be made, the first for the French, the second for the English. Humour should never be confused with what initiates laughter, nor mistaken for irony or wit. Humour and laughter are two different phenomena; Bergson's demonstrations only tangentially concern humour. On the other hand, wit and irony are far too intellectual to be identified with it, for humour demands the sympathy of a witness or accomplice. To the pleasure solitarily enjoyed by the 'wit', self-satisfied, convinced of his intellectual superiority, the humorist prefers the sympathetic wink, the sentimental connivance. He appears humble, only too willing to hand the fruits of his labours over to the invisible interlocutor who he himself has conjured up beforehand for his own purpose and pleasure. In this respect, humour (which has been described as a current passing between two poles) diverges aesthetically, because of its deep affective roots, from wit and irony (which cut the current between two people).

When successively reading *Decline and Fall, Vile Bodies* and *A Handful of Dust*, one cannot but be struck by the drastic evolution of Waugh's tone and humour induced by the trauma of his divorce and the revelation of the Roman Catholic faith. After the callous, careless impertinence of the first novel and the first half of the second, humour suddenly becomes the touchstone and the instrument of the writer's wounded affectivity, directly debouching on to bitterly heartfelt satire. This affectivity provides the next novels with their peculiar atmosphere, a *sui generis* flavour whose infinite nuances range from rosy to grey and black. When the tender element dominates, rosy humour prevails, as in the following passage in which the writer himself admits his sympathy for the tourists he describes.

> The word 'tourist' seems naturally to suggest haste and compulsion. One thinks of those pitiable droves of Middle West school teachers whom one encounters suddenly at street corners and in public buildings, baffled, breathless, their heads singing with unfamiliar names, their bodies strained and bruised from scrambling in and out of motor charabancs, up and down staircases, and from trailing disconsolately through miles of gallery and museum at the heels of a contemptuous and facetious guide. How their eyes haunt us long after they have passed on to the next stage of their itinerary – haggard and uncomprehending eyes, mildly resentful, like those of animals in pain, eloquent of that world-weariness we all feel as the dead weight of European culture . . . And as one sits at one's café table playing listlessly with sketch book and apéritif, and sees them stumble by, one sheds not wholly derisive tears for these poor scraps of humanity thus trapped and mangled in the machinery of uplift.[7]

In many cases, one observes that affectivity is neither openly didactic nor sentimental, it thus steers clear of the potential dangers of cheap, impersonal moralism or mawkishness which Evelyn Waugh deeply mistrusts. Father Rothschild's famous speech on the Bright Young Things' being possessed with an almost fatal hunger for permanence [8] is at worst a minor flaw, but, seen in a more positive perspective, it provides a moral standard by which to judge their behaviour.

Waugh's art may also serve, by dint of his humour, to numb his reader's sensibility. Then, in the case of such exemplary occurrences as Little Lord Tangent's or Simon Balcairn's deaths, humour turns grey. It is born not so much of the narrator's dehumanising detachment as of the fact that the reader, not allowed to feel that those are real people's deaths, smiles at happenings which, in other contexts, would be deemed tragic but here become essentially fantastic. The second epigraph of *Vile Bodies*[9] gives the key to this type of humour. The writer quells moralism by resorting to modern techniques – montage, collage, intertextuality – which generate humour in as much as they allow the reader to distance himself from his reading. In the epigraph, the moral slant is concealed by an apparently casual, or jocular, attitude. But, in most cases, the technical skill hides a hopeless or desperate brand of immorality. It is prominent in the pranks and hoaxes of the Bright Young Things and particularly in Agatha Runcible's adventures culminating in her untimely, but inescapable, and ultimately tragic, demise.

When the realistic element supersedes the 'Alice-in-Wonderland' atmosphere, merrymaking turns sour, bitterness sets in, and grey humour is strengthened. The older generation, a constant butt of Waugh's humour, illustrate this aspect; the description of their gathering at Anchorage House belongs in such a category.

> She [Lady Circumference] saw . . . a great concourse of pious and honourable people . . ., uncultured, unaffected, unembarrassed, unassuming, unambitious people, of independent judgment and marked eccentricities, . . . that fine phalanx of the passing order . . .[10]

Here the profusion of mostly negative adjectives turns them less into laughing stocks than creatures of a bygone age, grotesque characters in a sad fairy tale. The humour has turned dark grey in the melancholy realisation that the former rulers are both out of touch with the modern world and unconscious of it – in a word, decadent. Darker – for symbolic of the hero's misconceptions, – is the reality of the pseudo-refuges, the 'Lush Places', which the Younger Generation and their like wrongly consider as genuine shelters immune from the aggressions of the outside world.

> The immense trees which encircled Boot Magna Hall, shaded its drives and rides, and stood tastefully disposed at the whim of some forgotten, provincial predecessor of Repton, single and in groups about the park, had suffered, some from ivy, some from lightning, some from the various malignant disorders that vegetation is heir to, but all, principally, from old age. Some were supported with trusses and crutches of iron, some were filled with cement . . .
>
> The lake was moved by strange tides . . .[11]

Boot Magna Hall fares no better than the members of the Older Generation, is no better fortress than Oxford, Mataudi or Hetton

Abbey ever were. The humour, in its grey, dull melancholy, springs from the personification of a place victimised by the passing of time; more essentially and obliquely, it mocks the delusions of the protagonists and the responsibility they bear for their own misadventures.

When directed at the characters, humour varies with the degree of naivety or cynicism, innocence or perversion which they display. It may range from the tender to the sarcastic and the downright cynical, from rosy to grey or black again. Tenderness is the keynote to Nina Blount's shyly admitting to her lack of experience in amorous matters.

> Adam undressed quickly and got into bed; Nina more slowly arranging her clothes on the chair . . . with less than her usual self-possession. At last she put out the light.
>
> 'Do you know', she said, trembling slightly as she got into bed, 'this is the first time this has happened to me?'
>
> 'It's great fun', said Adam, 'I promise you.'
>
> 'I'm sure it is', said Nina seriously, 'I wasn't saying anything against it. I was only saying that it hadn't happened before . . . Oh, Adam'.[12]

It is remarkable that, after this scene, Waugh will never again present a perfectly innocent character, but here the gap existing between the bold situation and the reserve, coyness or self-consciousness which characterise the two lovers at this turning point of their lives is both touching and amusing. On the contrary, with Colonel Blount, Nina's father, the humour becomes jarring as one realises the nefarious treatment to which he submits historical truth. When his film, ambiguously entitled *A Brand from the Burning*, is presented on a Christmas Day desecrated by Adam and Nina's adultery[13] and the declaration of war, it appears exactly to reflect the downright cynical mood and utterly deleterious atmosphere prevailing in England. The darkening humour of the novel evidently coincides with the breakdown of the author's marriage and personal values. In the 'Happy Ending', Waugh, who has hit the bottom of despair, resorts to the blackest kind of humour he has used so far.

When all references to sentiment are erased, when the writer wavers on the brink of despair or sadism, when his comedy opens on to the absurd, then black, kafkaesque humour crops up. The most numerous instances are to be found, not innocently so, in *The Loved One*. There the decadence of the British exiles in Los Angeles can be classified as grey humour. It merely concerns the uprooted, self-deluding British colony. Sir Ambrose Abercrombie, its leader, paints it in a ludicrous, but not wholly humourless, profession of faith.

> We limeys have a particular position to keep up . . . It's a responsibility, I can tell you, and in various degrees every Englishman shares it. We can't be all at the top of the tree but we are all men of responsibility. You never find an Englishman among the underdogs – except in England of course.[14]

This debased 'White Man's Burden' type of speech, the deluded (and deluding) assertions, the self-imposed blindness of Sir Ambrose associated with his use of American slang ('limeys'), contrasted with the typically English metaphorical understatement that they are not *at the top of the tree* bring out the reader's compassion for, and amusement at, the plight of the Britisher in Hollywood. Black humour develops when more serious subjects are concerned – religion and interment rites in particular – in the juxtaposition of Whispering Glades, the Hollywood cemetery, and the Happier Hunting Grounds, its counterpart for pets, and its sombre implications of a society forsaking its most sacred values. The Biblical parody and the reversal of Christian values are central to a novel in which the notion of human death is sacrificed to that of efficacy, pleasure substituted for pain, merrymaking for mourning, all religious references banned from the Service of 'the Loved Ones' but reinstated for defunct animals.

> Dog that is born of bitch hath but a short time to live, and is full of misery. He cometh up, and is cut down like a flower; he fleeth as it were a shadow, and never continueth in one stay . . .[15]

The parody of Job (14, 1–2), under the imperturbable mask of ignorance, obliquely conveys the indignation of the author at what appears to him as an evil perversion of the sacred texts in the same way as the Entrance Poster to Whispering Glades[16] exudes humour in its lyrico-biblico-prophetic style, its caricature of the Creation and the Revelation wryly denouncing the debasement of the most sacred Christian values. Different, but as subtle and efficient, is the type of humour presiding over Tony Last's punishment. Condemned to read Dickens for ever, to live vicariously in the petit-bourgeois Victorian universe he abhorred, imprisoned in a jungle which negates the City he envisioned, Tony Last finds Hell because he had rejected the realities of the world, refused the primordial necessity of religion. In both *A Handful of Dust* and *The Loved One*, black humour (obtained through intertextuality) is resorted to to create a hellish universe which *a contrario* imposes the absolute necessity of religion in human existence.

THE CONDITIONS OF HUMOUR

Humour, whatever its coloration, requires a proper soil, special conditions to strike root in the substance of the literary work ('substance' is the proper word as a concrete basis is necessary to its growing, blooming and bearing fruit). Oxford, Mayfair, Abyssinia, Fleet Street, California, the Army provide the soils in which Waugh plants it. Unlike wit, humour thrives on the immediate observation of, and response to, the surrounding universe. It never focuses on a single word, phrase, paragraph, but suffuses the deep layers of the work of art. Waugh, a genuine humorist, patiently conjures, and bolsters, up an 'atmosphere', a 'climate' through his technique of writing and composition. He relies on a gradual refining of the raw, immediate impressions. The very genesis of the novels shows how he uses them as foundations for his fiction. His literary creation develops in three successive stages, the initial and personal experience, later transcribed into a diary or travelogue, and finally refined into an imaginative fiction which creates a new reality coloured by the writer's humour. The situations lived at the first degree are revived and transposed at the second. In order to preserve the appearance of realism, a number of 'serious' passages are inserted within the plot and serve as touchstones, foils or guide marks to the invented stories. The 'Guidebook' style for the introduction to Hetton Abbey, or the 'History' style for the Ishmaelia of *Scoop* play this role.

Ishmaelia, that hitherto happy commonwealth, cannot conveniently be approached from any part of the world. It lies in the North-Easterly quarter of Africa, giving colour by its position and shape to the metaphor often used of it – 'the Heart of the

Dark Continent'. Desert, forest, swamp, frequented by furious nomads, protect its approaches . . .

Various courageous Europeans in the seventies of the last century came to Ishmaelia, or near it, furnished with suitable equipment of cuckoo clocks, phonographs, opera hats, draft treaties and flags of the nations which they had been obliged to leave. They came as missionaries, ambassadors, tradesmen, prospectors, natural scientists.

None of them returned . . .[17]

These passages are characterised by a meticulous presentation of apparently historical or technical details, by the dignified, un-ruffled attitude of a narrator intent on brushing up the setting of the plot in as rigorous and scientific manner as possible. For a brief moment, the moralist dons the garb of the scientist. Devoid of indifference, close to the passion of the scholar, Waugh's humour-ous fictions are always founded on realistic observation either personally acquired or invented for the sake of the cause, more frequently half-way between the two. In all cases, his realism is suddenly and brutally, but cleverly and consciously, destroyed. It hardly needs the next few words 'They were eaten, everyone of them; some raw, others stewed and seasoned . . .' for the truth to jump to the reader's eyes and mind, and the writer's position to be clearly defined.

In this respect, one can say that affectivity is a second necessary ingredient of Waugh's humour. Although it primarily rests on the concrete, the affective quality is essential to its development. Again it adheres to a precise pattern. Waugh's humour – humour in general perhaps – develops in three successive stages. First the reality of a social group is subverted, which provokes the reader's confusion or distress; then, a few hints dropped by the writer relieve the reader who, confronted with the mind-boggling ab-surdity of the proposed scheme, bursts out laughing and thus comes to share the author's humorous criticism. The way in which Lord Copper selects his journalists, Seth his personal advisers, the workings of all institutions in Britain and abroad – staff an students at Oxford, the diplomatic corps in Azania, the Pre gossip-writers and foreign correspondents, the Army – all par¹ of the utmost absurdity.

A third condition, the most specific, must be added: two p⟨ – actor and witness, author and reader – must be invol⟨

humour to appear. Actor and witness may coincide, in which case first-degree humour is achieved. Oxford students, Fleet Street journalists, Army officers are so many alter-egos of a self-mocking Waugh who, having at one time of his life lived his characters' experiences, laughs no less at himself than at those he caricatures – Paul Pennyfeather at Llanabba, Gilbert Pinfold on a cruise among others re-enact the author's past experiences. But Waugh can also create a kind of 'foil', when second degree humour is conjured up. The foil may be totally irresponsible, dull-witted and passive (Paul, Seth, William) or, on the contrary, clever, cunning and prepared to go all lengths to accomplish his aims (Basil, Julia Stitch etc . . .). Waugh plays freely on both alternatives, but the important fact remains that, owing to his personal commitment in his novels, a close relationship is set up between the work of art and the intellectual or sentimental response it rouses in the reader, hence, between the writer and his public. Obviously such a relationship is not easy to establish. Being linked with an 'aesthetic response', it can only be appreciated by those who are willing to collaborate. The hostility which some people have to the so-called defects of Waugh (a cad, a Papist, a conservative, a fascist!), a hostility which feeds on the multifarious provocations of a man who relished aggravating people, nips in the bud not the writer's humour but the very sense of humour of a reader overwhelmed by a devastating phobia for the writer or his writings. Naturally the phobia often derives either from personal prejudices or from a first degree analysis of oblique writings (is it not both easy and tempting to mistake Waugh for a racist?), or from the utter refusal to have anything to do with a man one abhors. Humour, let us repeat it, presupposes the reader's collaboration; it rests on his capacity to understand obliquely presented truths through an intimate knowledge of their contextual frames and/or his thorough adherence to the writer's *angst*. To read, for example, the conclusion of *Remote People*[18] is enough to wash Waugh of the accusation of racialism so often directed at him.

> On the night of my return I dined in London . . . I was back in the centre of the Empire, and in the spot where, at the moment, 'everyone' was going. Next day the gossip writers would chronicle the young MPs, peers, and financial magnates who were assembled in that rowdy cellar, hotter than Zanzibar, noisier

than the market at Harrar, more reckless of the decencies of hospitality than the taverns of Kabalo or Tabora . . .

> Why go abroad?
> See England first.
> Just watch London knock spots off the
> Dark Continent.[19]

For humour to operate we must then agree that some *modus vivendi* has to be worked out between the artist and the more perspicacious reader, better still, connivance will add spice to the scandalous impact of pages that may be shocking or meaningless to the unsophisticated or unprepared public. Hence the fact that Waugh, like all satirists, has either bitter enemies on whom his humour is lost or unconditional defenders who feel his humour is supreme. Either one fights him to the bitter end or one accepts and is carried away, surrendering unconditionally to his humour.

HUMOUR, WIT, IRONY

The notion of complicity opposes humour and wit. Wit strives towards dazzling phrases, mesmerising formulas. It is not so much linked with a context as with the genius, the essence of the language. As such, instead of establishing a current between two poles, it provokes a short circuit.[20] A fire is suddenly set ablaze, and quickly put out. Wit obviously exists in Waugh's writings, but it never informs them (as it does, say, Aldous Huxley's earlier novels). Waugh prefers to set up links, to switch on the current so to speak. In this respect the irony he directs at characters whose innocence, ignorance, nay imbecility, are palpable, is not far removed from humour. It stimulates the reader's response, obliges him to pass a personal judgment on the actors of the novels and their actions. All satirists – Montesquieu in *Lettres persanes*, Voltaire in *Candide*, not to mention Pope or Swift – have drawn on this technique propitious to the flowering of humour. Paul Pennyfeather, Adam Fenwick-Symes, William Boot, Dennis Barlow, Guy Crouchback here replace Usbek, Rica or Candide.

The 'suspension of evidence', a subtle derangement of the natural order, which turns the world upside down and eradicates reason from the human organisation, is another source of humour pervading Waugh's novels. *The Loved One* provides the perfect illustration of a religion absurdly turned awry, in which the instant is made more important than eternity, sensual gratification more central than the soul's salvation.[21] As a corollary to this topsy-turvy world, demanding the reader's 'suspension of evidence', Waugh's humour assumes a new acumen when it allows reality, which the fantastic adventures and preposterous fancies of the characters had blotted out, to reassert itself dramatically in the nightmares of protagonists whose minds have been deranged (Agatha, Tony and Brenda, Gilbert Pinfold). The world then is felt to be truly out of joint, only the most severe shocks may set it right, but without the protagonists ever realising it, and consequently ever becoming conscious of their own errors and responsibilities for the misfortunes which befell them. The humour springs from the unreal atmosphere surrounding events which the reader alone can appreciate at its face value once the suspension of evidence has been annihilated by the drama.

> D'you know, all that time when I was dotty I had the most awful dreams. I thought we were all driving round and round in a motor race and none of us could stop, . . . and car after car kept crashing until I was left all alone driving and driving – and then I used to crash and wake up.[22]

Let us note at this point that, Waugh's humour transcending the comic and arising from almost any situation and technique, from language to structure, Bergson's comic hierarchy, which ranges from the mechanic to verbal and psychological devices, is of little avail to analyse it.

Humour indeed can occur when the writer uses his style pleasantly enough to convince the reader of his good sense. It is universally acknowledged that Waugh ranks among the best stylists of modern British literature. He himself claimed that, for the novelist he was, style was primordial

> Properly understood style is not a seductive decoration added to a functional structure; it is of the essence of the work of art.[23]

or

One thing I hold as certain, that a writer, if he is to develop, must concern himself more and more with Style . . . a writer must face the choice of becoming an artist or a prophet.[24]

Countless examples of humorous style can illustrate our purpose. Tony Last's Sunday ritual

Tony invariably wore a dark suit on Sundays and a stiff white collar. He went to church, where he sat in a large pitch-pine pew, put in by his great-grandfather at the time of rebuilding the house, furnished with very high crimson hassocks and a fireplace, complete with iron grate and a little poker which his father used to rattle when any point in the sermon excited his disapproval . . .[25]

is a pastiche of Addison's well-known portrait of Sir Roger de Coverley at church. The squire, vested with the remnants of feudal power, suffers no inattention from the parishioners for whose moral health he feels responsible . . . but he allows himself occasionally to doze off during the sermon. Humour then proceeds from the identification of Tony with Sir Roger, from the stereotyped, unconscious archaism of an attitude out of keeping with modern times and revealed through style. At bottom it opens onto Waugh's critical awareness of his hero and of his times. At this level the writer's specific humour may rightly be said to depend on his perception of an historical and political background, the past historical grandeur, the decadence of the ruling classes, the degenerescence of the religious and political leaders. Style has transformed Waugh into a prophetic artist. At the level of the overall structure, the final retribution of the hero-victims (Adam, Tony, Ambrose, Guy) introduces a tragic element in which *pathos* and *eiron* are associated, whereas the apparently successful characters only duplicate their preceding errors and are taken back to their starting points. *The more you run, the more you stay in the same place.*

At the elementary level, the most innocuous puns or euphemisms become significant. In *Vile Bodies*, for instance, the vocabulary often opens up ironic vistas. *Divine, just too divine* the characters exclaim at the very moment they enter Hell. Toponymy (Sink Street) and onomastics (the angels' names) partake of the same epiphanies. Occasionally the play-on-words is merely an affair of humorous backchat. The play on the different meanings of the French verb *baiser* (to kiss, but also 'to screw') in *Scoop* is immediately perceptible to French readers as a simple joke.[26] Superficially amusing, it is nevertheless connected with the desecration of Christmas, eight years earlier, by the adulterous protagonists of *Vile Bodies*.[27] The central, most serious reflexion of *Black Mischief*,[28] [Prudence] 'I'd like to eat you', takes a threefold meaning. It suggests Basil Seal's physical attraction to Prudence, foreshadows the nature of their amorous activities, and eventually, with the heroine's tragic demise, illustrates the deep nature of Azania. The humorous play-on-words all function as the euphemisms of human manners. The germ of the humour basically lies in the distanciation created by the style between the reader and the text. Whether spatial or temporal, it is primarily created by a clever handling of language, style, structure, and their hidden potentialities.

In some cases, when exceptionally tender feelings are involved (Paul for Margot, William for Kätchen), a dash of pseudo-lyricism allows the reader to escape from the bleak reality. Descriptions break the dramatic rhythm, the action stops in a stasis which is a mere structural lull, a dreamlike interval in a world whose harsh nature cannot but reassert itself in a brutal way. In such cases the humorous effect resides in the momentary (but deceptive) dissipation of the prevalent dullness into a fireworks of shimmering images, in the gap between reality and dream.

A week of blue water that grew clearer and more tranquil daily, of sun that grew warmer, radiating the ship and her passengers, filling them with good humour and ease; blue water that caught the sun in a thousand brilliant points, dazzling the eyes as they searched for porpoises and flying fish; clear blue water in the shallows revealing its bed of silver and smooth pebble, fathoms down; soft warm shade on deck under the awnings; the ship moved amid unbroken horizons on a vast blue disc of blue, sparkling with sunlight.[29]

Obviously such an escapist passage is not humorous *per se*, but it is based on a pathetic fallacy soon to be dispelled, when the drab aspects of the world will predominate again . . . i.e. very soon

Muddy sea between Trinidad and Georgetown; and the ship lightened of cargo rolled heavily on the swell.[30]

This type of humour is basically structural and essential to the emergence of the message. It springs from the confrontation of the passages, from the illusions harboured by the characters (and presumably the reader) that *all may be well*, that the interlude may last for ever. But a close attention to style and context reveals the vanity of the dreams, and the writer's intentions are clarified by his structural humour.

It has often been noticed that polarisation and counterpoints are constant features in Waugh's fiction. According to G. McCartney[31] they are 'the structural analogues of the divisive tensions he sensed both within and outside himself', but they go beyond the personal idiosyncrasy and concur in the structural development of humour. By juxtaposing scenes, applying in the process the discoveries of modern art (collage, montage etc. . . .), Waugh may exert his humour at the generational division, the faults of the couple, the city and the jungle (the banquet and the cannibal feast, war and racket, phony war and phony games etc. . . .). Amusing as they are the counterpoints or montage effects confront the reader with unmistakable, but hitherto unrealised, discoveries.

Another source of humour lies in the apparent indifference of the narrator to his story which he interrupts with great disdain for his plot. The humour lies in the fact that in their own bizarre way the apparent digressions turn out to be absolutely pertinent to the novel.[32] In *Vile Bodies*, the disquisition on 'Being and Becoming'[33] parodies the argument about the ontological primacy of essence on existence. In *Decline and Fall*, the Big Wheel at Luna Park stands for Silenus's metaphor of life. In the process, the reader is led to realise the insignificance of modern man caught in the infernal machinery of a world running loose or mad. Metaphors of this plight abound in all the novels (the film and the car race in *Vile Bodies*, the funeral parlour in *The Loved One*). Humour conceals Waugh's didactic stance; the mask it provides does not need to be elaborately contrived, but it is essential to the writer's strategy. The humorous (apparent) detachment of the narrator strengthens the situation of the writer as producer. Detached, unmoved by his characters' misfortunes, reluctant to get the readers involved, he all the same suggests a moral. He draws on the strategies of modern art to ridicule the 'modern' way of life. The humour lies in the ridiculing through which he demonstrates the failure of a feckless and faithless world, the futility of a society which has lost its fundamental values. Later, Waugh will switch from humour to realism, from detachment to commitment in an attempt to offer positive solutions to his drifting contemporaries. The humour will die in the process, to the regret of the readers who had not grasped the didactic nature of the early novels or enjoyed its discretion.

The didactic nature of the novels, essential as it is, does not suffice to make of Waugh a major novelist. Waugh's originality does not lie so much in the denunciation of an insane society as in a new form of humour; or rather the emergence of a demented or corrupt language initiates another species of humour designed to set off the degraded nature of contemporary society. Language becomes the mirror of society, the demented language rubs out reality and substitutes the Verb to it, becomes a possible key to the nature of Seth and his like whose estrangement from reason it symbolises. Seth's humorously unreasonable decrees fail because of the perversion the king imposes on language, in the same way as the utopian dreams can be said to represent another perversion of language.

Such phenomena culminate in what may be called corrupt language, which, once a meaning and desire to communicate have been eradicated, ultimately boils down to mere gibberish and jargon. The characters then forget reality, take refuge in an imaginary universe of their own and avoid contact with others. Humour, at this level, emerges in the superabundance of tags: 'so', 'then', 'now', 'presently' establish links whose logic is merely apparent.[34] The language, severed from reality, functions as a humorous code devoid of any significance. Dialogues disappear, there only remain incoherent phrases muttered by characters wrapped in their own obsessions. The humour of it all carries the message that the Babel cacophony is the objective correlative of a society disintegrating in insanity. It allows both reader and writer to smile at the simultaneous discovery of the mad ways of the world, and, in the eloquent silences between the corrupt dialogues, it carries the message that societal energies must be mustered to fight the spreading anarchism and dementia, to set up a wall against the proliferating jungle.[35]

Ironically enough, one should keep in mind Waugh's own experience: there was a Waugh idiom made fashionable by the 'Hypocrites' Club'. As W. Bogaards shows in her 'Waugh and the BBC' (above), only a few intimates understood it and it did imply scorn or pretended scorn for anything or any person outside the circle. Another miracle of humour is that it urged Waugh to transpose a negative personal habit into a positive element of his fiction. The humorist runs with the hare, and never hesitates to castigate the pack of hounds in which he once belonged.

To round up this essay, three things must be said. Firstly, if humour can proceed from the complete identification of the writer with his subject, this is not always the case with Evelyn Waugh whose brand of humour is often marked with ambiguity. He asserts what he apparently denies in his novels (that 'Lush Places' are no real shelters) and constructs what he pretends to destroy (religion, essential for man's salvation, never directly appears as a recourse in most of the novels). A new outlook on life resulting from this ambiguity pushes his comedy to open on to the tragic as apparently comic actions entail disastrous consequences. For Waugh, the prime function of humour consists less in propagating ideas than in setting off their relativity (Rosa, the Macushi woman, is more dependable than all the Mayfair 'ladies'), in showing that the ambiguity of things often debouches on a form of nonsense illustrating the absurdity of contemporary mores. But, more important, the relativity it introduces improves the lesson, makes it more efficacious. '"Oh! please God, make them attack the Chapel," said Mr Sniggs'[36] (the Junior Dean of Scone College). The message is coded (as satire demands) but the important point is that the satirical lesson is always tinged or suffused with humour.

Secondly, the concrete and affective elements humour contains also make it reversible so that the heroes can be mocked without weakening the message. Surely to don a mask of innocence, or to have an incompetent fool (Paul), a blissful imbecile (William) or an archaic moron (Tony) playing the role of hero, are brilliant ways of ridiculing social mores. Through the outsider – who never suspects the schemes wielded behind his back – the reader may form the weirdest impressions of the characters and social sets he meets (Margot and Chokey, the Bright Young Things, Lord Copper and Fleet Street, British exiles in Hollywood etc . . .). A subtle power of correction goes hand in hand with the reversibility of humour. It steers clear of the pitfalls of puritanical morality. The seduction of Prudence by Basil might have inspired a sermon, Waugh succeeds in making it authentic satire, matching in excellence T.S. Eliot's 'Seduction of the Typist' scene.[37] The bitterly humorous clash between the 'love scene' (as seen by Prudence) and reality, i.e. 'The Burma cheroot . . . slowly unfurling in the soapy water . . ., the soggy stub of tobacco emanat[ing] a brown blot of juice',[38] allows the writer to avoid moral indignation and to find an objective correlative to his disgust and reprobation. Thus the blackest humour arises of a situation which encompasses in a nutshell (or more precisely here in a bathtub) the faults, vices and blemishes of modern and western life, whose horrifying reality is never directly attacked but always, indirectly, denounced.

Thirdly, humour acts as an authorial catharsis. It does not only purge the writer of the moral or sentimental temptations, it also refines the whole gamut of his emotions. Waugh's sadistic tendencies, destructive leanings, suicidal attraction are refined into positive creations. The catharsis operated by humour helped Waugh to forget, if not to heal, the wounds of his divorce, and, in the fifties, those of his physical decrepitude. It freed him from himself, as it were. It somewhat smothered nostalgia and sentiment and invited him to assert his liberty to the face of the world. Thus it eventually achieves a twofold effect, heal the writer, touch or teach the reader.

As a conclusion, we can say that humour, within its possible combinations, remains relatively stable in its matter, although the manner in which Waugh shapes it remains specific of his creative imagination. Waughian humour, although it may verge on the most scathing irony, also includes affective elements which illustrate an extreme sensitivity and shed light on the innermost recesses of the writer's personality.

We must also add that ironically, in the course of his career, Waugh ceased to be the youthful humorist of the twenties to become a genuine 'humour' in the medical sense. In the fifties an unfortunate identification of the ageing man with the artist reinforced the clichés, stereotypes, and blatant untruths which are occasionally retailed in the general public and against which critics have fought in order to restore Evelyn Waugh to his true status as one of the greatest of English humourous writers. In this sense, the lines he wrote in his private diaries[39] pathetically demonstrate his thirst for the absolute and the constant fight he had to wage to be of use in this trite age of ours.

> To make an interior act of renunciation and become a stranger in the world, to watch one's fellow countrymen as we used to watch foreigners, curious of their habits, patient of their absurdities, indifferent to their animosities – that is the secret of happiness in the century of the common man.

Fortunately Waugh's incapacity to resign himself to indifference, to watch his fellow countrymen as foreigners, is a blessing which begot his humour for our pleasure and moral edification. But for his humour (and his religious faith), his would have been held a pessimistic, almost nihilistic vision of man. One can at times see him as a desperate man, but his good sense allied to his sensibility made him favour the smiles and benevolence of ravaging humour and reject the wailing and gnashing of teeth of black melancholy. To this humour Evelyn Waugh owes his status as a major novelist and satirist of our times.

NOTES

1. Cf Jaques' famous monologue, 'It is a melancholy of my own . . . in which [my] often rumination wraps me in a most humorous sadness', *As You Like It*, IV, I, 15–19.
2. Ben Jonson, *Every Man Out of His Humour*, (Oxford, Herford and Simpser, 1927, Vol. III), Prologue, I. 88–219.
3. *Guardian*, N* 144, 26 August 1713.
4. These preliminary remarks find their basis in the works of R. Escarpit (*L'Humour*, (Paris, PUF, Que Sais-Je? N* 877, 1960), and A. Laffay, *Anatomie de l'humour et du nonsense* (Paris, Masson, 1970).
5. M. Serres, *Le contrat naturel* (Paris, François Bourrin, 1990).
6. *American Journal of Psychology*, XVIII, 1918, 420–1. Quoted by A. Mavrocordato, *L'Humour en Angleterre* (Paris, Aubier bilingue, 1967), p. 45.
7. *Labels* (London, Duckworth, 1930), pp. 44–5.
8. *Vile Bodies* (London, Chapman and Hall, 1930), pp. 131–2.
9. 'If I wasn't real', Alice said . . ., 'I shouldn't be able to cry.' 'I hope you don't suppose those are real tears?' Tweedledum interrupted.
10. Op. cit., pp. 126–7.
11. *Scoop* (London, Chapman and Hall, 1938, 1964) p. 26.
12. *Vile Bodies*, p. 82.
13. Adam bought back Nina from her husband Ginger with a bad cheque.
14. *The Loved One* (London, Chapman and Hall, 1948, 1965, 1969) p. 15.
15. Ibid., pp. 97–8.
16. 'Behold I dreamed a dream and I saw a New Earth sacred to HAPPINESS. There amid all that Nature and Art could offer to elevate the Soul of Man I saw the Happy Resting Place of Countless Loved Ones . . . And behold I awoke and in the Light and Promise of my DREAM I made WHISPERING GLADES. ENTER STRANGER and BE HAPPY.' (ibid., p. 35.)
17. *Scoop*, p. 91.
18. *Remote People* (London, Duckworth, 1931).

19. Ibid., pp. 239–40.
20. Cf. A. Mavrocordato, *L'Humour en Angleterre*, (Paris, Aubier, 1967) p. 84.
21. Cf. description of Whispering Glades: 'Water played everywhere . . . out of which rose a host of bronze and Carrara statuary, allegorical, infantile, erotic. Here a bearded magician sought the future in the obscure depths of what seemed to be a plaster football. There a toddler clutched to its stony bosom a marble Mickey Mouse . . .' (*The Loved One*).
22. *Vile Bodies*, p. 186.
23. 'Literary Style in England and America', *Books on Trial*, October 1955, p. 65.
24. Ibid., p. 66.
25. *A Handful of Dust* (London, Chapman and Hall, 1964), p. 34.
26. 'et ça c'est pour tuer les serpents et ceci est un bateau qui collapse et ces branches de mistletoe sont pour Noël, pour baiser dessous . . .' *Scoop*, p. 66.
27. 'Next morning Adam and Nina woke up under Ada's sprig of mistletoe to hear the bells ringing for Christmas across the snow.' *Vile Bodies*, p. 210.
28. *Black Mischief* (London, Chapman and Hall, 1962).
29. *A Handful of Dust*, p. 188–9. Cf. also *Scoop*, p. 65, 'The machine moved forward . . . in the high places'.
30. Ibid., p. 193.
31. G. McCartney, *Confused Roaring: Evelyn Waugh and the Modernist Tradition* (Bloomington and Indianapolis, Indiana University Press, 1987).
32. Ibid., p. 38.
33. *Vile Bodies*, p. 160.
34. Cf 'So Miles Malpractice became Mr Chatterbox', *Vile Bodies*, p. 151.
35. This brief analysis of language owes a great deal to Y. Tosser's brilliant study (Y. Tosser, *Le sens de l'absurde dans l'œuvre d'Evelyn Waugh*, Lille, Atelier de reproduction des thèses, 1976). Yet where Tosser sees the emergence of the Absurd, I would rather speak of a humour which reveals not so much the absurdity of existence as the need for a religion and a faith which alone can help Man to endure and survive.
36. *Decline and Fall*, p. 14.
37. *The Waste Land*, Section III, 'The Fire Sermon'.
38. *Black Mischief*, p. 144.
39. Michael Davie, ed., *The Diaries of Evelyn Waugh* (London, Weidenfeld and Nicolson, 1976) 2 May 1962, p. 787.

7

The Being and Becoming of Evelyn Waugh

George McCartney

Ever since Aristophanes made Socrates look ridiculous, satirists have been in the habit of mocking philosophers and their notions about reality. It comes as no surprise, then, to discover Evelyn Waugh took his place in this tradition. Of course, as we would expect of Waugh, he gave this long-standing custom his own patented twist.

Satire has frequently found philosophers guilty of excessive intellectualism. Swift's unworldly sages on the floating island of Laputa were so consumed by metaphysical speculation that their servants had to slap them to attention with inflated bladders lest they run afoul of such pedestrian perils as cliff edges. Voltaire's Dr Pangloss polished his Leibnizian optimism so vigorously that its glare was able to keep him comfortably blind to earthly horrors, even those of the Inquisition. In our own century, Aldous Huxley and George Orwell dramatised the ruthless consequences of unchecked ideology. Samuel Beckett's characters indulge in a form of intellectual masturbation that leads them inexorably into the solipsism of a Cartesian void.

Waugh also dealt with the intellect's place in modern life, but he did so with a difference. His fiction reveals a world in which the source of human woe is not too much but rather too little mind. In a typical Waugh narrative the intellect neither imposes itself on the world nor sets up an alternative reality. Instead, it finds itself cowed into retreat, if not full-fledged rout. To create this world, Waugh drew upon contemporary critiques of reason, especially those of Henri Bergson and his fiercest critic, the painter-novelist-essayist, Wyndham Lewis. The polemical clash these two figures suggested – Bergson the intuitionist, Lewis the rationalist – is echoed in the collision of impulse and reason that reverberates as a 'confused roaring' in his first novel.

Decline and Fall begins with an unequal battle between rational order and wilful energy, embodied respectively by the prudent Paul Pennyfeather and the wanton Bollinger Club. An Oxford theology student, Paul lives a meticulously managed life of serious scholarship, relieved by precisely measured indulgences – three ounces of tobacco a week, a pint and a half of beer each day. Like others in Waugh's gallery of well-intentioned, well-bred young men, he is a dim representative of the middle classes who takes his orderly, civilised surroundings for granted. He reads Galsworthy's *Forsyte Saga* in nightly instalments and subscribes to its vision of a benevolently progressive world achieved and maintained by moderation and industry. But his Edwardian dream is dashed one evening as he returns from an improving lecture on Polish plebiscites. On his quad he encounters the members of the aristocratic Bollinger club in the advanced stages of their annual dinner. Their drunken revelry fills the night with the 'confused roaring' of 'English county families baying for broken glass' (pp. 1–2)[1] as they rampage through the college destroying any evidence of disciplined order they happen upon: china, pianos, paintings, and manuscripts. In no time at all, Paul finds himself helplessly engulfed by the 'kaleidoscope of [their] dimly discernible faces' (p. 2) emerging a few moments later without his trousers. The reasonable individual is overwhelmed by the anarchic horde, his unique and meticulously constructed identity compromised as he is sent scurrying across the quad, his common humanity clearly exposed.

Waugh handles this episode so that we understand that Paul himself is largely responsible for his humiliation at the Bollingers' hands. When he first sees the revelers, we're told he 'had no particular objection to drunkenness' and 'had read rather a daring paper to the Thomas More Society on the subject'. But, as it turns out, he is 'consumedly shy of drunkards' (p. 5). Paul, the would-be intellectual, is comfortable in the realm of ideas, but he has no stomach for the breathing, brawling reality of the twentieth-century anarchy. It is precisely this disjunction between idea and reality that fascinated Waugh. In his fiction, actuality almost always proves too turbulent to be managed by the intellectual categories that had once seemed to make sense of it.

Waugh traced this failure of mind to the culture of modern thought. He was particularly concerned that in our age intellect itself had become complicit with the forces that threatened rational order in both art and life. Accordingly, his satire is more occupied with metaphysics than morals. To see how Waugh drew upon contemporary philosophical issues to organise his fiction, we must first accompany him on what he once called his 'unguided and half-comprehended study of metaphysics'.[2]

Some of Waugh's critics have emphasised his intellectual limitations, one going so far as to call him a 'brainless genius with a gift for satire',[3] an opinion still in circulation among many of his readers. The evidence simply won't support such a view. Waugh always concerned himself with the intellectual and cultural issues of his time and, as we might expect, his thinking on these matters found its way into his fiction.

Although usually brief and journalistic, Waugh's articles on literature, painting, architecture, and film can still be read with pleasure and profit largely because they are informed by his abiding interest in philosophy. He comments on this interest in several places. In 1949 he recalled his initial schoolboy study of metaphysics which left him so 'muddled about the nature of cognition' that he prematurely concluded 'man was incapable of knowing anything'.[4] By 1923, however, he had apparently revised his position. This was the year he became one of the contributors to Harold Acton's *Oxford Broom*, an undergraduate publication that took a decided if precocious philosophical stance in its first issue. In an unsigned manifesto entitled 'A Modern Credo', the editors brashly asserted that

> human nature requires an absolute. The exquisite chaos of modern thought offers this one incomparable opportunity – the creation of new absolute values. Recent intellectual sap has yet to vitalise any adequate forms of existence, and an imaginative apathy is still in vogue. But what sporadic imagination has survived is inevitably God-seeking.

The manifesto goes on to patronise Plato as one who had supplied a useful 'life-concept' for earlier ages but could no longer be taken literally. There must be a quest for a modern 'life-concept', one that 'can scarcely come about merely through the cerebral or sensual irritations of our usual existence. Something slightly less primordial is required and more sufficient . . . The ultimate requisite is always idealism incarnate'.[5] Whether or not Waugh had a hand in drafting this piece of undergraduate self-importance, it certainly reflects the longing for certitude that would dominate the novels he began publishing a few years later. We can hear something of the voice of Father Rothschild in the manifesto, the enigmatic Jesuit of *Vile Bodies* who tries to warn the uncomprehending powers-that-be of the 'radical instability in our whole world-order' that has whetted a 'fatal hunger for permanence' (pp. 185, 183).

With the possible exception of this 'Credo', Waugh never expounded upon his philosophical views at length. He did recur, however, to one name, and that was Henri Bergson's. In 1921 we find him writing his brother Alec a facetious birthday poem entitled 'Ode on the Intimations of Immaturity' which includes these lines: 'Let Bergson prate of Memory, / Potential Relativity, / Whatever that may be, / Alec's twenty-three'.[6] Diary entries in 1925 report his continuing interest in Bergson.[7] He doesn't pass judgment on Bergson's thought, but we can make some deductions from his fiction and also from his interest in Wyndham Lewis. Lewis probably served Waugh as an interpreter of Bergson's thought, and he would also have been useful for his discussion of Bergson's influence on the modernist movement that had taken shape in the preceding generation.[8] There is ample reason to believe Waugh owed both Bergson and Lewis a hefty creative debt. His familiarity with them seems to have helped him clarify his earlier muddlement and focus his satiric objectives.

Lewis comes into the picture in a 1930 review of Lewis's essays on the novel *Satire and Fiction*, where Waugh praised him for displaying 'the finest controversial style of any living writer', quite a tribute coming from one who was himself so preoccupied with style. He went on to hail Lewis as the Samuel Butler of his age. Like Butler, Waugh argued, Lewis was a valuable 'critic of contemporary scientific-philosophical systems'.[9] This assessment seems to have been directed less at *Satire and Fiction* than Lewis's 1927 treatise against modernist thought, *Time and Western Man*. So impressed was Waugh, he even set himself to imitation, telling his literary agent he was ready to write more 'Wyndham Lewis stuff' for the magazine editors he was cultivating at the time.[10]

Lewis's argument in *Time and Western Man*, published a year before *Decline and Fall*, would have been particularly useful to Waugh. In this flagrantly unfashionable treatise, Lewis defended traditional Western philosophy, providing a rationale for a continuing commitment to the kind of Platonic absolutes Waugh and his circle at Oxford had called for. Had Lewis ever seen their manifesto, he would certainly have endorsed its description of modern thought as chaotic, although there's some doubt he would have called the chaos 'exquisite'. Lewis was never one to pay tribute to the enemy, and that is how he regarded the process philosophers whose influence had taken hold in the first decades of this century. He felt no compunction about viciously attacking thinkers as distinguished as Samuel Alexander and Alfred North Whitehead, both of whom he grouped with his *bête noire*, Bergson. The influence of their metaphysical speculations, he alleged, threatened to subvert Western order. They were promoting change at the expense of stability, the will at the expense of the intellect, collective feeling at the expense of individual judgment. For Lewis, the cost was intolerably exorbitant.[11]

Of these figures, Lewis considered Bergson the most influential. According to his findings, the philosopher of Becoming was 'more than any other single figure . . . responsible for the main intellectual characteristics of the world we live in', and this, he argued, was cause for alarm.[12] Certainly, Bergson presented both Lewis and Waugh with a convenient target. His work distilled and popularised intellectual trends that traditionalists such as themselves naturally abhorred. Lewis found Bergson's valuation of feeling and intuition especially suspect. It was worse than unphilosophical; it seemed to him a campaign to undermine reason itself.

Needless to say, Lewis's response to Bergson is founded upon a misreading. Bergson's arguments are much subtler than Lewis would have us believe. He clearly was not the simple-minded romantic we discover in the pages of *Time and Western Man*. Like some other creative misreadings, however, Lewis's seems to have the virtue of revealing his own predispositions and, indirectly, Waugh's. But before we consider these predispositions and how they affected Waugh's fiction, we should recall Bergson's central argument in *Creative Evolution*. Doing so will help us understand what Lewis and Waugh were reacting against.

Bergson was trying to place metaphysics on a new footing. He wanted to dissolve what he considered to be the artificial distinction between the perceiving subject and perceived object implicit in the essentialist metaphysics of the West. In their quest for the bedrock certainty of timeless Being, essentialist philosophers, he argued, had been chasing a will-o'-the-wisp. Reality was not to be discovered in supposedly timeless ideas, but rather in the ceaseless process of evolutionary growth he called Becoming. The reason this had not been understood previously was the Western tendency to place exclusive trust in the analytical, labelling intellect when making metaphysical inquiries. Philosophers had traditionally assumed that reality was only that which the intellect could objectify and communicate by means of representation in language and symbol. They had ignored the fixative property of language, the tendency of words to segment and hypostasise reality's processes. This oversight permitted them to assume that true knowledge could only be grasped with the aid of named and therefore seemingly immutable categories.

Bergson reminded his readers that the intellect's prized version of reality was, after all, an abstraction from immediate experience. Since the intellect traffics in representations, it is always and necessarily at one remove from concrete experience. It is as though the mind were only able to apprehend the discarded shell left behind by the numinous principle of reality. In order to think or speak about experience at all, we enter into a collaborative fiction. We label the fossil remains of direct experience and regard them as reality itself. But the thing-in-itself, life itself, which is fundamentally a process of Becoming in time, always eludes our static categories.

According to Bergson, the essentialist's purely intellectual approach to experience inevitably produces a dislocating sense of homelessness. By standing apart from its object of thought, the mind necessarily feels itself to be alienated from the world it perceives. He wanted to close this alienating distance between self and world. We need only let go of our hypertrophied intellect, he urged, and 'install [ourselves] within change'. We must allow ourselves to experience the moment directly without the intervention of analytical judgment, without questioning its significance. In the moment of intuitive experience, there is no gap between the perceiving subject and perceived object. Instead, the mind joins its object in simple, unreflective apprehension. Since this experience is nonverbal, there can be no slippage between signified and signifier, to borrow the formula from recent critical theory. Indeed, questions about significance are beside the point. The experience *is* the significance. This total immersion in the immediate moment instils a confident awareness of the irreducibly real and puts us into emotional and imaginative harmony with our world. This is the incommunicable, almost mystical experience of *durée* in which we unmistakably contact the numinous principle of existence: Bergson's unbounded, evolutionary Becoming.[13]

Bergson's thought is romantic, optimistic, and egalitarian. These were precisely the qualities that Lewis found objectionable. In his reading, Bergson is too soft-headed to make anything like the discriminations necessary for orderly thought. Again and again, Lewis stresses Bergson's apparent reluctance to make value distinctions. And, it must be acknowledged, Bergson's arguments supplied Lewis with his ammunition. Bergson often seems to be saying that virtually any and every experience is a potential occasion of ecstatic *durée*. Lewis, drawing his inferences from Bergson's own words, demonstrates that for the process philosopher time is democratised, each instant necessarily fulfilling itself in the universal Becoming. There are no declines, no falls from anterior ideals as there are in an essentialist metaphysics. At times Bergson seems to be saying with Leibniz and Alexander Pope, 'Whatever is, is right'. In existential Becoming there are no privileged moments from which to measure improvement or deterioration. Each existent is no more nor no less than it can be in each successive phase of its Becoming. Each new moment collects and advances all previous moments. There are no highs nor lows, no worse nor better, no befores nor afters, just the ceaseless climax of the now.[14]

Such easy tolerance of the actual could not have failed to provoke Waugh's satiric sensibility. His misanthropic nature must have delighted in the opportunity Bergson afforded, especially in the light of Lewis's trenchant criticism.

Lewis's charge was that Bergson had abandoned reason in favour of emotional whim, and that this was a dereliction of the philosopher's responsibility to locate an intelligible order in the world. Only a return to essentialist metaphysics could restore the balance. By insisting that essence precedes and defines existence, essentialist thought makes it possible to impose boundaries on experience and render the world manageable, he explained. Into the bargain, it provides the grounds necessary for individuals to sustain a sense of continuing identity. Rather than the existentialist's dynamic, unstanchable flow of *durée*, the essentialist's reality is founded upon the sculptural stasis of Platonic forms glimpsed at just those moments when the object of perception most realises its Being. In this epistemology, the mind is discriminating rather than passive in its pursuit of understanding. It actively seeks the essential nature of things by isolating what is humanly intelligible in them. Lewis approved of this deductive approach to knowing because it adhered to 'classical science' in which an object 'realises itself, working up to a climax. . . . It is its apogee or perfection that is it, for classical science. It is the rounded thing of common sense'. This, Lewis claimed, was what was missing in contemporary art. Bergson's influence had encouraged a sloppy, formless subjectivity when what was needed was a hard-headed, decisive objectivity. A passive, impressionistic mind had no chance to make sense of an increasingly confusing world. To do that, one required a confident intellect ready to apply the leverage of fixed principles. One recalls Waugh's remark in 1932: 'It is better to be narrow-minded than to have no mind, to hold limited and rigid principles than none at all'.[15]

Bergson and Lewis, and the conflict they represented, clearly captivated the young Waugh's imagination. Why else would he have introduced them into his narratives? In *Decline and Fall*, for instance, the avant-garde architect Otto Silenus, sounding very much like Lewis in one of his more dyspeptic moments, indicts human nature on the grounds of its inveterate Bergsonism. Between 'the harmonious instincts and balanced responses of the animal' and 'the inflexible purpose of the engine', he intones, human beings are 'equally alien from the *being* of Nature and the *doing* of the machine'. They are 'the vile becoming' (p. 160). Apparently just in case his readers did not see the connection the first time around, in his second novel, *Vile Bodies*, Waugh included a footnote to Lewis's Vorticist journal, *Blast*. The note explains that the innovative graphics and *ex cathedra* judgments for which Lewis had become famous served as the model for some absurdly avant-garde party invitations that appear in the course of the narrative.

Elsewhere in *Vile Bodies*, Waugh makes his most explicit use of Bergson and, the evidence suggests, he does so through the eyes of Lewis, his chosen critic of 'contemporary scientific-philosophical systems'. In this episodic novel, the one chapter that might be thought pivotal concerns an automobile race. As was his manner in this period, Waugh has his narrator interrupt his story and, with apparently sublime indifference to the unfolding plot, indulge in what seems at first to be a ludicrous digression. In the midst of describing the race's preparations, he pauses to meditate with Olympian aplomb on the philosophical differences between passenger and race cars. 'The truth is that motor cars offer a very happy illustration of the metaphysical distinction between "being" and "becoming".' Ordinary passenger cars, he continues, 'have definite "being"'. They maintain their essential 'identity to the scrap heap'. Race cars, however, are in a state of continuous Becoming.

Never quite the same machine from one moment to the next, they exist in a 'perpetual flux; a vortex of combining and disintegrating units; like the confluence of traffic at some spot where many roads meet, streams of mechanism come together, mingle and separate again', their various parts undergoing a ceaseless process of removal and replacement with each pit stop that interrupts their mad career around the track (pp. 227–8). This may seem no more than some by-the-way comedy, but, in fact, it is central to Waugh's concerns, as we can see when we consider how he developed this metaphysical conceit and applied variants of it elsewhere.

Waugh's parody of Bergson too closely resembles Lewis's attack on the concept of Becoming in *Time and Western Man* to be merely coincidental. According to Lewis, Bergson's 'reality is where things run into each other, in that flux, not where they stand out in a discrete "concreteness."'[16] Waugh's cars of Becoming translate Lewis's comments metaphorically, even borrowing his vocabulary: they are in a 'perpetual flux' and they 'come together', mingling promiscuously. Their 'streams of mechanism' even form a 'vortex', a key word in Lewis's lexicon. With Ezra Pound, Lewis had founded the short-lived but influential Vorticist movement on the eve of the Great War. It was supposed to promote the idea that an artist's achievement is directly proportional to his or her ability to reach the still centre of an experience's whirling vortex and from this position contemplate the surrounding confusion with the poised equanimity necessary to esthetic creation. It is Lewis's Vorticist theories that Waugh must have had in mind when he had Silenus compare life to 'the big wheel' at an amusement park, 'a great disc of polished wood that revolves quickly'. People pay their money and ride the wheel as best they can, Silenus explains. Many 'enjoy scrambling on and being whisked off and scrambling on again. How they shriek and giggle!' Others find their way to the rim and 'hold on for dear life'. Still others are best advised to stay in the observing stands and not get on at all. Silenus himself has Vorticist aspirations. He is in search of the centre. As he observes, the closer one comes to the middle, the slower the wheel moves and the 'easier it is to stay on. . . . Of course, at the very centre there's a point completely at rest, if one could only find it', he reports, adding with his characteristic self-assurance, 'I'm not sure I am not very near that point myself' (pp. 282–3).

However the currents of influence ran, one thing is certain: both Lewis and Waugh thought Bergson not merely mistaken, but, along with other process philosophers, a dangerous influence whose arguments supported the growth of relativism and were therefore inimical to the rationality they prized.

This is why, when Waugh envisions Becoming as the 'perpetual flux' of his race cars, he takes elaborate care to drain his conceit of any vestige of Bergson's optimism. The cars of Becoming are 'masters of men . . . vital creations of metal who exist solely for their own propulsion through space, for whom their drivers, clinging precariously at the steering wheel, are as important as his stenographer to a stockbroker' (pp. 227–8). No longer mediated by intellectual categories, the experience of Becoming overwhelms the individual mind just as the Bollingers' 'kaleidoscope of dimly discernible faces' had swallowed Paul Pennyfeather's identity in its blur. In Waugh's hands, Becoming is not the liberating concept Bergson had described, but rather a dehumanising assault on the rational self.

Waugh's cars of Becoming serve as an emblem of diminished individuality that presides over his early fiction. Until his later novels, his characters are generally abstract, insubstantial. Like Paul Pennyfeather, whose three-dimensional self mysteriously disappears and is replaced by a shadowy two-dimensional surrogate, his characters often seem hardly there at all. They flicker dimly in the middle distance, little more than the words they dazedly utter as they submit passively to one outrage after another. In this, Waugh seems to have turned Bergson's prescription on its head. Having installed themselves within change, his characters no longer know their own minds. As a consequence, they lack both the intellectual leverage and, more importantly, the personal confidence to shape the world around them. Their identity drowns in the flow of events over which they have relinquished control. Instead of finding themselves in the experience of Becoming, they merely fade from Being.

In *Vile Bodies*, we meet Adam Fenwick-Symes upon his return to England where, passing through customs, he is peremptorily stripped of the autobiography he's been writing in France and his copy of Dante. 'I knows dirt when I sees it or I shouldn't be where I am today', as one of the officers explains (p. 25). Thus deprived of his personal and cultural identities, he is transformed into a creature of Becoming, shuttling haphazardly from one role to the next – aspiring author, gossip columnist, vacuum salesman, impromptu pimp, finally becoming a soldier lost in the uncharted landscape of 'the biggest battlefield in the history of the world' (p. 314).

Motifs of disguise and mistaken identity also contribute to Waugh's sense of modern anomie. Although he works as a butler, Philbrick in *Decline and Fall* may be a gangster, an inn keeper, or Arnold Bennett. We're never sure. In *Scoop*, a reclusive nature columnist on the staff of the *Daily Beast* is mistaken for a globe-trotting war correspondent and, much against his polite protests, is rushed to Africa to cover the supposed outbreak of civil hostilities, a perilous mission for which he is singularly unsuited. In *The Loved One* the success of Juanita del Pablo's acting career depends upon her protean ability to submit to one identity change after another as she goes along with her studio's tireless quest to market her to a fickle public. By virtue of dyes, dentures, and pronunciation drills, she's a Spanish spitfire with 'a truly horrifying natural scowl' one year and an Irish colleen expected to 'laugh roguishly all the time' the next (pp. 8–9). Finally, her agent presses 'the metaphysical point, did his client exist? Could you legally bind her to annihilate herself? Could you come to any agreement with her before she had acquired the ordinary marks of identity?' (p. 25).

Many of Waugh's characters lack the ordinary marks of identity. Like the cars of Becoming, they are never quite the same from one moment to the next. They live in a blurred now in which there are no befores or afters, passively accepting their status as interchangeable commodities.

Waugh's strategy for characterisation ironically echoes Lewis's complaint that modernist fiction, under Bergson's influence, no longer troubled itself with constructing solid, identifiable human beings. Lewis had argued that, instead of an objective rendering of the external world and the individuals who inhabited it, the modernist novel typically celebrates subjective impressions; rather than characters, it dwells upon fleeting states of mind.[17] Waugh's momentaneous characters of Becoming could have served Lewis as an apt parody of the modernist preoccupation with the discontinuous self. Certainly, his charge that, under Bergson's influence, modern art had chosen to locate reality in the shapelessness of the passing moment found its incarnation in the wild and apparently aimless confusion of Waugh's early narratives.

One can see why Waugh was fascinated by Bergson. Had he not existed, Waugh would surely have invented him. With some strategic distortions – such as those suggested by Lewis – Bergson is easily, if unfairly, transformed into a modern Pangloss and, as such, presents a perfect foil against which to score satiric points. Waugh, like Lewis, seems to have considered Bergson's Becoming a philosophical justification for what he took to be the headlong mindlessness of the twentieth century. In one way or another, the Being-Becoming argument serves as the central tension in all of Waugh's early work. Being stood for reason, order, stability; Becoming, for a wilful disregard for consequences and a mindless abandonment to the anarchy of impulse.

But it must be added that Waugh's handling of this tension was neither facile nor moralistic. Nor did he indulge in the hectoring diatribes Lewis was too often too given to. Contrary to some readings, Waugh's satire does not fasten upon the will and instincts as though they were the exclusive source of the world's evil. If he had, his rogues wouldn't be so engaging and his innocents so tedious. We're invited to laugh at Captain Grimes, the bisexual bigamist of *Decline and Fall* who leaves schoolmastering in Wales for pimping in South America, but the anemic decency of the law-abiding Tony Last in *A Handful of Dust* elicits our scorn whenever we're not feeling sorry for him.

The primary target of Waugh's satire is not immorality, wilfulness, or disorder. Instead, he took aim at the contemporary refusal to sustain a dialectic between intellect and will. It seemed to him that those equipped by background and education had abdicated their responsibility to temper the extremes of both reason and impulse, or in Bergsonian terms, Being and Becoming. This is developed quite powerfully, if briefly, in a passage from 'Charles Ryder's Schooldays', the fragment of a novel that was to depict the youth of the character who narrates *Brideshead Revisited*.

When young Charles wilfully steps from the prescribed path of his public school's routine one day, his state of mind is described with an unusual allusion.

Today and all this term he was aware of a new voice in his inner counsels, a detached, critical Hyde who intruded his presence more and more often on the conventional, intolerant, subhuman, wholly respectable Dr Jekyll; a voice, as it were, from a more civilised age, as from the chimney corner in mid-Victorian times there used to break sometimes the sardonic laughter of a grandmama, relic of Regency, a clear, outrageous, entirely self-assured disturber among the high and muddled thoughts of her whiskered descendants. (p. 282)

The reversal in this passage reveals an essential component in Waugh's vision. To see what this is, we must ask the obvious question: in what sense could Jekyll be thought subhuman and Hyde civilised? This seems merely perverse until we reconsider Robert Louis Stevenson's late Victorian parable and discover that Waugh has gotten the tale's meaning perfectly in his seemingly casual allusion. Once suggested, it is obvious. Of course Jekyll is the real monster of the story and Hyde his maddened victim. Jekyll is a monster of rationality and good intentions whose belief in man's perfectibility requires that he brutally deny the Hyde in himself. For Hyde is not the product of repression, psychoanalytically understood. His appearance is not the result of Jekyll's unconscious denial of his unacceptable impulses. Long before Jekyll concocted his transforming potion, he had been acting quite deliberately on the promptings of his Hyde-nature, philandering furtively when he had opportunity. But he found his hole-in-the corner game tiresome. Though necessary to protect his respectability, it had become much too inconvenient. The purpose of his experiment is neither to repress nor sublimate his troublesome Hyde-self. He wants instead to purge and ignore it so that he can pursue his ambitious programme of scientific research and social reform undistracted. Hyde, then, is the product of Jekyll's refusal to take responsibility for the flawed condition of his human nature. Undirected and unleavened by a morality that accepts sin as an inevitable, even salutary, part of human experience, he splits in two. There is the noble, intellectual Jekyll, well-meaning but ultimately irresponsible, and the wilful, impulsive Hyde, growing more uncontrollable with each new outrage. Despite his anguished handwringing, Jekyll must bear the responsibility for the Hyde he has created by turning his back on his wilful nature.

Waugh's Jekyll is modern secular society whose moral relativism and progressive materialism require that it ignore a difficult truth: the energy that sometimes erupts as feral viciousness is somehow the same that can at other times spring forth as moral virtue. Swift had made the same point in the voyage to the Houyhnhnms where Gulliver becomes so seduced by the dream of pure reason that he does everything in his power to deny his Yahoo humanity. Jekyll and Gulliver suffer from moral immaturity. They desire nothing less than a shadowless life in which choice is invariably uncomplicated. The point of both characters is that they reject the moral adventure implicit in being creatures endowed with free will. Each would rather forfeit his freedom than face the anguish of ambiguous moral decisions. They long for a sunny world of childish irresponsibility, their lives laid out, every wrinkle anticipated and smoothed in advance.

Waugh directed his satire at just this sort of irresponsibility. Both in his fiction and his journalism, he attacked those who relied on reasonableness and decency alone to face an increasingly uncivil world. His Paul Pennyfeathers and Tony Lasts are muddle-headed Jekylls, naive enough to behave as though good intentions alone could banish the Hyde both outside and inside themselves. Waugh's argument was always that people who persist in the simple-minded belief that unaided decency will prevail in human affairs must continue to be at the mercy of the savagery they refuse to acknowledge.

It is the mind's temptation to shy from a confusing and corrupt world that was at the heart of Waugh's interest in the argument Lewis had waged against Bergson. He was drawn to this debate, no doubt, because, as his diaries make abundantly clear, he himself was divided between retreat and engagement. It was in large part the tension within himself that predisposed him to polarise his personal experience along the axes of Being and Becoming, stability and anarchy. This is vividly apparent in a scene close to the conclusion of *Vile Bodies*, the genesis of which can be traced to events in his life as recorded in his first travel book, *Labels*. To follow the process by which he translated his experience into fiction is to gain unusual access to his mind and method.

In 1929, Waugh flew to Paris where he visited an art exhibit in the rue Bonaparte entitled *Panorama de l'art contemporain*.[18] When he came to record his impressions a year later, he dwelt on two paintings that had been hung side by side. 'It was very French', he wrote in *Labels*:

[Francis] Picabia and [Max] Ernst hung cheek by jowl; these two abstract pictures, the one so defiant and chaotic, probing with such fierce intensity into every crevice and convolution of negation, the other so delicately poised, so impossibly tidy, discarding so austerely every accident, however agreeable, that could tempt disorder, seemed between them to typify the continual conflict of modern society.[19]

Waugh mentions other works, but it was the contrast of these two paintings that particularly intrigued him. In their juxtaposition he discovered a nearly perfect illustration of his theme.

He doesn't identify them by their titles and the only extant review of the exhibition does not itemise individual canvases, but Picabia and Ernst had their own unmistakable styles and we can be reasonably confident of the type of painting with which each would have been represented in a fashionable showing of 1929. Picabia had become known for his blend of cubist abstraction and futurist drollery; Ernst, for his fevered surrealism. Picabia's work suggests a mind that has turned from reality to seek relief amidst the timeless Being of geometric form; Ernst's paintings seem like a wilful plunge into the anarchy of Becoming. While we can only guess, Waugh probably neglected to name the paintings because he was more interested in the contradiction they suggested than in the individual merits of either. This would explain what seems to be an obvious discrepancy in the passage just quoted. Although Waugh mentions Picabia first, the sequence of his impressions does not follow this lead. His description of Ernst's 'fierce intensity' comes before his assessment of Picabia's 'delicately poised' order.

Waugh may have arranged his comments negligently, but they are too much to the point to have been carelessly composed. Few sentences could have caught so accurately the essential difference between these two painters. The sureness of his response suggests how fully their works engaged his imagination. And how could it have been otherwise? Put side by side as they were, they visually portrayed the antagonistic extremes of Being and Becoming with which he was preoccupied at this time in his career. The 'continual conflict' they suggested to his mind exemplified once again the incompatibility of rational order and wilful energy in a world that had lost its sense of purpose, a world in which mind had retreated from experience.

Picabia's paintings in this period resemble diagrammatic drawings of machines to which, perversely enough, he assigned human titles such as *The Infant Carburettor*, *Universal Prostitution*, and *The Daughter Born without a Mother*.[20] These canvases suggest the bright colour-coded illustrations to be found in *Popular Mechanics*. They portray sanitised machines unsullied by oil or grease, as if to suggest the triumph of the mechanical over the biological. With whatever mixture of irony, Picabia's vision reveals a self-contained technological world sealed off from dirt and decay, a Futurist celebration in which geometric design liberates us from the uncertainty of organic nature.

Ernst's surrealism, on the other hand, displays a world as distant from Picabia's as can be imagined. Between 1925 and 1928, he was painting his forest series – *Forest, The Grey Forest, The Great Forest*, and *Forest, Sun and Birds* – canvases crowded with fierce, writhing vegetation.[21] Through dense shadows, the spectator glimpses wriggling shapes that seem familiar enough at first but, upon closer examination, elude identification. The wild organic vitality of these paintings defeats the mind's inclination to name and categorise. Their world is one that evades definition at every turn.

The contrast of these two paintings suited Waugh's satiric purposes completely. Given the emblematic significance Waugh attaches to them, it is not surprising to see them echoed in *Vile Bodies*. Near the novel's conclusion, he presents two contrasting pictures of his own. Like the Picabia and Ernst canvases, they hang 'cheek by jowl', one following the other without benefit of any transitional signals. In the first, Nina Blount sickens at the strange perspectives of her first airplane ride, in the second, Agatha Runcible drifts into hallucination as she lies in her hospital bed dying of injuries she has sustained in a race car accident. But before nausea and death intervene, each gains a privileged if unsettling glimpse of the world from the perspective of modern art. Nina's aerial view of the countryside recalls a Picabia canvas; Agatha's hallucination echoes an Ernst forest.

Nina looked down and saw inclined at an odd angle a horizon of straggling red suburb; arterial roads dotted with little cars; factories, some of them working, others empty and decaying; a disused canal; some distant hills sown with bungalows; wireless masts and overhead power cables; men and women were indiscernible except as tiny spots; they were marrying and shopping and making money and having children. The scene lurched and tilted again as the aeroplane struck a current of air.

'I think I'm going to be sick,' said Nina.

'Poor little girl,' said Ginger. 'That's what the paper bags are for.'

There was rarely more than a quarter of a mile of the black road to be seen at one time. It unrolled like a length of cinema film. At the edges was confusion; a fog spinning past, *'Faster, faster,'* they shouted above the roar of the engine. The road rose suddenly and the white car soared up the sharp ascent without slackening of speed. At the summit of the hill there was a corner. Two cars had crept up, one on each side, and were closing in. 'Faster,' cried Miss Runcible. 'Faster.'

'Quietly, dear, quietly. You're disturbing everyone . . . .'

They were trying to make her lie down. How could one drive properly lying down?

Another frightful corner. The car leant over on two wheels, tugging outwards; it was drawn across the road until it was within a few inches of the bank. One ought to brake down at the corners, but one couldn't see them coming lying flat on one's back like this. The back wheels wouldn't hold the road at this speed. Skidding all over the place.

'Faster. Faster.' (emphasis Waugh's.)

(pp. 284–5)

The descriptions of these two scenes are inescapably analogous to Waugh's impressions of the Picabia and Ernst paintings. Nina's countryside is as 'impossibly tidy' as the geometries of a Picabia canvas; Agatha's hallucination has as much 'fierce intensity' as any of Ernst's scenes of organic anarchy. Nina reduces the countryside to an intellectual diagram; while Agatha plunges wilfully into the confusion of Becoming.

In addition to the internal textual evidence that links these fictional scenes with Waugh's comments on Picabia and Ernst, two non-literary considerations support this reading and further emphasise how much Waugh had invested in the Being-Becoming argument. First, there is their closeness in time: the comments in *Labels* must have been composed between 1929 and 1930, the same period in which Waugh was working on *Vile Bodies*. Second, this same travel book includes what must have been his source for Nina's distressing aerial vision. A few pages before he makes his comments on Picabia and Ernst, he describes the flight that brought him to Paris for the exhibition. It was unpleasantly memorable. He became air-sick and had to use a vomit bag. Afterward, however, he was able to appreciate the view which, he reports, was fascinating for the first few minutes we were in the air and after that very dull indeed. It was fun to see houses and motor cars looking so small and neat; everything had the air of having been made very recently, it was all so clean and bright. But after a very short time one tires of this aspect of scenery. . . . All one gains from this effortless ascent is a large scale map.[22]

Waugh's flight to Paris is certainly the personal experience on which he drew for his description of Nina's plane ride. Granted this, it would be reasonable to expect that he incorporated some of his other travel experiences into his fiction. So it is not surprising that his comments on Picabia and Ernst a few pages later can be applied with equal justice to Nina's sickening prospect and Agatha's fatal hallucination.

Nina views the twentieth century done in the Futurist mode. The unnatural perspective of airflight has distorted the conventional countryside so that it reveals its distressingly modern condition. This is a world in which standard expectations have been turned thoroughly inside out. Even the usual distinction between the organic and inorganic can no longer be taken for granted. From Nina's plane people seem to be no more than the nearly indiscernible dots one might find on a statistician's graph. The inorganic structures, however, have been invested with an eerie vitality: roads have become 'arterial', bungalows are 'sown', factories are 'decaying'. Compared with them, human beings have faded into their faceless functions, 'marrying and shopping and making money and having children' with mechanical regularity. The peculiar arrangement of this last clause reinforces Waugh's point. We would expect to hear that these people are marrying and raising families, earning and spending. By shuffling these activities and adding an extra coordinate conjunction so that first 'marrying' and 'shopping' are linked and then 'making money' and 'having children', Waugh suggests syntactically that there are no value distinctions among these activities. In the twentieth century people are reduced to the measurable functions of an economist's report in which love and consumption are of equivalent importance. In the foreground of Nina's vision, 'wireless masts and overhead power cables' form the technological grid under which the century takes its shape. This is a world in which things, especially mechanical things, are more alive than people. Like the geometric poise of a Picabia painting, the scene is 'impossibly tidy' and thoroughly synthetic. Little wonder that Nina must resort to the vomit bag. Coldly impersonal, her vision registers the essence of Waugh's twentieth century; it speaks of a world in which human sentiment can never be anything more than a bad joke.

From Nina's distress, Waugh abruptly turns to Agatha's death-bed nightmare. In the hallucinatory chaos of Agatha's mind, consciousness has been reduced to the rush of black road over which her imagined race car speeds at an uncontrollable velocity. The world has been reduced to a blur of 'fog spinning past' her. Like an Ernst painting, it is filled with shapes without recognisable forms, experience without defining categories. There is no perspective, no past, no future, only the confused sensation of each new moment as she rushes into it. The experience is unquestionably vibrant, 'probing', as Waugh had said of Ernst's work, 'into every crevice and convolution of negation'. It is also fatal. Agatha's nightmare course resembles Lewis's version of the Bergsonian flux, a stream of unordered sensation that first knocks her on her back and then overwhelms whatever ability she once might have had for directing her life. As she speeds toward the final nothingness of death, she has no chance to make sense of her experience. There is only the exhilarating but mindless imperative to go 'faster, faster'.

These are the choices in Waugh's twentieth century: impotent observation or mindless participation. Confronted by modern reality, his characters either retreat into Picabia's lifeless order or wander blindly through Ernst's chaotic forest. The traditional dialectic between intellect and will has all but ceased because the civilised mind has given up trying to discover any fundamental purpose in daily experience. It is this vision that gives Waugh's early novels their special bitterness. If the mind has despaired of making sense of the world, then human effort has no consequence.

For Waugh there was but one way out of this impasse. As he had written in 1946, human nature could only achieve 'its determining character' in the recognition 'of being God's creature with a defined purpose'.[23] Only in light of this purpose could the mind hope to address reality confidently and effectively. This is the burden of his 1950 novel, *Helena*.

Waugh liked to say *Helena* was his best novel.[24] Very few have agreed with this estimate. Of course, we should not overlook the possibility that Waugh made this claim in order to provoke his audience. He enjoyed disturbing the unwary. Whatever the case, in retelling the story of St Helena, mother of Constantine and finder of the True Cross, Waugh plays fast and loose with history and legend in order to make his didactic point. The narrative is sprightly and always entertaining, but it displays nothing like the literacy power of his best work. What it does display, however, is the motive for Waugh's conversion to Roman Catholicism. And this makes the novel very interesting indeed.

In Waugh's version of the legend, Helena's first promptings toward Christianity are much the same as his toward the Roman church. He invests his character with his own distaste for intellectuals who delighted in speculation for its own sake but were unable or unwilling to commit themselves to any definite principles. Marcias, the eunuch slave who was once Helena's tutor, is just this kind of intellectual. After achieving popular and well-paid success as a professional Gnostic, he returns to Helena's court to give a lecture on the mysteries of the fertility goddess, Astarte. At his recital's conclusion, Helena demands, 'When and where did all this happen?' Marcias tells her that her question is childish. 'These things are beyond time and space' (p. 121). Helena concludes, 'It's all bosh' (p. 123). Marcias is as sterile intellectually as he is physically.

Marcias is portrayed as an irresponsible intellectual – a clever, talented man who knows much but cares little for the consequences of his knowledge except as they help or hinder his own interests. When things become at all difficult, he simply retreats into his mind, 'sailing free and wide in the void he made his chilly home' (p. 9).

We meet variations of Marcias's type throughout Waugh's fiction, Mr Samgrass in *Brideshead Revisited*, for instance. An Oxford don, he enjoys an encyclopedic grasp of history and culture, but he is, for all his intellectual attainments, an essentially shallow man. We're told that although 'not a man of religious habit, . . . he knew more than most Catholics about their Church; he had friends in the Vatican and could talk at length of policy and appointments, . . . what recent theological hypothesis was suspect, and how this or that Jesuit or Dominican had skated on thin ice or sailed near the wind in his Lenten discourses; he had everything except the Faith' (p. 110). Samgrass, or Sammy as he is called by condescending acquaintances, is a little man who makes his way in the world by toadying to the whims of his aristocratic patrons. Despite his erudition, he is no more than a soulless flunkey, at best an object of scorn, at worst an interfering nuisance.

A more pathetic version of this type can be found in Mr Prender-gast, the parson of *Decline and Fall*, who suffers from 'Doubts', as he puts it. Finding he can no longer 'understand why God had made the world' (p. 38), he eventually becomes a prison chaplain. The post, happily, does not require that he hold any particular beliefs at all. Such agnostic felicity cannot last, however. Among his caged flock there is a religious lunatic wholly unhindered by doubt. Convinced – with good reason – that Prendergast lacks faith, he murders the well-meaning but ineffectual chaplain by sawing his head off. Prendergast's grisly end provides Waugh with another metaphor of his central theme: twentieth-century man decapitated, his intellect severed from his will. Reason abdicates its reign only at its peril.

These figures and others like them have an identifiable source in Waugh's life. Looking back in 1949, he tells us of the theologian who 'inadvertently made [him] an atheist' the day he informed his public-school class that none of the Bible's books were written by their supposed authors and then inviting his students 'to speculate in the manner of the fourth century on the nature of Christ'. Once this worthy had 'removed the inherited axioms' of his faith, Waugh found himself quite unable 'to follow him in the higher flights of logic by which he reconciled his own scepticism with his position as a clergyman'.[25]

Like his Helena, Waugh was repelled by such subtle evasiveness. Either there was a truth to be found or there was none at all. Either the human mind could discern a purpose to existence or life was meaningless. There was no middle ground. The choice was 'between Christianity and Chaos', as he put it in 1930.[26]

In telling the tale of Helena's discovery of the True Cross, Waugh was testifying to his conviction that we are meant to discover our purpose not in sophisticated metaphysics or other worldly mysticism, but in the ordinary world of the senses. When Helena undertakes her mission, she has no interest in metaphysical speculation or the many mystery cults of the fourth century. Nor does she care for theological niceties concerning Christian dogmas such as the hypostatic union. Her search is directed wholly outward. Her vindication is to be achieved not by retreating from but rather engaging with the ordinary world. She senses that once she finds the 'solid chunk of wood' (p. 196) on which Christ was crucified, she will have also reached a crucial intersection of time and eternity. This plain, homely artefact will prove that the world responds to our longing for meaning and that our thoughts and representations, from the most pedestrian to the most sophisticated, can never be wholly futile because they always carry with them revelatory potential.

Helena's mission speaks of Waugh's belief that in the beginning was the Word and the Word was made flesh, which is to say, among other things, that the original sign and its referent were one and the same. It followed for Waugh that, however uncertainly and fleetingly, language must have the power to put us in touch with the Real Presence of reality's eternal Being, no matter how confusing our day-to-day Becoming. Truth was to be located neither in the mind nor experience but rather at their fruitful intersection. It was no idle remark when Waugh commented in 1946 that his future career would be preoccupied with literary style and 'man in his relation to God'.[27] In his mind, language and belief were inseparable.

One need not have much interest in theological issues to see the appeal of Waugh's position, at least as far as it regards our ability to achieve certainty about the world around us. This is especially so today when fashionable intellectuals have advanced a new gnosticism. For the past twenty-odd years, critical theorists have been instructing us to give up our nostalgia for presence, to recognise that the search for a reality outside our various semiologies is futile. Any such reality would be by definition inscrutable. In all seriousness, we have been urged to cut anchor and drift among our signifiers as they float above the void of our unknowing.

Could it be that such Laputan logic has inadvertently stimulated the growing critical interest in the satirist of the mind's malfeasance?

NOTES

1. References are to the Little, Brown edition of Waugh's works and will appear parenthetically in the text.
2. 'Come Inside', collected in *The Essays, Articles and Reviews of Evelyn Waugh*, ed. Donat Gallagher (Boston: Little, Brown, 1983) p. 367. In subsequent references this collection will be identified as *Essays*.
3. Sean O'Faolain, *The Vanishing Hero: Studies in Novelists of the Twenties* (London: Eyre and Spottiswoode, 1956), pp. 68–9.

4. 'Come Inside', *Essays*, p. 367.
5. 'A Modern Credo', *Oxford Broom*, 1923, I, unpaginated. A copy is held by the Harry Ransom Humanities Research Center, University of Texas at Austin.
6. Document held by Harry Ransom Humanities Research Center.
7. *The Diaries of Evelyn Waugh*, ed. Michael Davie (London: Weidenfeld and Nicolson, 1976) p. 218.
8. For an instance of Waugh's interest in Lewis, see 'Satire and Fiction', *Essays*, p. 102.
9. 'Satire and Fiction', *Essays*, p. 102.
10. *The Letters of Evelyn Waugh*, ed. Mark Amory (New York: Ticknor and Fields, 1980), p. 30. This is an undated note to Waugh's agents, A.D. Peters. Amory places it between 1928 and 1929.
11. In *Time and Western Man* (Boston: Beacon Press, 1927, 1957), Wyndham Lewis argues throughout against Bergson's tenets but considers his thought most closely in Book II, 'An Analysis of the Philosophy of Time', pp. 131–463, which also includes discussions of Samuel Alexander, Alfred North Whitehead and Oswald Spengler among other 'time-philosophers', as Lewis called them.
12. Lewis, *Time and Western Man*, p. 162.
13. Henri Bergson, *Creative Evolution*, trans. Arthur Mitchell (New York: Random House, 1911, 1944), pp. 330–87.
14. Lewis, *Time and Western Man*, pp. 162–259.
15. Lewis, *Time and Western Man*, pp. 162–82, 163; Waugh, 'Tolerance', *Essays*, p. 128.
16. Lewis, *Time and Western Man*, p. 164.
17. Lewis, *Satire and Fiction* (London: Arthur Press, 1930), pp. 51–3, see especially 'An Analysis of the Mind of James Joyce', Chapter XVI in *Time and Western Man*, pp. 75–113.
18. The exhibit was reviewed by Charensol, 'Les Expositions', *L'Art Vivant*, February 1929, with some general comments about the artists.
19. *Labels: A Mediterranean Journal* (London: Duckworth, 1930), p. 20.
20. See reproductions in William Camfield's *Francis Picabia* (Milan: Galleria Schwarz, 1972), unpaginated.
21. See reproductions in Pamela Pritzker, *Ernst* (New York: Leon Amiel, 1975), unpaginated.
22. *Labels*, p. 14
    (note: no footnote 23 & 24 & 25. 'Come Inside', p. 367.
23. 'Fan-Fare', p. 302.
24. See letter to Nancy Mitford, 16 November 1949, *Letters*, p. 313.
25. 'Come Inside', p. 367.
26. 'Converted to Rome', *Essays*, p. 103.
27. 'Fan-Fare', *Essays*, p. 302.

Select Bibliography

PRIMARY SOURCES

Novels

Decline and Fall (London, 1928; New York, 1929).
Vile Bodies (London and New York, 1930).
Black Mischief (London and New York, 1932).
A Handful of Dust (London and New York, 1934).
Scoop (London and Boston, 1938).
Brideshead Revisited (London and Boston, 1945).
The Loved One (London and Boston, 1948).
The Ordeal of Gilbert Pinfold (London and Boston, 1957).

Travel Books

Labels: A Mediterranean Journal (London, 1930).
Remote People (London, 1931).
Robbery Under Law, The Mexican Object Lesson (London, 1939).

SECONDARY SOURCES

M. Amory, *The Letters of Evelyn Waugh* (London, 1980).
H. Carpenter, *The Brideshead Generation: Evelyn Waugh and His Friends* (London, 1989).
W.J. Cook Jr., *Masks, Modes and Morals: The Art of Evelyn Waugh* (Rutherford, N.J., 1971).
M. Davie, ed., *The Diaries of Evelyn Waugh* (London and Boston, 1976).
R.M. Davis, *A Catalogue of the Evelyn Waugh Collection at the Humanities Research Center, The University of Texas at Austin* (Troy, N.Y., 1981).
R.M. Davis, *Evelyn Waugh, Writer* (Norman, Oklahoma, 1981).
P.A. Doyle, *Evelyn Waugh* (Grand Rapids, Michigan, 1969).
D. Gallagher, *The Essays, Reviews and Articles of Evelyn Waugh* (London, 1983).
J. Heath, *The Picturesque Prison: Evelyn Waugh and His Writings* (London and Montreal, 1982).
G. McCartney, *Confused Roaring, Evelyn Waugh and the Modernist Tradition* (Bloomington, Indiana, 1987).
D. Pryce-Jones, ed., *Evelyn Waugh and His World* (London, 1973).
J. St John, *To the War with Waugh* (London, 1974).
M. Stannard, *Evelyn Waugh: The Early Years 1903–1939* (London, 1986).
C. Sykes, *E. Waugh: A Biography* (London and Boston, 1975).
Y. Tosser, *Le Sens de l'absurde dans l'ceuvre d'Evelyn Waugh* (Lille, 1976).

GENERAL WORKS

H. Bergson, *Creative Evolution*, trans. A. Mitchell, (New York, 1911, 1944).

T.L. Bouscaren and A.C. Ellis, *Canon Law: A Text and Commentary* (Milwaukee, 1951).

N. Bransom, *Britain in the Nineteen Twenties* (Minneapolis, Minnesota, 1976).

A. Briggs, *The History of Broadcasting in the United Kingdom*, 3 vols., (London, 1965).

R. Escarpit, *L'Humour* (Paris, 1960).

A. Fowler, *Kinds of Literature: An Introduction to the Theory of Genres and Modes* (Cambridge, Mass., 1982).

J. Goodman, ed., *The Master Eccentric: The Journal of Rayner Heppenstall, 1969–1981* (London, 1986).

A.P. Herbert, *Holy Deadlock* (London, 1934).

H. Hopkins, *The New Look: A Social History of the Forties and Fifties in Britain* (Boston, 1964).

A. Jolles, *Formes simples*, trans. A. Buquet (Paris, 1972).

A. Lafay, *Anatomie de l'humour et du nonsense* (Paris, 1970).

W. Lewis, *Time and Western Man* (Boston, 1927, 1957).

W. Lewis, *Satire and Fiction* (London, 1930).

B.B. Lindsay and W. Evans, *The Companionate Marriage* (London, 1928).

A. Mavrocordato, *L'Humour en Angleterre* (Paris, 1967).

C.L. Mowat, *Britain Between the Wars: 1918–1940* (Chicago, 1955).

S. O'Faolain, *The Vanishing Hero: Studies in the Novelists of the Twenties* (London, 1956).

C. Segre, *Structures and Time Narration, Poetry, Models*, trans. K.J. Medemmen (Chicago, 1979).

M. Serres, *Le Contrat naturel* (Paris, 1990).

Index